She should have recognized the signs, but she'd just been so tired and lonely...

Knowing she wouldn't sleep, Sydney rented a car, deciding to go to an antique flea market in Long Beach. It was crowded, and the constant noise battered ears accustomed to the mountain stillness. In one small booth, she found a chunk of high quality Baltic amber, with darker streaks inside, proof of ancient life, almost as beautiful as Devin's eyes. The fine gold chain held it against her heart.

She searched for a place that was quiet and cool, but everywhere there were even more people than she remembered. At the arboretum, her favorite quiet spot, she found herself dodging wedding parties and photo sessions. Finally, she gave up in favor of an early dinner. At least Los Angeles had a lot to offer food-wise.

She didn't recognize this restlessness in herself. It wasn't like she wasn't used to spending a lot of time alone. It was just that she had become accustomed to spending so much time with someone very special. During her solitary Japanese dinner, she studied the amber, and tried to ignore her memories. If this was what being lonely was all about, no wonder people wrote so many songs about it.

Still deep in thought and mentally miles away, she returned to her motel room as the setting sun was making silhouettes of the palm trees and power lines. Her normal cautious nature had been softened by the time spent in New Mexico.

That was the only excuse she could come up with for not noticing something wasn't quite right until after she stepped into her room.

Sydney Castleton has worked hard to put her less than savory past behind her...until her sister asks for her help. Devin Starke has fought too many battles, seen too many deaths, to look forward to a peaceful future...until his best friend and partner asks him to help return the horse his wife, Sidney's sister, took when she left.

Stormhaven, a ranch in northern New Mexico, has become a place for fighting men to readjust to the world, a sort of decompression chamber for those who have seen too much. Devin Starke is such a man. And Sydney isn't far behind him.

When the sparks ignite between them, Devin and Sydney fight the attraction, as neither one is good at relationships. But when Sydney is attacked and fighting for her life, Devin realizes things aren't quite what they seem. Can these two overcome the issues from their past, or are they doomed to lose any chance for love in the future?

In *A Question of Honor* by Mona Karel, Sydney Castleton has a past she's not particularly proud of, working with her father as a soldier of fortune. Now her father is dead, and Sydney is trying to start over. Wanting to right a wrong committed by her sister, who may also be dead, Sydney agrees to take a stolen horse back to its owner at Stormhaven Ranch in New Mexico. The horse's owner doesn't want Sydney driving alone, so he sends his right hand man, Devon Starke, to California to bring both Sydney and the horse back to the ranch. But trouble is following Sydney and her life—as well as that of anyone she cares for—is now in danger. This book, like the others Karel has written, shows a depth of understanding of people and their relationships. You can't help but root for her characters as they struggle to find their way through unique trials and tribulations. The story has a good strong plot that will keep you turning pages, but it's the charming, heart-warming love story that will have you reading this one again and again. ~ *Taylor Jones, Reviewer*

A Question of Honor by Mona Karel is both a suspenseful spy thriller and a captivating romance. Our heroine, Sydney, is a former mercenary who worked with her father, a legendary operative known as "The Rook." When her father is killed by an act of vengeance and his team disbands, Sydney tries to start over, but her past haunts her. She is convinced that she will never find anyone to love her enough to overlook her shady, less-than-legal past. Our hero, Devon, is a veteran of the Special Forces and has seen way too much death and tragedy. All he wants now is a little peace. Devon's boss at Stormhaven Ranch in New Mexico sends him to meet Sydney in California and drive her, and the horse her sister stole from

Stormhaven—which Sydney tracked down and recovered—back to New Mexico. A tough, seasoned cowboy, Devon tries to ignore the sparks igniting between him and Sydney. He's convinced he'll never find anyone to love him enough to overlook his none-too-subtle scars, both physical and emotional. Karel is one of my favorite authors, and this book doesn't disappoint. One of the things I like best about her work is that her , both male and female, are not the "mass-produced" incredibly beautiful hunks and hotties we see so much in romance fiction today. Karel's characters feel like real people and the obstacles they face are tough, intriguing, and complicated. Not that I have anything against beautiful people. I enjoy drooling over a hunk as much as the next red-blooded female. But Karel brings an authenticity to her characters that pulls you in and tugs at your heartstrings page after page.

ACKNOWLEDGEMENTS

This book would not be here without the wisdom and support of my editor Lauri Wellington, and the staff at Black Opal Books. From that first acceptance through a long dry spell, they have been there for me. Thank you.

A
Question
Of
Honor
By

Mona Karel

A Black Opal Books Publication

GENRE: ROMANTIC SUSPENSE/WESTERN ROMANCE/WOMEN'S FICTION

A QUESTION OF HONOR
Copyright © 2015 by Mona Karel
Cover Design by Jackson Cover Designs
All cover art copyright © 2015
All Rights Reserved
Print ISBN: 978-1-626942-70-7

First Publication: MAY 2015

Published by Black Opal Books **http://www.blackopalbooks.com**

I would like to dedicate A Question of Honor *to Elizabeth Lowell, who encouraged me to write the books I want to read and whose generous sharing of knowledge gave me the tools needed.*

Chapter 1

She knew that walk. With a slight hesitation in one leg, he prowled like a wounded predator, conditioned to succeed against the most dangerous game of all. Even limping, his reactions would be instantaneous, his balance superior. By itself, his body would be a weapon. He'd be the best man to have on your side in a battle. After the battle, he'd unwind with a drink and a woman. The drink would be strong and straight. The woman would be bosomy and not too bright. He'd very likely spend more time with the drink than the woman.

Sydney Castleton let her mind drift through bitter thoughts and buried memories as she waited for the man who proclaimed danger with every step he took toward her. He was no different from the men who'd worked with her father: soldiers of fortune, whose luck could run out at any minute.

What trouble had her sister gotten her into this time?

This late at night, the Long Beach Airport was far quieter than its Los Angeles counterpart to the north. Weary passengers straggled across the large hallway, looking for friends, for family, for signs guiding them to their luggage and the end of their trip. The surrounding crowd would see only the man's height, the breadth of his shoulders, perhaps the dark hair under his wide-brimmed hat. His distinctive gliding walk might seem merely athletic, and who else would notice his awareness of everything around him?

Sydney knew these skills demanded a greater price than most would willingly pay. What had his payment been? She shook her head to dispel the thought and quell her imagination. He was just a man, after all, here to help her move a horse. She put aside her memories and stepped forward to greet him.

He didn't seem to notice her at first, his attention on the rowdy returning youth sports team about to overrun the lobby. With a quick step to the side, he slowed down and put himself behind a young mother pushing a stroller, until the swarm separated around them without incident. Then he looked over at Sydney and tilted his head, indicating a door leading to the outdoor baggage claim area.

When they were both out of the air conditioning and fluorescent lights and she could get a closer look at his face, she saw his eyes more clearly. Amber. His eyes were like the finest Baltic amber, translucent, with darker streaks that had once been alive. Now the darker streaks were suspended in the depths of eyes that had seen too much, surrounded by a face that had experienced too much. Small lines on his face marred the healthy tan of an outdoorsman. One of those lines had cut deeper, too near the memory-shadowed eyes for anyone's health.

She shook away the impression. Now wasn't the time for any distraction.

"Mr Starke?" She waited a beat for his reply, then forged ahead. "I tried to call the ranch, but you left early. Something's come up. I won't be able to leave as soon as I'd hoped." She looked closer into the shadow cast by his hat brim, gauging his response. "It might be as much as a week."

He stared at her in silence, obviously trying to filter her words through layers of exhaustion and what looked like a nasty headache.

"Is the coffee in here any good?" His voice rasped in the best Marlboro man accent. "The stuff on the plane tasted like it was strained through old socks."

"I've always suspected the coffee here is what they can't get the passengers to drink on the plane." She tilted her head, judging how badly he needed coffee. "A couple places nearby make it fresh every hour or so. Would you like to try one of them?"

"If that's your best offer, I'll take you up on it, Ms. Castleton."

"Sydney, Mr. Starke. Ms. Castleton is someone who has to work for a living. I try to leave her at the job site." She turned toward the outside baggage claim area. "Do you have any luggage to pick up?"

He shifted his carry-on bag and settled his hand in the middle of her back, urging her away from the door. "Just this bag. And no one's called me Mr. Starke since I spent the night in the county jail for busting up a bar. Devin'll do just fine for me, Sydney." He matched strides with her, and she couldn't help noticing how much better his longer legs looked in worn jeans than hers.

✧✧✧

The coffee might not have been French roast, or whatever was trendy today, but it was fresh and strong and hot. Devin held it in his mouth long enough to burn his tongue then let it slide down his throat, obviously enjoying every aromatic sting. Even as he seemed to lounge on the restaurant's turquoise vinyl bench, seat he remained balanced, his senses alert. Sydney remembered men who sat like this, the power in their hard bodies barely leashed. Their eyes had spoken of pain deeper than any scar. She remembered sitting that way herself, more than once, her every sense tuned to survival. But that was in a lifetime she'd left far behind.

No wonder the pretty blonde waitress hovered, re-filling coffee cups, bringing water and, in general, stalling as long as possible while she waited for Devin to shift his attention away from the fresh strawberry pie and steaming black coffee. An aura of menace always attracted the foolish young.

Devin lifted his head only to scan the meager crowd before returning his attention to the strawberry pie. Sydney indicated no further need, and they were left alone.

"That was good." He pushed away the empty plate. "Our fruits are just barely starting to flower."

"One of the few advantages of being in Southern California. We've had fresh strawberries for most of the last two months. Mosby thinks they're special."

"You're wasting strawberries on that stud horse?"

"He likes them, almost better than carrots."

"Never said he was dumb." He took in a healthy swallow of coffee. "You actually keep Mosby in the back yard? In Los Angeles?"

"County, not city. The house is east of the city in a more rural area near the San Gabriel river bed. Maybe an hour away from where I'm working."

"You ever been in New Mexico?"

"Just the weekend in Santa Fe, when I met Ty at the wedding party. I was looking forward to spending more time there. I haven't had a vacation for years."

"It's the least he could do, after you took care of his stud. You're talking like you can't come out—does it have to do with that delay at your job?"

He'd been listening, of course. He'd know how to control the topic and answer when he chose. Sydney allowed herself a small smile and let him wait while she sipped at her coffee.

"As I told Ty, I won't be ready to leave for at least a couple of days, maybe a week. The best thing would be for you to take Mosby back to the ranch yourself. After you rested up, of course. There are several decent motels nearby."

"What'd Ty have to say about you not coming out?"

Devin's face and voice had taken on a polite, noncommittal tone.

"To talk it over with you."

"The only thing I hate worse than airplanes is motels, and I'd rather not pull a horse trailer that far by myself. You didn't say if there was another choice."

She hesitated, searching for the best words "It's late tonight, and I have to work tomorrow," she heard herself say and wondered at her rashness. "You can stay with me, if you don't mind roughing it. We can figure the rest out tomorrow. You can use the bed. You're too tall for the couch."

"You're awfully ready to trust someone you barely know."

His voice was deep, gravelly, ineffably sexy. He wasn't coming onto her, was he? No, she'd imagined the flash of interest in his eyes. He just looked tired. Tired, edgy, and out of place in the impersonal coffee shop glare. She understood and, for the first time in years, wished she could reach out and offer comfort. She didn't have time for this. Not now, when every moment wasted could lead into potential danger for anyone around her.

"Ty Randolph wouldn't send someone I couldn't trust to move his horse." It was an incomplete answer, but the best she could offer for now.

જ⁄૩જ⁄૩

Devin studied her while he took another gulp of the coffee he really didn't need. Now he understood Ty's insistence that only Devin could be trusted to deal with Sydney and found himself wishing he and Ty weren't such close friends. He also wondered what had brought the flash of wariness to her face.

"Ty'n I've been partners for years. He's a helluva guy," he said, as much to remind himself as her. Before he could signal, the waitress was there with a refill and another series of eyelash flutters.

The blonde was too obvious, and as cheap as the perfume she'd reapplied in the last few minutes. Any perfume on the woman perched on the bench seat across from him had long since blended with her personal scent. Even from this distance she smelled fresh, spicy, and undeniably arousing.

When he'd questioned her invitation, Sydney had looked annoyed, a flush highlighting her cheeks while she narrowed her eyes at him. Didn't she know she was too cute to boss anyone around? A strand of hair brushed her cheek and her mouth primmed up, daring him to kiss it soft. Damn, he'd been on the ranch too long.

"Too bad Ty hooked up with the wrong woman," he said, probing for a reaction. "I'm glad to see he finally wised up."

"I'm afraid I don't follow you."

"He married the wrong woman the first time. Looks like this time he's going about it the right way."

"That woman is my sister, Mr. Starke."

"Don't worry, honey, I won't hold that against you." The reaction was more than he'd expected. She straightened out of her tired slump, growing a whole quarter of an inch. Whatever problems Lana Randolph had dumped on her, Sydney wasn't about to let anyone dump on her big sister. Misplaced or not, Devin admired that kind of loyalty. He also admired the spark she got in her eyes at the casually drawled endearment. Damn, she'd be fun to tease.

"Trouble is, Sydney," he went on, trying to convince his body to let him get down to business, "I'm not a sightseein' kind of guy. Unless you're plannin' to leave real soon, I don't know what I'd do with myself in the city."

He could see Sydney was no more taken in by his country bumpkin approach than she had been by his headache-induced rudeness. Suppressed annoyance showed in the set of her mouth.

"I'm sure you could find some way to occupy your time," she said, a dangerous edge to her smooth voice. "Or someone."

She obviously meant the waitress who'd done everything but write her telephone number on the back of the check. Did Sydney really think he was the kind of bum who'd hit on another woman while he was with her? Devin scanned the shifting restaurant crowd.

"She'd be disappointed if I took her up on what she thinks she's offering and her boyfriend didn't try to beat the stuffin' out of me. You wouldn't want me to upset her, would you?"

She turned her head slightly, checking out the crowd much as he had himself. He knew when she spotted the glowering, shaggy-haired man at the counter. Not content with one flirtation, the waitress now flaunted herself in front of a group of truck drivers.

"It's sad she thinks she has to resort to such cheap tricks." Sydney frowned, obviously upset by the situation, and perhaps by some memory it sparked.

Devin remembered more than one time a woman had tried to pull cheap tricks like that to get her way. Lana'd been a master at the game. Sydney took a final sip of water while she reached for the check. Her attention flickered back to the counter, and she tensed.

"Who the hell do you think you are, cowboy?" The sneered words came from across the room, followed by heavy footsteps.

Devin straightened, ensuring his body was between the rapidly advancing unkempt young man and Sydney, but he stayed in his seat. Best would be not to encourage the fool.

The waitress rushed across the room, grabbing the young man's arm.

"Billy, what in the world are you doing?"

"I saw you slip him your number."

"No I didn't. Stop being stupid." She pulled at his arm, digging in her heels to attempt to stop him.

"Oh, bad move," Sydney muttered, seeming to try to make herself smaller.

Devin stood. No reason to let her be any more worried than she already was. He straightened to his full height, braced his shoulders, and was happy to see awareness seep into the young man's face.

"Son, I don't know what's goin' on with you and your girl, but I suggest you take it outside."

Before he could say anything else, the front door swung open, and two policemen stepped through. Obviously realizing he was surrounded, the boyfriend stopped moving forward and gave in to the waitress's pull. In the resulting confusion, Devin slid the check out from under Sydney's hand. Quick reactions were good for more than doing a job better and faster than anyone else.

"Your place'll do for tonight." He urged her toward the exit, letting his hand settle lightly on her back. Just enough to tease himself with the subtle shift of her spine. Not enough to crowd her. "Be kind of silly to waste time flying back and forth. Besides, it's a big city. Maybe I'll find something I want to do."

He still hadn't figured out why he wanted to spend any more time than he absolutely had to in Los Angeles. One thing for sure, he wasn't about to put Sydney out of her bed.

⌘⌘⌘

The bed smelled of her. Even with fresh sheets that had obviously been dried outside on a less smoggy day than average, the damned bed smelled of her. So did the pillows she'd left when she went to make up the couch for herself. He couldn't sleep for thinking about how she'd calmly and sweetly steam rolled him into her bed.

There wasn't much else in the little house. More of a bungalow than a real house, the ceilings were so low he found himself ducking if he turned around too fast. There was the bed and a dresser in here, a ragged couch and chair in the living room, and a battered table with two chairs in the galley-sized kitchen.

Except for shelves holding the television, some books, and a radio, it was a pretty damned depressing place. She'd read his expression, shrugged with a funny little smile, and said it was a good place for the horse. He listened for any sounds from the living room. She slept quietly, only an occasional slightly deeper breath showing where she was. Did she favor sleeping in the raw, like he did? She probably wore a flannel nightgown she thought hid everything from view, when it actually just teased him to hunt for the treasure underneath. He laughed quietly at himself, and wondered when he'd lost touch with reality. Of all women to turn him on—a pint-sized career woman interested in his partner. Life could be a real bitch sometimes.

ⱭᴥⱭᴥ

The jungle underbrush rustled in stealthy whispers around him. They were out there, just beyond the range of his senses, watching him. They were small and quick and had knives that could cut a man in half if—

ⱭᴥⱭᴥ

Devin came awake with a start, every muscle tensed. Light filtering around the edges of the blinds made a subtle pattern on the wall. It was before dawn and this room, wherever it was, faced east. *There was someone in the room with him.* He could sense them, hear their breathing, smell them. No, what he smelled was the damned bed. Then he realized the fresh scent on the air was the same scent that had plagued him throughout the night.

Sydney was taking something out of the dresser. She wasn't sneaking in, peering at the bed every few steps, but stood at the dresser pulling out lacy feminine things. A dark suit covered her arm. She'd already gone to the closet. He must've been more tired than he thought to not have heard her before.

He watched her through slitted eyes. A plain, dark blue robe covered her slight figure and her golden brown hair was pinned up in a prim knot. He was glad to be lying on his side, or he would've tented the bed covers. It made no sense.

"I have to go in for a half day," she said from the doorway in a normal tone of voice, not turning around. She knew he'd been watching her. He liked that. "I've taken care of Mosby for the morning. There's coffee left. Help yourself to whatever you can find to eat. If you need to rent a car or call a cab, I've left money on the table. I'll call if anything comes up." She slid out the door, letting it close soundlessly behind her without ever turning in his direction.

ↄ৩ↄ

Much later that evening, Sydney eased the extended

cab pickup truck to a stop outside the wooden gate in front of her temporary home. For a moment, she leaned forward, resting her head against the steering wheel while she gathered strength to open the cumbersome barrier. The half day had stretched into nine hours, complicated by multiple problems. Scant, restless sleep the night before and retrieving her clothes with Devin in her bed had done nothing to ease her state of mind, and she still hadn't figured out how to convince him to leave sooner rather than later.

"Sydney?"

The voice near her elbow and a rap on the truck window jerked her upright. A shadowy figure stood a few feet away, its size and uncompromising stance potentially alarming. She'd almost fallen asleep in the driveway. She shook the cobwebs from her mind and partially rolled down the window.

"Sorry, the day caught up with me." She looked ahead at the opened gate. "Oh, thank you. That gate gets heavier every day."

As he stepped away, Sydney slipped the truck into gear, letting it glide forward into the customary parking space beneath a mulberry tree. She was out of the truck, gathering up her briefcase and purse before she heard the rattle of chain wrapping around a heavy pole, securing the gate. It was a safe, comforting sound. Ridiculous.

Delicious odors reached out to her as she stepped inside the front door. She stopped, sniffing deeply. Devin took the heavy leather briefcase from her and settled his hand in the small of her back. Sydney had never known the comfort of a strong man's gently guiding hand. Then again, no man had ever gotten close to her who hadn't known enough about her to believe she needed guiding.

"You fixed dinner?" It seemed a safe enough topic. Turning to face him as she asked the question made it possible for her to step away from the warmth of his hand. If she felt suddenly bereft, she could blame the impossibly long hours she worked.

"I found some meat in the freezer. When you called to say you'd be late, I started a stew." He moved past her to set the briefcase down next to the couch. "It'll be ready any time."

"I have to change and take care of Mosby." Not even her father had ever fixed her dinner. Men didn't take care of women that way.

"The nice thing about stew is that it just keeps getting better, the longer you cook it. I cleaned Mosby's pen and tossed him some hay a while ago, but I wasn't sure what else you were feeding him." The corners of his mouth twitched briefly before he turned to check the gently bubbling pot, almost as though he really had a sense of humor. "You go on ahead and change."

℮℘℮℘

Two days later, Devin sipped rich, dark coffee, savoring the difference freshly ground beans made. The tap water here tasted just this side of poison, but Sydney bought bottled water, especially to make coffee. In the short time he'd spent in Los Angeles, he'd at least learned that much about her.

Sydney was gone from dawn until well after dark. They saw so little of each other, moving to a motel seemed foolish. While she worked, Devin managed to keep himself busy. He'd done some simple repairs around the ratty old house, walked to the dry river bed, fussed with Mosby, checked out the horse trailer, and rested enough for the next ten years. The old leg injury he'd aggravated back home had finally eased into a standard level of discomfort. How in the world did city folk survive having so little to do day after day?

From things Sydney mentioned, the little they talked, she'd supervised projects around the world. Yet she now worked a temporary job any decent secretary could do, lived in a dump of a house in a neighborhood one arrest away from an all-out police crackdown, and drove a truck that had to make the hour long commute seem endless. All to help out a someone she insisted she barely knew.

There'd been no more early morning forays, but he was always aware of her. His errant mind provided pictures to go along with the muted sounds she made. More than one restless night found him heading for the door and the relatively open air outside. Seeing her cocooned on the couch, blankets pulled up over most of her face, guaranteed he would stay outside even longer.

A sound at the front of the cottage drew him away from the kitchen. She was early today. Muttering a half-formed curse, Devin tossed the rest of his coffee down the drain. That old wooden gate was too heavy for such a little woman to move.

By the time he was out the door, Sydney was back in the truck, driving forward enough to be able to close the gate. She saw him through the deepening gloom, raised an acknowledging hand, and continued on behind the house.

She'd pulled up near the horse pen before he could secure the gate and follow her. When he rounded the corner of the house, he hesitated and felt the corners of his mouth twitching. Sydney had gone around to the side of the truck bed. As she leaned over the side, small, furry felines appeared, rubbing themselves along her arms and head in obvious delight. The feeling seemed to be reciprocated. Trying to wrestle feed sacks became more of a chore when she had to stop and provide equal time to all her little friends.

"I wondered where they kept themselves. I saw the bag of food, but no pans and no kitties."

At the sound of his masculine voice the cats scattered, tumbling over each other to get away. Sydney turned, a sack of feed on her shoulder and a guarded smile forming on her face. He relieved her of the sack and watched her smile slip away.

"I'm perfectly capable of carrying that sack. It wouldn't be the first one."

"I'm sure it's not," he said in a level, non-confrontational tone. "I'm also sure it's the last one you'll ever carry." With no further comment, he took the feed into the small storage shed. He turned back just as she reached for the next sack. "Put that down, Sydney. Take care of your kitties."

"Being small and female is no more a sign of weakness than being large and male is a sign of stupidity." She reached for the next sack. She had no more luck lifting this one to her shoulder than she had the first one.

"Has anyone ever mentioned you have an overdose of stubborn in your make-up?" He tried to keep the humor out of his voice.

"Isn't this a case of the pot making color references to the kettle?"

This stopped him cold. Feed bag perched casually on his shoulder, he tipped up his hat brim to look more closely at her stormy face. "Sydney, it's just a feed sack. It's no big deal."

"If it's no big deal, why can't I help unload? And don't you dare tell me this is men's work, and not to worry my little head about it."

That killed one argument before it had a chance to draw a breath. Her chin tilted up as she watched him try to come up with a logical reason why she shouldn't be doing what was, in his opinion, a man's job. At least, not while a man was around to do it. He looked her over, from the restrained knot she was keeping her hair in to the low heeled shoes that gave her a much-needed fraction of an inch more height. He grinned.

"Well, for one thing, you could break a nail."

Sydney transferred her glare from his face to her hands. The small fingers ended in perfect ovals. It was an exquisitely feminine touch. He wondered how those ovals would feel trailing down his body—and wrenched himself back to the current situation.

"Heaven forbid I should harm a nail." She spun away. Reaching down to yank a handful of long grass from along the fence, she headed toward the gray stallion that stomped its feet and tossed its head for her attention.

There were only a few more bags of feed in the truck, enough to take with them to ease Mosby's change to a new diet. While Devin transferred them into the shed, he watched Sydney's stiff back and high-held head. She'd lost the serenity that seemed so much a part of her. For the life of him he couldn't figure out why.

Once he'd finished unloading, he hesitated. Natural inclination told him to just walk away and let her work out her own problems. Women had a tendency to be moody, and there wasn't much a man could do about it. It was simply the way they were. But this woman had shown no previous sign of moodiness. Leaning back against the truck, he crossed his arms and waited.

It seemed the cats decided once he stopped moving around he ceased to exist. One tiny feline after another emerged from around the shed, whiskers twitching and ears at the alert. Without fail, they headed toward the woman rubbing the horse's neck, her back uncomfortably straight.

Sydney gave the gray stallion a final ear scratch, drew a deep breath, and turned back to the house. Late sun filtering through the thick trees feathered shadows across her face, almost hiding her expression. She took an awkward step forward as if to distract him from the expression she hadn't hidden soon enough.

"I'm sorry if I upset you," he said, not shifting from the side of the truck. "But you might as well get used to it. Outside of Ty, I'm the most liberal man on the ranch. You'll be lucky if anyone lets you pick up a napkin."

"My fault." She buried the threatening emotions beneath a professional calm. "Being tired makes me over-sensitive." She brushed past him, reaching into the truck cab for her jacket, purse, and briefcase.

ᏋᎦᏋᎦ

"Where'd the cats come from?"

Sydney looked up, obviously startled. She'd changed into old jeans and begun dinner in a silence charged with emotion. He'd started a fresh pot of coffee then puttered around outside while it brewed. By the time he came back in and poured coffee for both of them, she was acting like they'd never disagreed. Wonderful thing, denial.

"They were here when I moved in. I trapped the ones I could to have them neutered. Fortunately they don't seem to hold a grudge."

"Will you take them with you?" he asked, wanting to nurture the tender expression he saw on her face.

"I can't. Once Mosby's out of here, I'll go on to my next job. There's a place in Fullerton that takes in stray cats and tries to find homes for them. They'll have a slightly better chance there than with the animal shelter."

For a moment she forgot he was looking, forgot to control her reactions. Then she shook back her hair, reaching for her coffee, while she stirred the soup heating on the stove.

"I bet you had a lot of pets as a kid."

"Not hardly. Pets take up time and room that can be used in more useful ways." She seemed to be quoting something been said to her times without end. "Lana had pets. I didn't."

"Your sister seemed to have a lot of things you didn't have," Devin ventured, watching her closely. Had she brought up her sister to discourage his conversation? "Like a husband."

"I had a husband, Mr. Starke," she said, preserving a cool distance between them. "Marriage is a vastly overrated concept. The few benefits were outweighed by the effort it took to keep my husband amused."

The primly delivered words stung, even if he did agree. "Couldn't keep him in your bed?"

It struck home. He'd wanted only to irritate some answers out of her. For a moment her composure crumbled, and Devin found himself peering into the coldest depths of hell.

"No, as a matter of fact, I couldn't. Nor could I keep him out of any other woman's bed. I finally decided I didn't want to keep him at all."

Setting down the coffee cup, Sydney pushed away from the counter and started to walk out of the room. Then she took a deep breath. "I took the truck in today for a final checkup. It's ready to go, any time you want to leave." The comment seemed to come out of left field, and her expression had gone politely blank.

"When are you going to be ready to leave?"

She frowned, picked up the coffee cup, put it back down. "If you left this evening you could get out during the slow traffic. Otherwise you have to leave extremely early in the morning."

"Sydney, what aren't you telling me?"

"I just think it would be an extremely good idea for you to leave as soon as possible."

Now he took her arm, and turned her to face him. "You've been acting like you expect a bomb to go off since you got here today. What the hell is up?"

"I really can't explain it. Not now. There's no time. But if Mosby's not here, I don't need to be here. We don't need to be here."

"And that would be a good thing?"

She nodded, watching his face as if gauging his reaction. Obviously she wasn't going to say anything more.

"Okay." he ran his hand through his hair, searching for the right words. "Okay. I'll leave if you come with me."

"But I—"

"No buts. You come with me, and not just to another part of Los Angeles. You come with me to Stormhaven. Whatever the hell you're running from, you'll be better off there."

She stared up at him in silence and he wondered what thoughts she kept hidden behind her blank expression. Then she nodded again and he felt the pressure release from around his heart.

Chapter 2

They worked quickly, packing up what absolutely needed to go, and by sunset Sydney had her bags and boxes filled, her computer secured, and everything that could be traced to her removed while Devin worked out by the horse. Even so, by the time she had her bags by the door it was fully dark. When she didn't turn on the outside lights, Devin looked over but didn't question. He'd hitched the trailer, loaded the supplies, and was by the pen when she stepped out. Her things were stowed in the second truck seat and in the truck bed.

"I'll just need some help with his leg wraps. We use Velcro wraps at the ranch, and I only saw these." He indicated a box on the fender of the trailer.

"The vet said flannels with cotton underpadding were safest, especially in the beginning, when he was so restless."

"You mentioned getting him over that. What kind of magic did you use, anyway?"

Her voice drifted up from near Mosby's rear legs. "No magic on my part. I just spent two days at a seminar, a couple hours of an expert's personal attention at the boarding stable, and about a week practicing. He was afraid of small spaces. Once he got past that, he was fine."

She stood, reaching into the box for another halter, this one equipped with a padded leather attachment which would go over the top of the horse's head. Seeing the expression on Devin's face, she shrugged. "I know, it seems like overkill. But he wasn't my horse and I didn't want to take a chance on him being hurt before I could track down Tyler Randolph."

"How did you finally manage—want me to do that for you?" This last as Mosby decided, just as Sydney almost had the head guard adjusted over his ears, to be interested in a noise a few blocks away. In the process, his nose hit Sydney square in the chest, propelling her back into Devin. He closed an arm around her, steadying her while he settled the horse with his other hand.

Sydney felt him from the back of her head to the back of her thighs, and where her bottom nestled could well bring the blush back to her cheeks. Even through the layers of jackets and denims, he was strong, warm, male. She felt an almost overwhelming urge to simply give in and melt against him. Almost. She'd learned her lessons in a harsh school, and it would take more than a temporarily excited male to change her boundaries. Then tiny mewling sounds, clear in the unusually quiet night, distracted her.

"The cats! Dev—" She pulled away from the enticement of his body and headed in the direction of the shed.

He caught her arm before she could get out of reach. "Don't worry about the cats. Get this lunkhead loaded so we can get on the road."

Sydney jerked her arm out of his grasp, but nodded in agreement. She'd felt the quiet on the edges of her perception. Now she directed her attention beyond her immediate surroundings to the world outside the ivy-covered perimeter fence.

It was quiet. Too quiet. Not the quiet of peaceful rural lanes, but the quiet of an impending disaster. Old instincts listened, catalogued, evaluated. She didn't care for the conclusions she drew. Without another word, she took the lead, turning the gray stallion toward the trailer.

"Stand back. He fusses about his wraps." As always, Mosby lifted each leg in turn, stretching it away from his body until he was comfortable with the supporting flannel. Then he followed peacefully toward the ramp of the trailer.

"Want the light on inside?"

"No. Just give him a minute. We practiced night loading."

In spite of the impending conflict they could both now almost taste, they waited in a semblance of patience while the stallion inspected the ramp leading to the dark hole he was supposed to enter.

For a long minute, he sampled the air, tasted the straw thrown down to cushion his ride, nudged the center divider, which had been pulled to one side to give him plenty of room. Then he snorted softly, as though he too understood the need for quiet, and bumped Sydney's shoulder. She rubbed under the protective leather cap, and faced the front of the trailer.

"Don't get behind him until he's all the way in. He still backs out if he thinks someone's going to force him." She took the first step onto the ramp herself, not looking at the horse. After a moment, seeming to be fascinated by the slack in the lead rope, Mosby lowered his head and followed, hesitating only once, when he looked into the other side of the trailer. Then they were in, the rear guard was secured, the ramp was up, and Sydney was outside the trailer, reaching in through the side escape door to finish snapping shipping chains to the halters.

Once the escape door was closed and latched, Sydney brushed past Devin, heading for the other side of the trailer. Murmuring a soft warning to the stallion, she eased open the small metal door.

"Devin," she whispered, the need for quiet not dimming the emotion in her voice. "Now I feel like such a creep for yelling at you."

Devin had followed close behind her, and looked in over her shoulder. Secured against the front of the empty trailer stall were two large cages, occupied by five irate feral cats, their eyes gleaming in the dim light. Each cage had food and water containers attached to the sides, with a small litter pan at one end of the cage and empty burlap feed sacks at the other end.

"When did you—how did you—" she stammered,

then turned to face him, leaning back to look directly into his shadowed eyes. "Thank you," she said simply, reaching up to touch his cheek lightly with one small hand.

Devin shrugged. "It won't hurt to have more mousers at the ranch. All I had to do was put some food in the cages and stand back. They jumped right in."

Sydney smiled, but didn't press the issue. She stroked the cheek her hand was cupping, relishing the rasp of his night beard, then turned to close the door.

"You drive," he said abruptly, as though denying any reaction to the brief moment of closeness. "I'll get the gate. We can switch off once we get into a better area."

Sydney hesitated then followed his directions in silence. If Devin felt the situation was too precarious for her to close the gate, she would defer to his instincts. She swung open the driver's door, bracing a hand on the seat to step into the truck. They had a long drive ahead of them.

ぐろぐろ

"So how long did it take you to convince that lunk-head that trailers weren't carnivorous?"

The lazy question took Sydney's attention briefly away from the road. Lit by the early sun, the truck cab held a warm intimacy. Devin pushed his hat back as he straightened some in the seat.

"Those clinics were for people who didn't know much about horses. I found out real fast that I was nowhere near strong enough to out power Mosby, so I had to out think him."

"He try smashing you into a fence?"

"Just before he dragged me about twenty feet."

That brought Devin upright, his hat jostling to one side. "When did that happen?"

"The day I picked him up. It took four hours and a lot of help to get him into the trailer."

"Did the owners of the stable help you much?"

"Not hardly. The owners were Lana's friends."

That brought a typical pall of silence to the conversation. There just wasn't much positive he could say when her sister's name came up. The freeway continued to glide beneath the truck tires while he tried to come up with something to explain his point of view.

"Your sister had a lot of friends," he ventured. "Mostly men, who were willing to do things for her. It's a mystery how a man like Ty could get himself tangled up with a woman like that." He stopped before he could say too much.

"I really don't know a lot about Lana's life, except for the times she would visit." Sydney's voice did not encourage further comment.

His partner deserved a special sort of woman, one like Sydney. It was good Ty had sent him to come help her. Some other man might forget how long they had been friends, and whose woman she was. However, until Ty could take over, Devin needed to establish a few ground rules.

"It's not safe for a woman like you to handle a horse like Mosby."

"There hasn't exactly been a mob of volunteers to help me," she reminded him.

"Well, there is now." Deciding from her silence that she understood, he relented. "You've done a great job with him, considering. Most women would have just boarded him out somewhere until they could get hold of his owner."

"Getting hold of his owner wasn't all that easy. The party was in Santa Fe, so I never really knew where the ranch was, and no one at the boarding stable was about to tell me. I finally talked to someone I knew who could research the VIN on the truck, since the registration was bogus. My sister didn't offer a lot of information when she called."

"What exactly did she say?" He tried to sound more interested than scornful, for which Sydney had to feel at least some gratitude.

"Just that she couldn't take care of Tyler Randolph's problems any more, and if someone didn't help her out, she would have to either geld the horse or have him shot. She sounded more stressed than I ever remember her being. When I asked her why she didn't just call her husband, she told me that he didn't care what happened to her or the horse."

"Maybe not to her, but Ty's been after that stud's bloodlines for years."

"I remembered how proud Ty was at that party, when he told everyone about the horse that was going to put his ranch on the map. I also remembered what Lana had always been like." She fell silent, concentrating on the holding the truck steady as an eighteen wheeler breezed past.

"Self-centered, grasping, and totally without morals or scruples."

The indictment, uttered in a flat voice from underneath the hat brim, wrenched her attention briefly from the road.

"How did you—"

"I spent entirely too much time around your sister. It didn't take long to figure out what kind of a person she was. What I still can't figure out is how you're so different."

"Simple. Lana is beautiful."

This time the hat fell back completely as Devin straightened, easing the seat belt until he could face her. Sydney had to feel the heated intensity of his gaze, but she kept her attention firmly on the road.

Devin looked closely at her. The early morning light washed mercilessly over her face. She hadn't slept much, hadn't put on any make-up, hadn't done much more than pass a washrag over her face and confine her shining chestnut hair in a fabric-covered elastic band. She wasn't classically beautiful.

She wasn't even conventionally pretty. She was simply, uniquely, Sydney.

"Is there any logic to that statement, or do you always start getting stupid when you're driving?"

She spared him an amused glance. Once he decided she really did know how to drive towing a trailer, Devin had let her stay at the wheel while he dozed in snatches. He felt like an out-of-sorts bear wakened in mid-January, and probably looked the same.

"No stupider than you get when you haven't slept. My parents divorced when we were young. Mother only liked beautiful things around her, so she took Lana and left me with Dad."

Devin forced the air out of his lungs, allowing only one sharply bitten-off word to escape. "I take it your husband was equally insensible."

"Equally observant. I hadn't realized you liked to wake up with a rousing game of twenty questions."

Now was not the time to discuss what he'd like to wake up with. Not when the skin was beginning to draw tight against her cheekbones and her full lips were compressing.

Not when she was still his buddy's woman.

"You ready for me to take over?"

"I can last a while yet. I imagine by the end of this trip we'll both have more driving time than we could ever possibly want." She resettled herself at a slightly different angle.

Devin reached behind him for his hat. "After a while, you begin to feel like you're pulling the trailer yourself."

"You've obviously done this before. No wonder Ty was upset when I told him I was going to do the drive by myself. I figured it for a fifteen hour drive or so, and I've done that alone plenty of times."

"More like twenty, by the time you add in rest stops for the horse." He stared at her for a long moment. "For someone who's never done this before, you were willing to make quite an effort for a man you barely know. Unless you wanted to get to know him a lot better."

"I told you before," she said, her voice tranquil, her gray eyes intent on the drive. "Lana behaved dishonorably when she took Mosby. When she turned the horse over to me, the debt of honor became mine."

"Where'd you get an idea like that?" he asked, his voice unusually gruff.

Sydney allowed herself a small smile. "My father attempted to raise me to understand honor, as well a mere female ever could. He was a man of honor, as is Tyler Randolph. As you are also, Devin Starke." She took her attention off the empty Interstate to study him. "Why else did you think I would invite you into my house, and my life?"

It was very quiet in the truck cab for a long while after that.

∽∾∽

"That your rig out there, honey?" the dark-haired waitress asked, pausing in her whirlwind circuit of the dining area.

Sydney nodded, sipping at what the truck stop swore was coffee while waiting for the monitor to finish tallying the gallons of gasoline being poured into the truck. They'd slipped across the state line into New Mexico a couple hours before, and this would probably be their last gas stop.

"Nice rig. *Nice* driver."

Sydney nodded again, smiling slightly. After another, longer, look the waitress sighed and went on with her duties.

What the coffee lacked in flavor it made up for in caffeine, intensified by sipping it through a notch torn into the plastic lid. With the stimulant singing in her veins, she would be able to drive her late night stint without a problem.

She looked forward to the end of the trip and a couple of weeks at the ranch with nothing to do but rest. Even more, she looked forward to getting to know Devin better. He intrigued her more than any job she had ever taken on.

Shaking her head at her own fanciful notions, Sydney looked out the window again, to see Devin striding across the pavement toward the coffee shop. While she waited for the credit slip, she studied his size, his carriage, the slight hesitation in his gait, and decided the waitress was definitely right.

e/oe/o

Devin held the door open for Sydney to slip through and wondered at the smile that lifted the corners of her mouth and brightened her eyes. "Something funny?" She shook her head while she sucked coffee through the lid of a styrofoam cup. "Coffee any good?" brought another head shake and more of a sparkle to her face.

He almost asked if the cat had her tongue, until he realized how much he wanted that warm, slick part of her, and where on his body he wanted it. A non-committal grunt seemed to be the safest response to her mood. That brought a bigger, saucier smile.

Devin felt the corners of his own mouth curling up while he went through the motions of washing the gasoline off his hands and getting his own coffee. This was the first time in his memory he wouldn't have minded a trip taking longer than planned. Unfortunately, so far everything had run smoothly, bringing them closer to the ranch and the suddenly unwanted intrusion of the only people he called friends.

He examined a display of junk food, decimated by the recent rush of long-distance drivers, while the waitress filled a take-out cup and the thermos with recently brewed coffee. Something outside the window attracted the tired brunette's attention, and she set down the coffee pot, hard.

"Mister," she called out, an edge to her Southwestern drawl. "You'd best get yourself out there. It looks like your woman needs some help."

The pack of chocolate donuts fell as Devin whirled. He'd pulled the truck and trailer off to one side, out of the way of the gas pumps but still in the lights. Four scroungy young men were amusing themselves by beating on the trailer with heavy sticks and tire irons.

From the way the trailer was rocking, it was obvious Mosby was not enjoying their rhythm. The truck door was closing behind Sydney as she exited in a rush to get to the trailer.

As the large man burst out through the glass doors, the waitress reached for the phone. There would be enough trouble tonight to need a patrol car, if one was in the area.

From the predatory look in the man's eyes, an ambulance might not be a bad idea, either.

෧෨෧෨

Four. Dammit. Sydney studied the men. They all looked dirty and tough, and strung out on something— enough to be dangerous. She had to get them away from the trailer before Mosby hurt himself. She flexed her hands, consciously easing her shoulders as she drew on the adrenaline for extra strength and speed. This might be fun. If only there weren't four of them. Waiting for Devin to notice what was going on never crossed her mind.

"Hey, guys, looky what we got here." The words were slurred, the eyes were bleary, but there was enough innate menace in the tire iron he swung to overcome the most inept handling.

At least they had stopped pounding on the outside of the trailer. Mosby was making enough noise on his own, rocking the trailer as he thrashed in the confined space. Thinking of how much time and effort had gone into getting the stallion to trust small spaces was enough to give her the last edge needed to face poor odds. Sydney waited for them to come to her.

Then there was no more waiting. A hot breeze flowed by her, made up of equal parts of angry male, deadly intent, and blinding speed. Two of the punks were on the ground before they realized they'd become prey themselves.

Breathing slowly in an attempt to dissipate accumulated adrenaline, Sydney eased around the milling group. Devin fought with power and agility, his style far more elegant than anything she'd ever learned. When you had that much strength to draw upon, you could concentrate more on form. She watched appreciatively, noting some moves she might try herself some time. The two punks on the ground were scuttling away without getting up while their companions tried to decide if this were as much fun as they had first thought it would be.

It was obvious Devin didn't need her help, but Mosby was a different matter. Sydney slid the keys from her jacket pocket, calling to the stallion while keeping part of her attention on the conflict. The lock yielded, and she eased the door latch open, speaking to the horse the whole time.

"Sydney, don't open that door!"

Devin's voice carried the whip of command, taking her attention away from Mosby as she reached in to lay a hand on him. She stopped, looking over her shoulder while holding the door open just enough to admit her arm. Then more than half a ton of terrorized stallion wrenched against the restraints holding his head in place. The chains held, and his body slammed once more against the padded side of the trailer. This time, there was an arm in his way.

Pain exploded in her wrist and radiated up her arm, wrenching a cry from her. Sydney retained enough sense not to jerk back, instead waiting until Mosby thrashed against the center divider before retrieving her arm, cradling it against her body while she fell against the side door, slamming it shut. A footstep behind her sounded unnaturally loud to her overcharged senses and when a hand fell on her shoulder she whirled, ready to do as much damage as she could with one hand.

If she hadn't subconsciously recognized his touch, she would still have known whose hand it was from the curses pouring over her like hot lava. At odds with the anger in his voice was the arm easing around her shoulders, cradling her while gentle fingers reached for her hand.

"You idiot! Why didn't you just stay in the truck? Damn all independent women! Don't you have the sense God gave a tree stump? Let me see your arm."

Shivers were beginning to chase themselves up and down her body, the after-effect of too much adrenaline and not enough outlet. Sydney worked to draw air into her lungs, holding herself very still in the shelter of Devin's body. It would feel so good to throw herself into his arms and let him take care of everything. It would make him feel good, too. Unfortunately, she wasn't made that way.

଼ଽ଼ଽ଼ଽ

Any other woman would be sobbing against him, begging him to hold her. Sydney stood very still, obviously in shock. Devin knew he shouldn't have let her see him fight, but there'd been no way to avoid it. It would be a long time before he forgot his rage when he heard her soft cry of pain. The punks had retreated as soon as his attention was divided. Now he had a bigger problem on his hand. Sydney was obviously afraid of him.

They would have to deal with that later. Once she was cared for and he'd gotten her away from the crowd now gathering around the trailer, they could discuss her reaction to his fighting.

☙☙☙

Moonlight filtered through sparsely planted trees at the roadside rest area. Devin eased the truck to a stop in the darkest corner, facing the window away from the few overhead lights provided by the highway department. He turned to Sydney, huddled in the seat next to him, her right arm held stiffly against her body. When the engine was switched off, she lifted her head from the seat back.

"What's up?"

"Rest time. The ranch isn't going anywhere, I need a couple hours shut-eye, and you need to give yourself a chance to relax."

He slipped out of the truck cab before she could dredge up another question. Sydney watched him open the trailer window to secure a bucket of water in front of Mosby before locking everything up. Her bruised arm, having been soaked in ice water then wrapped at the truck stop, gave off a steady throb which she could ignore. Harder to ignore was pounding of her blood. Too much. Too much excitement, too much repression, too much caring. Her skin felt too tight, and she was sure her hair no longer fit properly.

When it came, the crash would be appalling, but nothing she hadn't experienced before. Unfortunately, she couldn't deal with it by walking it off, talking it out, or becoming intimate with a good bottle of brandy. Devin still had his image of her as a frail flower of femininity. Eventually, he might find out otherwise, but she wanted to put that confrontation off as long as possible. It was a welcome change, to be treated like a normal female.

An influx of cold air cut into her musings as Devin opened the door, sliding under the wheel and quickly re-closing the door.

"You're supposed to be resting."

She shrugged, pulling her jacket more closely around her. Devin reached a long arm over the seat to where he'd packed the bedding, along with some of the suitcases. He eased back the seat as far as it would go and wedged a pillow against the door. Sydney pulled away, making as much room for his long legs as possible.

"Come over here."

Sydney tried to read his face under the hat brim. Throwing caution to the wind, she slid across the seat, and let him arrange her body for maximum support against his. Another pillow was placed on the steering wheel, to elevate her arm. Her head nestled cozily under his chin, and a quilt was settled over her. The instant comfort was beyond description. Particularly when his hands rubbed along her back, easing away the strain.

"Better?"

She nodded, enjoying the feel of his suede-covered shoulder against her cheek. The tension left her body on a long sigh, and she felt herself going boneless. Why had no one ever told her about the comfort possible between a man and a woman? Would she have believed them?

A distant light cut across the deep dark in front of the windshield, and a moan announced a train hurtling through the night. Sydney raised her head, letting the distraction ease her relaxation.

"I've always thought that would be a fun way to travel...just lay back, relax, and enjoy the rocking." She slid into sleep on that happy thought.

෫෩෫෩

Devin felt the sudden increase in her weight as she finally gave up the fight to hold herself away from him. He reminded himself to tell her how brave she had been, trying to help Mosby when it was so dangerous for her. All he'd done was yell at her, and she still hadn't fallen apart. Ty had chosen well. He decided not to think about how that no longer pleased him.

He shifted, trying to avoid the pressure of jacket buttons. It took only a brief argument with himself to decide both of them would be more comfortable with their jackets opened, and even less time to accomplish the task.

He almost groaned at the bliss of her soft breasts pressing into his chest as she nestled closer to him. A tiny sound escaped between her parted lips, her breath puffing warmly against his chest, when his hands drifted under her jacket, rubbing slow patterns over her back. He lost the argument with himself about unfastening her bra. There was a fine line between pleasant arousal and outright agony, and it was stretching finer by the moment.

Deciding it would be safer to be asleep himself, he took a firm hold on her body, tilted his hat further forward, and allowed himself a couple hours of sleep.

Chapter 3

The ride roughened as the truck eased off the state road. Devin glanced down at Sydney, nestled into a pillow propped against his thigh. In the soft predawn desert light she looked incredibly fragile and precious. Too fragile and precious for a used up warrior.

He felt a tightening below the region of his heart, but attributed it to the appallingly bad coffee they'd discovered on this trip. For once he was free of the irritating snug fit his jeans had given him lately. Then she stirred, pushing the pillow off his leg, and her cheek rested directly on his thigh. The damned jeans shrank again.

"Rise and shine, Sleeping Beauty." His voice was rough, but that was normal for this time of the day, wasn't it? "Dawn's coming, and we'll be at the ranch in a couple hours." It was past time to get back to reality.

⁐ෙ⌇

Sydney stirred, trying to orient herself. The pillow under her cheek was hard, and moving, the narrow bed vibrated. Was she in one of those tacky motels she had heard about? Then a large, warm hand settled on her shoulder, steadying her while shaking her awake.

"Come on, Sydney. The coffee's horrible, but it's still fairly warm."

With Devin's help, she managed to lever herself more upright on the seat, leaning against him when a yawn caught her halfway up.

Her body felt strangely stiff, and she dropped her hand to brace herself. Instead of the truck seat, her hand encountered a hard male thigh and enough pain to bring her fully awake. The wrapping on her wrist brought the immediate past back to her in a rush.

"We're almost there? Why didn't you wake me?"

"I just did. Don't worry. Bringing Mosby back is enough to impress Ty. How you look is a bonus for him." His voice and expression seemed unusually harsh.

Sydney didn't dignify that remark with a reply. Devin was obviously tired of her company. It was too bad he'd wakened her. She'd been having a wonderful dream about being held and stroked and petted until she relaxed against a big warm body.

Her fertile imagination had even supplied a strong, steady heartbeat and the regular rhythm of deep breaths under her cheek. She damned her imagination and looked resolutely out at the land emerging in the growing light.

இௐௐ

"Welcome to Stormhaven, Sydney." Ty opened the passenger door as he spoke, sounding unnaturally loud and cheerful to the two weary occupants of the truck.

Sydney blinked at him, trying to associate this tall, casually dressed man with the elegant host of a party so many months before. The light brown hair and sky blue eyes were the same. Perhaps the lines in his face were less severely drawn, as though he'd come to terms with life's small surprises.

After all that had happened, it was difficult to find her company manners. That proved unnecessary. When she didn't respond immediately, Ty reached for her right hand, ready to help her out of the truck whether she wanted to come out or not.

Before she could warn Ty, a long arm snaked past her, and a large hand clamped, onto the equally large hand reaching into the truck.

"She's been hurt," was all Devin said, in that rough, near-irritated voice he'd been using all morning.

Ty stepped back, deftly retrieving his hand and sliding it, along with its partner, into the back pockets of his jeans. A smile flirted around the edges of his mouth, deepening the lines etched there by many smiles before.

"What're you grinning about, dammit?" Devin slammed his door shut, stalking around the front of the truck.

"Good morning to you too, partner. Looks like you had an interesting trip."

A grunt was his only answer. Devin shouldered the other man out of his way as he opened Sydney's door completely. "Let's get the stud unloaded so we can get Sydney into a real bed."

No doubt as far from him as possible, and the sooner the better. Sydney allowed herself a mental shrug as she eased down from the high truck. Time for reality to take over.

෫ৎৎ෫ৎ

The kitchen was a nostalgic combination of battered, oversized furniture, well-used pots, and huge windows that filtered the early morning light through hand-woven hangings. Bunches of drying herbs hung from open beams, adding a piquant note to the promising scents of home baking.

The coffee smelled fresh and strong and was served in large mugs that fit well into a man's hands. Sydney had been offered a smaller mug, or even a delicate china cup, but refused. She felt at home with her hands wrapped around a mug of hot coffee, anchoring her to comfortable memories.

"So where'd the kitties come from?"

Sydney looked up from contemplation of the mug cradled between her hands. When she was a little more awake, and her brain was functioning just a little better, she would pick the mug up and take a sip. Maybe in an hour or so.

"They were at the house I rented, and I sort of adopted them."

"I'm surprised Dev let you bring them along. He hates

cats. Says they're too much like women. Dogs mind better. Male dogs, anyway."

"That's enough."

The warning in Devin's voice would be plain to the hearing impaired. Ty merely grinned wider, a devil dancing in his blue eyes. He opened his mouth again, and Sydney decided to head off any arguments.

"Bringing them saved me from taking the time to drop them off at a shelter." She didn't look at Devin as she spoke. She didn't need any more reminders that he was tired of her company.

Before Ty could get in any more digs, a buzzer sounded on the oven. Both men looked toward the kitchen door rather than getting up from the table. Sydney was gathering the energy to push back her chair when the door flew open to admit a whirlwind of colorful swirling skirts.

"Don't get up, I'm right here." The tiny dark-haired woman hustled to the stove, punched off the buzzer, and opened the lower oven door, releasing an enticing aroma of cinnamon and oranges. She slipped on oven mitts and reached in to pull out trays of steaming rolls. Only when the rolls were transferred to cooling racks did she turn to the silent group at the table.

"Good morning, I'm Maria Gladstone. You must be Lana's sister." Bright brown eyes regarded her from a dark complexioned face of few wrinkles and much character.

Sydney tensed, waiting for the inevitable comments, which only varied according to whether or not the speaker had liked Lana. The woman's age was impossible to guess, though no silver highlighted the dark hair worn in a thick bun at the base of her neck. She studied Sydney unwaveringly, seeming to note every sign of the long, difficult trip. Then she nodded, and a smile of amazing warmth spread across her round face.

"It is good you finally arrived."

Before anyone could speak, Maria was making the rounds of the table, dispensing fresh coffee and small plates. She then set a plate of the rolls in the center of the table.

"Eat now, and then you can rest. Tyler, did you tell Devin yet about the letter from Priscilla?"

"Cissy's my sister," Ty explained to Sydney. "She's in her last year at the Air Force Academy. Her letter came the day after Devin left for LA. Seems she's decided to apply to fighter pilot training."

He looked around the table expectantly.

"Fighters?" Devin's mug hit the table with a solid thump, sloshing coffee over the rim. "The Academy was bad enough. Where does she come up with damn fool ideas like that?"

"Probably from listening to us talk about a citizen's responsibility to defend his country," Ty said mildly.

"Well, she's way off base. It's a man's job to fight for his country's freedom. It's the duty of a woman to keep life good for her man."

"Don't you think that opinion is slightly outdated?" asked Sydney, as calmly as she could. "In Israel, women have been fighting alongside the men for years."

"That doesn't make it right. Real women don't fight wars."

Sydney attributed the tension she felt in the room to her own sensitivity and exhaustion. She could not be reacting to Devin's statement. If he felt that way about someone merely applying to jet school, how would he react if he knew the background of the woman he'd sought to protect since they met? This wasn't the time, and she wasn't in the mood to bring it up. She drew a deep breath and scrubbed her hands across her face to help herself come to her senses.

"I hate to break this reunion up, but I'm afraid I'm going to need to crash for a while. Ty, where do I put my stuff?"

Whatever tension she'd sensed before was nothing compared to what she felt now. It was as though everyone held their breath, purposely not looking at anyone else. She glanced at Devin, but he'd effectively removed any expression from his face.

ཀ✻ཀ

Ty grabbed for his coffee mug, sternly repressing the smile he knew was trying to take his mouth over. His buddy had it, but good, for the feisty little brunette. After that crack about a woman's place, it would be a long time before Sydney would be warming Dev's bed again. If she had yet. She was a little hard to read, but there was no mistaking the possessiveness in the looks Dev had been throwing her way until just a second ago.

"Miss Castleton," began Maria.

"Please, call me Sydney."

"This is the largest house on the ranch. For now, I have made up a room for you here. After you have rested, we can see about a more permanent arrangement."

Trust Maria to know how to handle a touchy situation, after nearly thirty years at Stormhaven. Sydney followed her with a studiously casual farewell to the men at the table. When Devin didn't respond, a brief tightness crossed her face before she turned away, missing the way Devin's gaze followed her. Ty hid his grin in the depths of his coffee cup. It was going to be a fine couple of weeks at the old ranch.

☙☙☙

"Take it easy, you little demons. I'll let you out in just a minute," Sydney chided the mewling cats as she eased open the trailer door. She paused to look around her appreciatively, drawing in a large lungful of air. The fresh evening air was a radical change from Los Angles, even with a day's residual pall of dust and ranch odors.

Since the cats had food and water, Sydney had decided to leave them crated until this evening. Actually, Devin suggested it that morning, and she'd been too tired to do much but agree with him. An afternoon spent in the cozy room Maria had shown her to helped physically, and she felt ready to take on any simple problem. Emotionally, she was as mixed up as ever.

"Guess that's what growing up is all about, huh, munchkins?" she crooned to the small, disgruntled felines as she unlatched their cage doors. The cages would remain open and the trailer door propped until they could settle in.

At first the cats hung back, staring out the side trailer door at the limitless horizon. Then a gray tabby, always a trifle braver than the others, slithered out and onto Sydney's arm, followed by an orange tabby. From this vantage point they could study their new domain. Needle sharp claws pressed rhythmically into her leather jacket, and minute rumbles showed approval.

"Tough kitties," she said, stroking along the flexing spines and rubbing erect ears. "Gonna whip your weight in gophers, aren't you?"

"That's not too many prairie dogs," drawled a deep voice from behind her.

Sydney pivoted, reaching out to secure the cats before they dug into her arm. She managed to catch the orange tabby, but the other one, farther up her shoulder, began to slide along the leather, scrambling frantically for purchase.

Before the cat could slide more than an inch, Ty's hand reached out and closed gently around the tense body. The cat was wise enough not to struggle against the hold, although it looked smaller than ever, secured within the large hand.

Sydney wasn't surprised at the speed of Ty's reaction. This man hadn't always been a rancher. There were too many memories in his eyes, and he was too aware of what went on around him.

Ty didn't move with Devin's stalking grace, but he still carried himself like a man who knew his body and trusted what it would do for him.

"Don't underestimate these guys. They came from a pretty tough neighborhood."

"So I heard." Ty set the dark cat on the trailer wheel well, grinning when it spat and scampered down to the ground, followed in short order by the rest of the undersized pack.

"In fact, we got a call from that agency you worked for. The man who called—Brian?—said the house you were in was raided by the police. Something about drugs?"

Sydney felt her brain go on alert. She turned away, busying herself with propping the trailer door open just far enough to let in a small feline, if they chose to return. Should she answer Ty's unspoken questions and reveal more of her background than she had so far?

It wouldn't be fair if she stayed quiet and trouble followed her to this ranch. Still, she didn't want to borrow trouble before it was absolutely necessary. It was interesting, to be around men who thought they had to take care of her.

"It wasn't the best neighborhood, although I really didn't expect anything like that to happen. Otherwise, I would never have moved Mosby there."

"Brian said it ended up being some kind of misunderstanding. Someone phoned in an anonymous tip, and they obviously got the wrong place. He said it was all taken care of."

"He's pretty handy that way. I'll give him a call tomorrow, when my brain is closer to actually working."

"Dev told me your trip was pretty rough."

Ty led the way away from the trailer toward the pen

where Mosby paced, stirring up dust while waiting for some notice from his adoring public.

"Long, definitely, and tiring. I'm glad I didn't do it alone." Even if she felt more alone now than she had in years.

They reached the gray stallion's pen, and Sydney reached into her pocket for the carrot ends she'd grabbed from Maria's salad fixings. The smaller woman had refused any help, but gave Sydney full kitchen privileges any time she, or Mosby, was hungry.

"I'm glad you finally made it out here. When you called to tell me you had Mosby, and he was safe—" Ty stared off at the distant mountains sheltering his ranch. "Well, you eased a lot of worries for us."

Now it was Sydney's turn to look away, staring at a corner of the barn cast in shadow by the setting sun. She'd never accepted praise well, especially when it was for something she considered her duty. Stalling for time, she dropped the carrots into Mosby's feeder. The stallion lunged for the treat eagerly, and the last few pieces bounced off his forehead.

Mosby raised his head, jaws working on the carrots while he fixed Sydney with what had to be an irate glare for being so careless. It was the light touch the moment needed. Both people broke into laughter and the horse snorted, obviously disgusted with the foolishness of humans.

"I'm just glad he's back here where he belongs, and nothing serious happened while I was taking care of him."

"You did fine with him. I hope you're planning to stay

long enough for us to make it all up to you."

"It's a beautiful place," she said, wanting to turn the subject to something a little less personal. "I've never been in this part of the country."

"You're welcome to stay here as long as you want. Consider this your home, Sydney."

There was no answer possible for that kind of offer. At least, not for someone who hadn't had a home for many years. She hesitated then accepted with a smile. After watching Mosby explore his new domain for a while, Sydney decided to go back into the house and clean up before dinner.

☙℆☙

"Enjoying your guest?"

"She's a fascinating woman," Ty said, easing his hands into his jean pockets. "You must have had an interesting time in the big city."

He smiled when Devin detached himself from the other shadows, coming forward in a controlled rush. There was danger in his movement, and in the hand gripping the upper rail of Mosby's pen. Ty ignored the implied threat, enjoying his partner's reaction. It had been years since he'd been able to get this kind of a rise out of Devin. The critical thing was knowing how much he could push. Still, you weren't really alive if you weren't willing to take chances.

"She not much like her sister, is she?" Ty probed, still maintaining his non-threatening stance.

"I can't really say. I spent as little time with your ex-wife as I could." Devin's voice was tight with control.

That had been a poor choice of topics. Ty didn't like to think about how badly he had misjudged the woman who had lived here, all too briefly, as his wife. It hadn't been the best of times for him. When Devin wasn't in the mood to be teased, he could draw blood.

"It's good to see this beast here," Ty said, turning back to look at his stallion now pacing restlessly around the large pen. "Place didn't seem the same without him."

Devin reached through the rails to scratch the stallion's back. "You were damned lucky."

"What are you going to do about her?" asked Ty, leaning against the pen and pushing back the wide brim of his disreputable working hat.

"It's done. I helped her bring your stud home."

"You always did have a way with conversation." Ty felt a hot breath on his neck and automatically reached up to push away the stallion's nose. Mosby was almost embarrassingly affectionate with the few men he liked. Idly rubbing the itchy spot between his stallion's powerful jaws, he glanced at his partner. "Charlie's gone."

Any pretense of indifference was dropped as Devin straightened away from the fence. "Since when?"

"Day or two after you left. He's up somewhere in Far Canyon."

"When were you planning to tell me?"

"Tomorrow morning, after you'd gotten a good night's rest." Ty didn't need to add that he had hoped Devin would not be sleeping alone. No sense pouring kerosene on the flames just yet. "He's okay for now. I tracked him to the canyon, and we've been leaving food where he can find it easily. Rations, mostly."

"What happened?"

"I think it just got to him again, like it has before. We had a pretty noisy storm, and he was gone the next morning. Set out on foot. When I asked the guys about it, they said he was restless, like he gets sometimes."

Devin cursed under his breath, the unconscious litany of a warrior who can't control the situation he's in. Charlie had been a friend while they were both in the service. Then Devin had re-upped and Charlie had retired from the military, opting for a higher profit fighting career.

Unfortunately, some of the things Charlie had seen and done had not left him as easily as he had left the Rangers.

"He seemed to be getting better, especially after he got that letter from one of the guys in his group. I thought it would be enough if we were here for him, let it work itself out."

"When we get him back this time, you know he's going to have to need professional care." Ty tried to sound casual.

Devin nodded. "I'll start up there at first light, make sure he hasn't hurt himself. Maybe he's ready to come back."

"Miracles happen, but not near enough." Ty dared a sly grin as he moved away, toward his house. "I'll take care of Sydney for you," he said, then burst out laughing at the growled reply.

လာလာ

Sydney leaned back against the tree trunk, enjoying the protection its thick branches offered against the sun, and casual glances. The air was scented with hot dust, filtered through the rich pine.

Nestled in a ridge at the base of the Rocky Mountains, Stormhaven escaped the worst of the high-altitude winters. Ty had mentioned a long history of shelter not only from the weather, but also from oppression and government interference. The Randolph family had always gone their own way.

The ranch hands were efficient, competent, and quiet. It was only the eyes of experience that could see that some of them were competent at more than just caring for livestock. Sydney doubted there was much hunting for sport done at Stormhaven. No one here needed to prove himself in that fashion.

She'd started to let the rhythm of the ranch ease some of the tension in her body for the last couple days. Though the guards were not obvious, she knew the ranch was a safe haven for her and the animals she'd brought. Unfortunately, she didn't seem to be settling in as well as Mosby and the cats had.

Ty spent as much time with her as he could while still running his ranch. She hadn't seen Devin. Ty had said he had a lot of catching up to do. Not that she cared. For the moment, she entertained herself with observing the ranch itself.

"'Scuse me, Miss Castleton?"

Sydney jerked upright as the quiet voice intruded on her warm afternoon musings. A tall young man stood not far away, a small cat cupped in his hand. When she raised her head, she heard his sudden intake of breath.

"I thought…Syd?"

She rose to her feet, the slope of the ground giving her a few inches advantage. The cowboy did not approach, nor did he take his gaze away from her face. He was young, at most in his mid-twenties, but there was an aged weariness to his eyes. At first she didn't recognize him as an individual. Then he pushed back his hat with his free hand to allow more light on his face and squinted slightly when the sun hit his eyes.

Memories crashed to the front of her brain and she sat down abruptly, her knees suddenly weak. It had been in one of the small, angry Central American countries, where she and her father had gone in to mop up someone else's botched operation. Most of the men had been dead, or too far gone down the road of senseless violence to be able to help. They had been able to salvage a few, most of them very young, on their first mission. She remembered one of them in particular…

"Jeff? No. James?"

A wide grin split the lower part of his face, taking away some of the strain around his eyes. "Jamie. You used to call me Laird Jamie, Highland berserker."

"As I remember, you were."

"I was a wreck." The cat shifted in his hand, mewing irritably, and he looked down. "Oh, is this one of yours? It was in the stall with the gray stud, and he's been restless since they started using him again."

"They're used to walking all over Mosby." She accepted the disgruntled feline, holding it gently until it got over its spite at being handled by a stranger. Then she looked back up at the hesitant young man. "How've you been, Jamie?"

"Alive." The simple word told a complex history. "I knocked around for a while after I got out of rehab, then heard Ty Randolph took people on who'd seen action and were tired of it. I've been working here for a couple years. I never would have made it without your father. How is he?"

"He died a few years back." She'd given up finding a way to say it gently. "He would have been glad to know you made it."

Jamie looked away, a young man still not quite strong enough to let his tears show. "He was a hell of a man."

Sydney had never been able to find a good reply to that statement, either. Her father had simply been himself, living life as he saw fit. She stroked the cat, giving Jamie a chance to pull himself together.

"Was that blonde bit—" He hesitated, glancing at her. "Was Randolph's wife really your sister? Do they know who you are?"

"They know I'm Lana's sister, not who our father was." She made her voice as noncommittal as possible, hoping to stop this line of questioning.

"You're Starke's woman, aren't you?"

"I don't believe I've had ownership papers signed out."

Jamie snickered. "You used to strip the hide off anyone who stepped out of line. Starke told us to leave you alone and watch our language while he was gone."

"And do you always do what Starke tells you to do?"

"We do when he's been like a bear that lost part of his body in a trap."

"Jamie, I think I'm capable of deciding whether or not someone's bothering me. Devin Starke has no say over what I do."

"You're his woman all right. Lucky bastard."

Sydney eased the cat into a comfortable position in the crook of her arm. This argument was one she would reserve for someone else.

"You said Devin was gone?" she asked in what she thought was an idle tone of voice as she led the way down the rise and toward the large barn.

Jamie fell into step beside her, not trying to hide his amusement. He'd obviously learned something in the last few years about reading the truth of people's reactions. As they approached the pens flanking the barn he slowed.

"Sometimes, one of the guys isn't ready even for this place, and he'll go off in the mountains to be alone for a while."

Sydney studied what she could see of the young man's face. Because of their shared past, Jamie might tell her where Devin had gone. But he wouldn't reveal any more than the absolute minimum about someone else's secrets.

"Is Devin looking for one of those men?"

"We know where he is, more or less, but he won't talk to anyone but Starke. They go back a long way." He turned away, looking up the driveway at a dark green vehicle that trailed a high plume of dust as it approached. "Looks like we've got company. Better find the boss."

Chapter 4

Hel—lo there. I don't think I've seen you here before." The man's voice was predictably deep and smooth, well-suited to his tailored western-cut suit and handsome, rough-hewn face. At another time, Sydney might have even found him attractive. Now, he was only an irritant. But she did like his truck.

She slowed as she walked past the dark green vehicle. From the mud on the winch and dust on the windows, it was obviously a well-used work vehicle. It was also one of the most expensive off-road models available. Obviously this cowboy didn't need to think about cutting any corners to help make it through the winter.

As she attempted to pass with a polite smile and nod, Ty came up between them. She could have pulled away from Ty's light touch on her arm, but there was no reason to cause a scene. A few minutes of polite conversation wouldn't be too much of a strain.

"Kyle, where've you been keeping yourself?" There was no doubting the sincere welcome in Ty's voice.

"Here and there. I heard you got your gray stud back, but I had a couple of board meetings I couldn't get out of. I just flew in a few minutes ago and came straight over." He removed his Stetson as he spoke, running well-manicured fingers through dark red hair before resettling the hat. "Didn't know you had company. I might've cut out a little sooner."

"Sydney Castleton, this smooth-talkin' guy's Kyle Jorden. His family has had a spread around here almost as long as mine has."

"Don't listen to him, Sydney. My great-granddaddy was waiting when his came over the pass. Helped him build the first house, up there among the pines." Kyle indicated a spot half-way up one side of the mountain.

"What he neglects to mention is that his great-granddaddy was the Mescalero brave who helped burn out the cabin before that, over by the river bank." Ty waved toward what was now a stand of fruit trees.

Sydney felt her irritation slip away like water through a screen. The two men had obviously been friends since before either one of them could walk. She wondered if Devin had known Ty then.

Then Ty was talking again. "Sydney kept Mosby in LA for me and brought him back just last week."

"You made a lot of ranchers happy bringing that stud back," Kyle drawled, flicking open the buttons on his jacket to rest his hands on his lean hips, emphasizing the fit of his expensive slacks. "A lot of mares, too."

She waited briefly for more of his "shucks, ma'am" routine. If he dared tack "little lady" on the end of a sentence, it would have been over, Ty's friend or not. Fortunately, Kyle only acted like a hick Romeo. When she didn't respond, he changed the focus of his attention to Ty.

"Kyle, if you have a minute, I want to show you some of the mares I'll be using Mosby on." Ty pushed himself away from the pen usually occupied by the gray stallion. "You coming, Sydney?"

She shook her head. Even if she wanted to spend time around Ty's neighbor, the only horse that interested her was not to be seen. A sudden banging in the stable gave her a clue, and she started toward the interior. It seemed dim in contrast to the sunshine, but she didn't need much light. She'd heard that particular pattern of kicking before, along with the grunted whinnies and heavy snorting.

Mosby had worked himself into a heavy sweat, pacing in the large stall. Each time he turned, he kicked out twice with one hind leg, making contact with the solid wooden walls. Equine rumbling punctuated his progress.

Thinking only to soothe the agitated animal, Sydney moved closer. She deposited the cat on a bench as she approached the stall, all the while speaking clearly and quietly. It was working, or at least Mosby slowed his charging around the stall long enough to flicker an ear in her direction. Heartened by this much response, she reached for the door.

She'd no more than taken hold of the steel latch than a large hand settled over her wrist, pressing just hard enough to cause her to relax her fingers. Sydney reacted instinctively, allowing herself to be pulled around, while she added subtly to the momentum. Her free hand formed into a fist, one knuckle slightly raised, her elbow braced against her side for greater strength.

"What the hell do you think you're doing, woman?"

Devin's growl betrayed the tension under his surface anger. Recognizing him as he spoke, Sydney relaxed her hand, laying it on his wrist in an attempt to remove his hold. She might as well have tried to remove handcuffs with her teeth. "I'm trying to help Mosby before he hurts himself."

"What about before he hurts you?"

"I might not have all your years of experience with other horses, Devin, but I know how to deal with Mosby."

"Not the way he is now."

"He gets upset like this whenever he's closed in. I told you he didn't like small spaces. He relaxed once I moved him outside."

"Yeah, but back then he wasn't working." Using the firm hold he maintained on her wrist, Devin pulled her away from the stall. He glanced quickly around the barn and, seeing no one, he called out for some help.

Two of the more experienced ranch hands came in to move Mosby. Once outside, the stallion visibly relaxed although he continued to pace, scenting the air and occasionally issuing a muffled whicker.

Devin kept hold of Sydney, dragging her into a corner of the stable until the stallion was moved. His hold changed subtly, fingers easing the iron grip on her arm. She could probably pull away from him if she really wanted. Instead, she stood obediently still, noting every new line and frown on his face while she tried to ignore the welcome warmth of his hold.

"From now on, stay away from Mosby."

"Why?"

"Because he's no longer a pet horse. Ty's started using him, probably this morning." Devin spoke as if to a dense child. His restless gaze flickered across her face, settling on her mouth, then looked away.

For a moment, she frowned, attempting to decipher his meaning. Then Kyle's comments came back to her.

"You mean you think he'll be dangerous just because he's been bred? Was he that way before, or are you making assumptions based on general knowledge?" She tilted her head to get a clearer look at his face. It was a useless effort.

Devin had effectively wiped out all expression except for stern patience. "It's the way stallions are, Sydney. During breeding season they can't be trusted."

"Male horses get cranky because they're getting sex? Isn't that contradictory?"

She raised her chin at an aggressive angle. Devin might think she had radical ideas about the place of women in society but she was too bright to be easily buffaloed.

For a moment, it seemed like Devin would have laughed if he hadn't thought it would destroy any minor control he had over her behavior, and his own.

"Just accept it as fact, all right? While you're at it, don't trust Kyle Jorden, either."

"Is that because he is or isn't getting sex? This western male stuff is really confusing, Devin."

As he had many times in the past, Devin mastered his impulses. He dropped Sydney's arm, turning away from her teasing.

"Is this a private party or can anyone join in?"

They pivoted at the laughing voice. Ty and Kyle stood in the doorway of the stable, silhouetted against the evening light.

"Jorden, good to see you."

"It's been a while. I understand you helped this little lady bring the stud back."

Sydney felt her back stiffen, and this time she didn't bother to hide her grimace.

"She didn't need much help, just someone to spell her driving," Ty said, not bothering to hide his smile. "You want to stick around for dinner, Kyle? I'm sure Maria made enough for an army."

"Let me take a rain check on that. I really need to get back to my place. I'll be seeing you again, Sydney?"

"If I'm still here when you come back by."

She made it obvious that seeing him wasn't high on her list of priorities. It was hard to say if Kyle took the hint. He winked at her and took one last look at Mosby before climbing into his truck and leaving in another cloud of dust.

Sydney shook her head, leaning over to scratch Mosby. "So that's the modern western male. I like his truck. Think he'd let me take a drive in it sometime?"

"From the way he was looking at you, he'd probably

take you anywhere you want to go," Ty said, around another grin.

"That's some line he has, isn't it? As smooth as he is, you wouldn't think he'd need to practice it on any available warm-blooded target."

"Kyle's a connoisseur, Sydney," Ty explained. "He just goes after the best looking women around."

"Then I must be lucky there aren't any other females around."

She spoke casually, looking over her shoulder, a wry smile taking any bite out of her words. For once, Ty had no answer, although he shot a questioning glance at Devin. But his partner was in a stone-faced routine.

"How'd it go up there?" Ty asked quietly. "Did you find that stray you were looking for?"

Devin shook his head and moved away from the group. "He's up there, but I couldn't get a line on him right away. He'll be all right for now. I'll probably go back up in a couple days."

"You coming over for dinner?"

"Not tonight. I've got some things to get done."

Devin left abruptly, offering a general hand wave. His things to get done were obviously far more significant than a plain female who couldn't resist challenging the proper masculine order of things.

"I guess it's just you and me for dinner," Ty said gently. "Unless you have other plans?"

"None I can think of at the moment. Although if I keep eating Maria's food and laying around like a slug, I'm going to have to indulge in a major shopping trip."

"I haven't heard any complaints about how your clothes fit, Sydney."

"You're a nice man, Tyler Randolph."

There was no real joy in Ty's smile. "Sometimes, maybe. Sometimes nice isn't quite enough, is it?"

Sydney shrugged and fell into step beside him, heading for the house. Close, but not quite touching. There was a bittersweet comfort in the distance, for both of them.

At the door, Ty turned toward her, his hand resting on the ornate handle. "If you're up to some real Western type exercise, we can see about getting you on a horse tomorrow."

"That would be a totally new experience. I think I might like it. Thanks."

"Thank me later, when you're heading for the liniment. Once you're riding well enough, you'll have more mobility around the ranch."

Sydney looked up at him, wondering again what had gone wrong between her sister and this essentially kind man. She wondered, also, why kindness didn't seem all that appealing at the moment.

ᏨᎧᏨᎧ

Lana would have liked the high proportion of fit, quick-moving men at Stormhaven, but the remoteness of the ranch could never have appealed to her. Sydney's sister had sought out large crowds of people who could convince themselves, and her, they were having a good time. Sydney wondered how Lana had lasted here, when no one had the time to cater to her. It was doubtful she'd made herself useful. That was not one of the lessons their mother had considered necessary.

Maria, who would have been her sister's most constant companion, made it obvious she neither liked nor respected Lana. Even if one of the ranch hands had been interested in Lana, they had too much respect for Ty, and an intimate knowledge of how much pain hurt. Lana had left with a man she met in town.

All this came out in subtle, and not so subtle, comments made while she was learning about the working capabilities of horses. For the most part, Jamie helped her when he had the time but any of the men were willing to lend a hand, a suggestion, or a comment. This was done in a respectfully impersonal fashion. Devin might not have considered her interesting enough for his company, but his word carried weight even in his absence.

෧෧෧

"So, how are things going with your houseguest?"

Ty knew better than to face Devin with the smile that once again threatened to break out on his face. It would take minimal encouragement for his friend to try a healthy swing. Instead, Ty continued to scan the cliffs with his binoculars, searching for cattle too wild, or too foolish, to stay with the others.

"If you stuck around the place longer than five minutes at a time, you wouldn't have to be asking that."

"I've got better things to do than sit around and watch you score on another city woman."

"I've got better things to do than listen to you belly-ache. For your information, I see very little of *our* houseguest. She's not usually up when I leave, and if we do happen to have dinner together, she leaves right after. I do know she's not sleeping well."

"You keeping her up, old buddy? Is she better than her sister?"

"I don't know, *old buddy*. Is she?"

Faced with the blunt, cool words, Devin turned away. For a long moment, neither of them spoke, being too strong, too male, to back down. Then Ty relented. Fun was fun, but there would be no pleasure in baiting Devin much longer.

"Her light's on when I'm done with the bookwork."

"Guess it's too quiet out here for a city lady."

"Could be. She generally goes out sometime after midnight. Morgan sees her running most nights." Ty referred to one of the men who preferred standing guard at night to sleeping.

"Alone?"

"No, she meets a motorcycle gang for a quickie out on the flat rock." Ty shook his head in disgust, then went on. "She stops there for a while before she comes in. Look, bozo, why don't you just give in and have dinner over at my place tonight? Maria's beginning to think you don't like her cooking any more. Tonight. Just bring yourself, and your manners, if you can find them."

ↄ⁄ↄↄ⁄ↄ

Sydney set heavy stoneware plates around the dining room table. The periwinkle blue sweater dress she'd found in town that day flared elegantly around her stockinged legs. It had been a very productive trip. Not only had she found a reliable dry cleaner and an excellent dress shop, she'd also had the acrylic renewed on her nails. The same shop offered pedicures, and she'd indulged herself a little further. All the tiny reaffirmations of femininity soothed her feelings of inadequacy about herself. It had been a lonely couple of days.

"You are not like your sister, are you?" Maria's softly accented voice cut through the comfortable silence between them.

Sydney concentrated on setting the plates in the exact middle between the silverware. Maria's question couldn't be ignored but, oh, she was tired of this subject.

"No, Lana was blonde and pretty, like my mother. I look more like my father's side of the family."

"I refer to the way you act, not your appearance." Maria's voice held a note of gentle rebuke.

"I'm sorry. My parents separated when I was young. Lana was raised by our mother, and I stayed with Dad." Sydney had the strangest urge to hang her head and beg forgiveness. She thought Maria would be as generous with her kindness as she was with her opinions. What would it have been like to be raised by a woman like this, instead of by a man who saw life in terms of obligations to be fulfilled? She shrugged mentally, throwing off the idea. As soon wish for the moon to come closer to earth so she could grab a ride to the stars.

"Well, well, well, what have we here? The help has improved drastically since the last time I patronized this establishment." Ty's booming voice preceded him as he sauntered through the dining room door, tossing his leather jacket onto an available chair. "Hel—lo there, Miss Sydney." He looked her over thoroughly, not missing any details of the drape of the new dress across her hips.

Sydney had to smile back. Ty's blatant flirting was almost as much of a pick-me-up as the new dress had been. At one time in her life, she might have been attracted to his bronzed good looks and merry blue eyes. The first time she met him, he'd been married to her sister. Now, her mind and heart were filled with the uncompromising harshness of a weathered, scarred face, ancient weary eyes, and a soul with a carapace acquired to shield it from the world.

"You know better than to drop your clothes in here, Tyler Randolph." Maria rapped out orders like a troop leader. "Put that jacket away and go wash for dinner. You too, Devin."

Sydney had been preparing a remark equally as outrageous as Ty's. She stopped, keeping her back to the door and to the man she could feel staring. The new dress suddenly seemed too warm for the room, and her legs felt very exposed below the long hem.

"If I'd known you were dressing for dinner, I would have come by sooner."

It was the same voice, but harsher and more condemning than before. Sydney braced herself before turning.

"So glad you could make it. I heard you were too busy to join us."

"That's what happens when you get involved with helping out a friend. You fall behind in your regular work."

There was no warmth in the predatory eyes that swept over her, noting every change from the last time they had met. The contrast was extreme, but she was not about to apologize or explain. Nor would she continue to search his face for any of the minute signs of softening she'd once imagined seeing there. Instead, she turned toward the kitchen, consciously keeping her balance in the heeled dress shoes.

"I'll need another place setting, if you're staying for dinner."

⁀ᔓᔒ⁀

Maria had produced a meal that would gladden the heart of any cattleman. Her roast was tender and flavorful, with the perfect amount of pink showing in the middle. The side dishes were simple and delicious, a rice pilaf with extra grains and spices, steamed broccoli, and home-baked dark bread. Maria excused herself early, wanting to set buns to rise for breakfast.

"I wish I'd learned to cook like this," Sydney said, reaching for another serving of rice. "My repertoire seems limited to stew and whatever's already made at the grocery store."

"I think Maria's aunt taught her, but she has a library of cookbooks in there."

"We moved around too much to collect many books. I'm afraid I wasn't much of a reader when I was a kid. My sister enjoyed books far more than I did." The observation came out before Sydney could stop it.

"That's certainly an understatement." Ty reached for the wine. "Lana had more books than most stores. Every time I turned around, she had her nose in another book. Damn near took out my chimney burning them after she left."

"Lana didn't take her books with her?"

"She took her jewelry and some of her clothes. She must've been in too much of a hurry to get away to pack more." Ty was not smiling now, nor did his tone encourage discussion.

"That's strange. She'd had some of those books since she was a teenager. She used to say they were her link to sanity."

"Yeah, they were pretty ragged. She probably figured she'd be able to get enough off Mosby to buy all the damned books she needed, if she was that desperate for fantasy."

"If you'd been raised by our mother, you would have needed some fantasy in your life, Ty." Sydney frowned. "Lana never left her books behind."

"Having gotten to know you better, Sydney, I can't help wondering how much different your sister would have been if she'd been raised as you were." Ty kept his attention on the dark red wine he poured into everyone's glass.

Sydney took a moment to sip her own glass of the potent cabernet. "Considering everything, Lana was a far better person than she might have been."

"She was good at a few things," Ty admitted. "Unfortunately none of them had much to do with living on a ranch."

"Why did you marry my sister, Ty?"

"The usual reasons. Mutual attraction, admiration."

"Did you meet her and immediately believe this would be the woman who would gladly follow you barefoot through the desert and bear your young without complaint?"

"God, no."

"Once you were introduced, did you believe she would be happy on a working ranch, and would willingly pitch in during the day, then have a hot meal waiting for you every night?"

"Not hardly. Lana didn't cook."

"While you were getting to know her better, did you become convinced she would sacrifice her comfort for yours without question?"

"No one who knew Lana would ever think anything like that." Red was beginning to work its way up Ty's neck, but he kept his replies in an even tone of voice.

"Or did you possibly take one look at Lana's long blonde hair, elegant legs, and voluptuous build and see a body you wanted in your bed long term, and you were willing to pay the ultimate price for that possession?"

Devin lounged back in his chair, watching her with narrowed eyes. "You sound almost jealous of your sister."

Sydney took a deep breath, trying to control the shaking in her voice. "Maybe Lana never learned to think of anyone before herself, but I don't think she completely deserves the bad rap she's been getting. At least she was feminine enough to attract the attention of the man she wanted." The chair tilted dangerously as she rose from the table. "If you gentlemen will excuse me, I believe I'm through."

ↄↄↄ

Her heels sounded loud against the wood floor, then muted by the carpet in the living room, and loud once again as she crossed the entrance way to her room. The only sound in the dining room was the scrape of wood on wood as Devin righted her chair and pushed it back into place.

"Leave it to a woman to interpret everything backward," Devin observed, reaching for his wine.

"I don't know. A lot of what she said made sense. I never thought much about Lana living here when I married her. I was too busy getting her to say yes."

"You never did explain why you fell for the married routine when you could have had everything you wanted by just bringing her back here for a while. Then when she left, she wouldn't have held title to anything."

Ty shrugged, obviously uncomfortable with the subject. "When I met Lana, she was beautiful and seemed interested in me and the ranch. I probably should have just brought her back here, but she told me she wanted the whole deal: marriage, kids, all of it. It was past time I was married."

"Are you planning to do things a little differently this time?" There was a sudden note of steel beneath Devin's casual voice.

"What the hell are you talking about now?"

"You planning to live with Sydney a while and try to get her out of your system? She's obviously interested in you. Why else would she have attacked you about her sister?"

"You damned idiot, how many times do I have to tell you? She has yet to see me, for looking at your ugly mug. She probably defended her sister for the same reason she took care of Mosby. Sydney has her own code of honor to uphold. Why don't you get smart for once? Get your butt out there and take care of her."

"I don't poach on my friend's property."

"You better never let her hear you talking about her as property. Sydney cares about *you*, Devin. Lord knows why. Don't be any dumber than you have to be about this."

There was less expression than normal on the scarred face. But deep within the gold of his eyes, a fire began to glow. He tossed off the rest of his wine, nodded once, and rose.

He hesitated when Ty spoke once more. "Just let me know where she's sleeping tonight."

"Don't mind if I do."

Chapter 5

If the stars were big and bright in Texas, they were awesome in New Mexico. Sydney arranged herself on the rock she'd begun to think of as her own and searched the heavens for an answer to her problems, much as philosophers had done for the past ten thousand and more years. She had no more luck than they'd had.

The stars did help dissipate whatever tension was left after her long run over the ranch roads, as the soft night breeze helped cool her skin. The run had become a necessary part of her evening routine. Only after expending energy was she able to sleep in the antique carved wood bed, under the handmade quilts. The bed was too strange, too large, and far too empty. She buried that thought as counter-productive to relaxation.

Sydney knew men. She'd worked with them, sparred with them, trained with them, talked with them, helped them through their problems. Never before had she felt a burning ache for one particular man, a need to touch and be touched. To care and be cared for. She was bothered by the intensity of her unrest, and by her lack of will when it came to Devin. Her loss of control tonight probably blew any chance to be with him one last time.

A sound, just an insignificant shuffle, brought her inner muscles into play. Someone stood off to one side, watching her intently. She knew someone had been aware of her every night, which was to be expected. But this was different.

The shuffle again, as though it were a deliberate action on the part of the watcher to let her know she was not alone. Sydney raised her face to the stars, breathing deeply, then let her head fall forward.

"Do you realize how dangerous it could be out here for you?"

"Do you realize there are more crimes committed in one weekend in Los Angeles than are committed in the whole state of New Mexico in a year?"

"It only takes one, Sydney." As he spoke, Devin moved closer to the rock. "Next time you want to go for a run at night, call me. You could trip while you're running and it would be morning before anyone would miss you."

Sydney doubted that, but she saw no purpose in the discussion. Instead, she turned away, resting her chin on her drawn-up knees. A slight shrug conveyed her opinion of his concern.

She heard his quickly indrawn breath and suppressed her impulse to smile. When he moved to sit next to her, his body heat reached out to the part of her that had become very lonely these last few days. The silence stretched between them.

"Sydney, why did you let me think you were Ty's woman?"

"I didn't. That was your decision. I simply didn't bother to argue with you about it."

"You're not."

"I know."

Both of them stared at the stars, and watched a sliver of the moon move across the sky.

"You're mine."

The benefits of hard exercise and meditating left in a rush. Whatever his game had become, Sydney saw no reason to stay around and find out. Uncoiling her legs, she pushed away from the rock, intending to hit the ground in stride.

Her feet never touched the ground. Devin's reach was long, his aim accurate. Almost lazily, he pulled her back against his broad, hard chest. A quick shift, and she was on her back on the rock, the sky blocked out by the width of his shoulders. His chest pinned her upper body and he supported the bulk of his weight on his forearms, surrounding her with his heat.

Feeling the tension in the body pressed against hers, she willed herself to be very still. Experience should have taught her to not aggravate a man like Devin when he was in this kind of a mood. But she'd never been one to take the easy way out.

"I'm not yours, Devin. I'm not a piece of property to be shuffled back and forth at the whim of anyone."

She didn't expect an explosion of soft laughter to shake his body and warm the breath ruffling her hair. Large hands framed her face, holding her still for his intent appraisal. His long, rough fingers caressed her neck and burrowed into her hair.

"You are mine, Sydney. It's about time you found that out."

She had that warning, and the tightening of his fingers in her hair, to prepare herself for the onslaught of his mouth. There was no hesitancy in his kiss. It was basic, primal, the action of the dominant male, seeking to establish authority over his female. His thumbs moved against her jaw, urging her mouth to open and accept his invading tongue.

Now, when it was too late, Sydney remembered old lessons she'd learned. This was Devin. It was his taste in her mouth, his weight on her chest, his aroused male body beginning to edge closer to its goal. But her body recalled other times. She prepared herself for the aggressive possession, for the act that would bring him relief and would leave her hurting in carelessly used places and aching in an untouched spot deep within herself.

❧❧❧

Devin shifted, attempting to ease some of his need by pressing himself against her thigh. She tasted so good, so clean and sweet, and her body felt so right against his. She wasn't fighting him off. She wasn't doing anything at all.

He tore his mouth away. Sydney lay still beneath him,

her eyes closed, her breathing shallow and even. Too even. He could feel the effort of the control she exerted over herself in the subtle trembling of her body. Frowning, he eased his fingers from her hair and stroked along her cheekbones. Her skin was cool, as though chilled from deep within.

"Sydney? Honey, what's wrong?"

Starlight glinted off the flat silver of her eyes as she stared at him silently. Her mouth, slightly parted, moist from his kisses, looked no less inviting than it had the night he met her. But there was no welcome in the stillness of her face. She looked ready for the worst.

Devin lifted his body off the soft temptation of hers and shifted to one side, bracing himself on an elbow. He continued to trace his fingers gently across the angles of her face, the softness of her neck. Finally, warmth began to flow beneath her skin, and her breathing deepened fractionally. Finally, the trembling stopped, and the tension eased out of the body so close to his, yet so far away.

"If you didn't want me to kiss you, Sydney, all you had to do was say no. You didn't have to make a sacrifice out of it."

For a long moment, she stared at him, unblinking. Then her lashes lowered. A deep breath eased into her lungs, bringing her breasts dangerously close to his arm.

"I wasn't saying no, Devin."

"You sure as hell weren't saying yes." Devin studied her face. There were none of the subtle signs of arousal he'd seen while they were in Los Angeles. He remembered the soft warmth in her eyes, the sidelong glances when she thought he wasn't looking, the slight color when he looked too obviously. She had the look now of a woman hurt badly by someone they had trusted. He knew he hadn't hurt her. Then, who—

"Sydney, what kind of a man was your husband?"

Once again, he held a rigid body against his side. There was caution in the look she turned on him.

"He was like you in many ways."

"What the hell do you mean by that?"

"He was a man's man. He believed women were put on earth to be decorative, and available when he wanted them."

"Is that what you think?"

"That's what you think, Devin. You're nicer about it, more civilized, and you don't seem to enjoy demeaning women…" She hesitated, a small frown forming between her eyes as she searched for words. "Still, you would prefer women on their backs, with their mouths shut and their legs open."

He squashed down the rumble of laughter threatening to rise from inside. "That position has some merit," he teased. Then he heard his own words, and the desire to laugh dissipated. Along with it went the last of his arousal. He rested his forehead against hers, cradling her body. "God, I have acted like that. What a bastard I've been."

Devin felt the tension slowly leave her. She lay against him, unmoving, but at least she was no longer rigid. He took a deep breath, daring to risk what little trust she offered.

"I do want you, Sydney."

"Devin, don't."

"Don't what? Don't want you?"

"Don't ruin it like this. You won't like it."

"Honey, if it's with you, I'll like it."

"No you won't, and then you won't like me any-more."

Finally, Devin understood the nature of her insecurity, and the cause. "Where is he now?"

"Who?"

"That bastard who called himself your husband." He didn't try to hide the menace in his voice, or the intent.

"He's dead."

"He's lucky. Damned lucky." Devin thought of the ways he would have enjoyed hurting the man who had so deeply wounded Sydney. All the while, he stroked her hair, her face, and wanted her desperately.

"Sleep with me tonight, Sydney."

"Dammit, Devin, we just went over that. No."

"I said sleep. We've already slept together. You do that very well."

At last some humor slid back into her, softening her mouth into a small smile. Still, she shook her head.

"I haven't slept worth a damn since we got here, and neither have you."

She couldn't argue with him about that. Not when the shadows beneath her eyes grew darker every day.

"Just sleep?" She couldn't hide the wistful note in her voice. It sounded so sweet, so tempting, he wanted to crush her against himself.

Instead, he cupped her face in his large palm, forcing her to look directly at him. "Just sleep."

ↄ✧ↄ✧ↄ

She huddled well to one side of his huge bed, only her chestnut hair showing under the dark patterned quilt. Stifling a chuckle, Devin slipped out of his clothes and into his bed, leaving on his snug briefs. It would take a while to bring his fox to hand, and he was going to enjoy every minute of it. Knowing she wore one of his tee shirts added spice to the game.

The bed shifted under his weight, and his rough, bare calf brushed against her smooth leg. She lifted her head, bracing herself to not roll farther in his direction. "Don't you have any pajamas?" she blurted then looked disgusted with herself as her face heated up.

"I usually sleep in my skin. This is a compromise," Devin murmured while he settled himself. The blush was more adorable than he'd thought it would be. There was little sign now of the self-assured woman. Now she looked strangely defenseless, peering through hair that had fallen into her eyes. After a slight hesitation, she lay back down, keeping a broad expanse of mattress between them. As though she thought he wouldn't want to touch her.

"Wrong, Sydney." Devin rolled onto his side and reached across the bed. "We're going to sleep together. I want to hold you while you sleep." At the thought of holding her warm, supple body against his, he felt himself grow hard.

She tensed like a half-tamed creature about to bolt. Devin hesitated, then slowly lifted his hand and fell over onto his back. He stared at the ceiling, forcing deep breaths and counting slowly until he felt confident he could speak without cursing. Only then did he turn his head on the pillow and look over at her.

"Did I scare you again?"

Soft chestnut hair flew around her strained face as Sydney shook her head abruptly. "No, I scared myself. I haven't—I don't—I've never wanted anyone to touch me before," she said in a rush, drawing in her breath quickly at the end.

"You weren't this spooky in the truck."

"There we shared a space. Here, we're—sleeping together."

"And?" Humor was beginning to soften his frustration. Even now, when his body felt like it was about to explode, she was as fun to tease as he had thought.

"I don't know. Since I met you I…Devin, I just don't know."

"Take it easy. It's not the end of the world. No." He lifted his hand, forestalling any further talk. "We're both too tired and too wound up right now to talk about it. Let's try something else." He shifted onto his side, stretching his muscular arm out along the edge of the pillows. "Lay your head on my arm, babe. Get as close as you feel comfortable."

It was a gradual thing, but eventually she was within feeling distance of his body. After shifting several times, she found the best way to rest her head on him. His arm embraced her unthreateningly when he bent his elbow and laid his hand gently, naturally, on her arm.

Once she was settled, once her cheek rested on his upper arm and her hair tumbled across his shoulder, Devin let out the breath he'd been holding. Any heat he may have felt was subdued as he realized how much of an effort it was for Sydney to trust him even this far.

The stiffness began to leave her slender body although her eyes remained opened, silver gaze fixed on his face. A tiny frown drew her brows together. Unable to help himself, Devin reached out with his free hand and touched that frown. How delicate she seemed next to him. She looked so alone, so tempting, curled up on her side, clutching the comforter under her chin. Not yet, he cautioned himself, his eager body. Wait.

"So serious. So sweet. Sydney, did your husband hurt you?"

The expected stiffness didn't develop, but he felt her mental withdrawal. He knew this wouldn't be something she'd be accustomed to discussing, so he practiced patience and waited for her to breathe again.

"What do you mean by hurt?"

"Mock you, belittle you, ridicule you, hit you, beat you. Did he hurt you in any way?"

"Yes."

"Yes, what?"

"Yes, sir?" She forced a tiny smile, but at least she was breathed more easily.

"Sydney," Devin warned, wanting to crush her against his chest for her attempt at a joke.

"I married Rick when I was still in college. No one had ever—Dad had never been much for emotional demonstrations, although he would never intentionally demean anyone. Rick started picking at me about my courses, my cooking, then about anything he knew made me sensitive. He was good at going for the jugular."

"Did he hit you?"

"One day he started an argument and—I lost my temper. I guess, since I flew at him, he decided he had the right to hit me. When he was done, he left. As soon as I could, I left also, and never went back." It was all said in as remote a voice as he'd heard in years, while she concentrated on a point just beyond his shoulder.

"You aren't blaming yourself, are you?"

At this, Sydney brought her attention to Devin's face. "I lost my temper, Devin."

"That don't mean diddly. No man has the right to hit a woman."

"Does a woman have the right to hit a man without expecting retaliation?"

"Must you always be so damned rational?" Devin shifted until he could look directly at her. He stroked her hair back with a gentle hand, enjoying the cool feel of it between his fingers. She nuzzled her cheek against his palm, and he felt himself harden dangerously. "No, a woman doesn't have the right to hit a man without expecting some kind of retaliation. But women are made smaller and softer so men can take care of them, not so they'll be easier to beat up."

Sydney grimaced, as though wanting to argue but not

sure how to convince him he was wrong. Devin knew his chauvinist opinions irritated her, but she was going to have to get used to it. A soft touch on her cheek intruded on her dilemma.

"Stop thinking so hard, honey. Just let yourself relax and get some sleep."

He felt her trust grow as he caressed the petal softness of her cheek and traced her lips. Once she settled against him, the dim light was turned off, and covers were pulled up over both of them, trapping in their body heat.

❦❦❦

Caught in the shadow land between sleep and waking, Sydney arched her back against the massaging fingers, edging closer to what her dozing mind identified as the source of the feelings. She felt trapped in a particularly realistic dream, a memory of something that had never really happened. The warmth enticed her, and she gave in to the temptation. She nestled into a body scent that had become as familiar as her own, sliding her fingers through thick hair to cup smooth skin over tense muscles. Still the hand stroked her back and the fingers played along her spine.

In an effort to get even closer, to merge with the body against hers, she drew her leg up over the hair-covered hardness of the thigh so close, so tempting. Then the ultra-sensitive inner surface of her thigh encountered a different hardness, a pulsing, shivering hardness barely enclosed in soft fabric.

No longer dozing, her mind sent out two commands: to wake up before she did something stupid, and to move her leg out of the danger zone. Before she could decide if she really wanted to obey either command, the hands once more swept down her back and up again, soothing and warming her through the T-shirt he'd given her to sleep in.

"Yes, I'm hard." Devin's voice rumbled under her ear, and his breath stirred her scalp. "I've been so hard for you, for so long, I've come to think of it as a natural state of being. No, I'm not going to do anything about it. Not tonight. Not now, at any rate. You just get back to snuggling up against me and making those sweet noises."

Sydney raised her head, striving to regain control of her mental faculties. She could barely make out his features in the dim light filtering through the windows. "Very good. Is that some kind of line you've developed to soothe nervous females?"

First the body beneath her became very still. Then she was rocked violently as Devin roared with laughter. His brawny arms encompassed her, holding her against him in an embrace that could have been painful, but wasn't.

"Do you always enjoy tormenting your men in bed?"

She hesitated, considering the question. "No, I don't think so. But I don't have any men."

"Not now, of course," he said with a broad streak of arrogance. "But surely you've had one or two lovers since..." His voice trailed off as Sydney shook her head slowly, in the negative. "Nothing since your husband? Why the hell not?"

She felt his question vibrate under her body as well as

hearing it roared from entirely too close. In spite of the power of his voice, he still held her gently against his body, and his hands never ceased massaging her back. If it hadn't been for the subject matter, and her knowledge of what could happen at any moment, she would have been a boneless puddle of contentment.

So she controlled herself and answered matter-of-factly. "Why bother? It was obvious where the dates were leading. Why should I waste my time when the culmination of the evening was messy and boring and—" Realizing where her burst of candor led, Sydney ducked her head, instinctively seeking shelter against his chest.

"Keep going, Sydney. This is just getting interesting." Devin threaded his fingers into her hair and lifted her head to stare directly into her eyes. "What else is it besides 'messy and boring'?"

"Painful." She pulled away from him, preparing to roll off his body. Again, he stopped her with an unyielding hold.

"No, you stay right there. I like having you for a blanket. Why was it painful?" His voice was as gentle as the fingers that sought out and eased the tension in her neck, and as inflexible as the arm that held her in place against the solidity of his torso.

"I don't know, it just was, okay?" She was in no mood to be soothed, especially not when the oddest sensations radiated from everywhere their bodies touched. Every time Devin shifted, every time he breathed, she felt his muscles flex against her. Her legs were still half on the bed, but she sensed the tantalizing hardness of him, so close to her thigh. "Devin, you've had your fun for tonight. Will you just let me get some sleep?"

Something, that could almost be hurt, flickered across his mind before he smiled and tightened his hold. "Wrong again, Sydney. My fun's not yet begun."

He watched her from between lowered eyelids. Under his old T-shirt was warm, smooth skin he ached to touch. But not yet. Not quite yet. When she relaxed, he resumed stroking her back.

"That's better. It looks like we both have some old baggage we'd like to dump." He rested his chin on the softness of her hair and looked along the body draped across his.

Their combined body heat had been uncomfortable to him, and he'd eased back the blankets.

The shirt Sydney wore, softened by many washings, faithfully outlined the slenderness of her back and the enticingly feminine flare of her hips. Her legs were still covered by the sheet, which was just as well. He was hard enough just imagining her.

"Sydney, let's forget, just for tonight, that we were ever hurt, ever knew someone who used us for whatever reason." He was shocked by the words coming out of his mouth, but not at the rightness he felt saying them. "Just for tonight, let's pretend we're two kids, and it's the first time for both of us."

She raised her head, regarding him warily between narrowed eyes. "Isn't that rather unrealistic?"

"I don't think so. I think we both need some good memories to overcome the ones we have. Just for tonight.

We were too embarrassed to stop at the drug store, so we can't go too far."

"If you're trying to tell me you missed out on some of life's finer experiences when you were a kid, I'll be happy to take your deposit on a bridge."

Again Devin shook with laughter, cradling her body against his, feeling a comfort and union he had never before experienced with a woman. "You are a treasure. I don't know how I kept away from you."

"Then we're about even. I don't know why."

It was flung at him in a quiet, even voice, as one would offer a challenge to duel. Devin studied the woman he held against his chest, seeing the honest confusion on her face.

"You puzzled me, Sydney. Right from the beginning, I wanted you, and you didn't seem unaware of me. I've known so many women who played games with men's heads, I didn't realize at first that you don't."

"You judged me by your extensive memories," she teased, but there was hurt underlying the light words.

"Have you been doing anything different? From the moment we met, you've been judging me against your ex-husband, or someone else from your past."

Sydney stared at him, speechless. He was right. She had seen him as part of the timeless tapestry of Warriors. He walked with the automatic grace of a predator, and she had categorized him as a creature of instinctive impulses he would not be able to control. At best, she granted him a limited emotional maturity.

As her thoughts raced, her mouth dropped open and

her tongue swept along her lower lip. Devin's eyes darkened to antique gold as he stared at her mouth.

Giving her every chance to retreat, he raised his head. It was a surprisingly chaste kiss at first, their lips seeking, heads tilting until they shared the feeling on every part of their mouths. His tongue slid out to touch and taste the inside of her lips then eased between her teeth.

A mutual sigh escaped them.

૯౨૯౨

This wasn't kissing, Sydney thought, stroking her tongue along the length of his. This was too beautiful, too arousing, to be merely kissing. She would find the right word for it. Later.

Too soon, Devin lowered his head, separating the perfect union of their mouths. After only a slight hesitation, Sydney followed him down, nestling her lips against his in an attempt to recreate the contact. Now she was a creature of instinct, seeking only to feel more of him.

She nibbled at his lower lip, holding it gently between her teeth and stroking with her tongue. So good. It felt so good to lie against him like this, sliding her tongue along his in a hot, gliding caress unlike any she had ever experienced. Devin gave back willingly every touch she offered. When she sought to wriggle closer he shifted his hold on her, helping until she lay fully on top of him, her legs resting along his. Sydney felt her bones melting in the heat rising from his body.

"Devin?" Sydney raised her head, crossing her forearms on his muscular chest and resting her chin on her clasped hands. "Any time you want to jump in, feel free. We're coming close to the end of my experience level."

Devin's deep, even breaths raised and lowered her like the ocean under a sailing ship. His large, calloused hands rested against her hips, holding her steady without pressure. If the smile on his lips was a bit pained, it was not overly so.

He was aroused. There was no way, lying together as they were, that he could hide the extent or heat of his arousal. Still, he made no move to deepen the kiss or take anything from her.

"You just keep right on with what you're doing, Sydney. I see nothing to complain about so far."

"Is this some sort of macho pop psychology game?"

"No, this is me, enjoying as much of you as I can get."

"Are you going to try that line about only wanting as much as I want to give?" She knew she was revealing a lifetime of bad experiences in her question.

"Damn, you *have* been around losers. No, Sydney, I want you to take as much as you want. I'll get my pleasure out of you finding yours."

It sounded enticing, and a little bit scary.

"What if this is all I want?"

"A little holding and some touching is all you want?"

"For now?"

"Your husband was one of those bastards who only touched you when he wanted sex." There was no question in Devin's voice, only cold certainty. He didn't bother to wait for her reply. "Honey, I won't lie to you. I'd like to take you now, so hot and deep you'll forget anything you ever thought you knew about men. But something tells me right now you need the comfort part of loving a lot more than you need the sex part." His hands resumed their soothing, arousing patterns on her back.

Devin felt himself fall under the spell of his own words.

Suddenly panicked, Sydney sought to push herself back from the brink she seemed to teeter on. "What makes you so damned smart?"

"If I said experience, you'd probably hit me. If I said I was born knowing what you need, you'd think it was a line. Let's just say my instincts are working overtime, and leave it at that."

He cradled her lush bottom in his palms, pulling her gently against his arousal, bringing himself to iron-hard readiness. Who would've thought he could find so much pleasure in teasing himself? The easing of the tension in Sydney's body as she melted against him, even going so far as to cradle him in the apex of her thighs, was almost as rewarding as fulfilling the fantasies he'd been weaving for a week. Almost.

After a moment, she rested her cheek against his chest and her hands reached up, her slender fingers threading through his hair. It wasn't a perfect union, but Devin found more pleasure in the almost-chaste contact than in hours of hot sex with other women.

Who the hell was he kidding? He was so hard he was about to explode. It was only his belief that Sydney needed this time that kept him from rolling over her and burying himself in the warm, moist heat he could felt against the agonizing sensitivity of his erection. That, and the certainty that any rushing now could ruin their chances for something better later. She had to learn he could be trusted to control himself.

It became moot very quickly. Soothed by the contact, Sydney fell sweetly asleep on top of him. What man could seduce a woman who lay against him so trustingly, and still call himself a man?

Chapter 6

A note on the neatly folded jeans and western-style shirt told her to take it easy until Devin returned. It had been many years since Sydney had waited on a man's whim. Now would not be a starting point. Nor did she want to be moping around his house while he was having second thoughts and avoiding her.

A walk in the mountains seemed to be the best idea. In spite of everyone's protective attitude, she'd managed to explore many of the trails at the ranch. She considered riding, but her running shoes were more suited to hiking, and she could easily out walk the horses they let her ride. Besides, if Devin weren't at the barn, the men there would probably have orders to not let her have a horse. For her own good, of course.

Sydney knew about rejection. What she hadn't picked up from her mother she'd quickly learned from her husband. For a brief time, the night before, she'd forgotten that she sometimes read too much into other people's reactions. What she'd seen as sexual attraction had been friendly affection. Not that there was anything wrong with friendship. But it was particularly galling when the most intimate part of your body was in close contact with a fully aroused male, and all he wanted to do was pet you.

The rational, scrupulous part of her did admit it had felt good to be held so closely, so tenderly. Another part questioned what was missing in her, if the only man who caught her interest took her to bed just to sleep with her? How much sleep had Lana ever gotten with a man?

Sydney made a rude sound at herself, startling a jackrabbit that, lulled by her stillness, had dared to venture into the meadow. The rabbit streaked for the safety of the high grass, then doubled back, going into hiding under a fallen log. Moving back, Sydney sank into herself, becoming one with the rocks around her.

"I thought I told you to stay put until I got back."

A night's sleep had obviously done nothing for Devin's attitude. Nor had it adversely affected his appearance. Sitting tall on the sturdy bay horse she'd seen him riding before, he emerged from the dark forest like one of the mountain men coming to conquer the land.

Sydney had chosen a high perch among the rocks. For once, she was on eye level with him. It wasn't quite the advantage she'd thought it would be. Even from ten feet away, his golden eyes pierced with the mesmerizing glare of a predator. This time, she would not let it affect her.

"I wasn't aware I was supposed to clear my day's activities with you." When the brooding silence stretched into an uncomfortable span, she added, "I suppose I have you to thank for the clothes."

∽∾∽

Sydney sat absolutely still, hugging her knees to her chest, tilting her chin up in that way she had that drove him wild. She looked so good to him, perched among the rocks and fallen trees, radiating insecure defiance. Wild flowers blossomed in stray patches of soil around her. Like the wild flowers, she could bloom in the weakest soil. How much longer was he going to be able to keep his hands off her?

"I had Maria bring over some things for you. We can go pack the rest later." He worked hard to make it a request, not a command.

"You're so sure I want to stay at your house with you?"

"I'm so sure I want you to."

"Why, Devin?" Using both hands, Sydney pushed her hair back off her face. "How will you benefit from where I stay?"

"You're judging again, Sydney. Would you rather stay somewhere else?"

"I didn't think what I wanted had anything to do with it."

"Now what the hell are you talking about?"

"Never mind." She stood and bent over to brush pine needles from her jeans.

"Typical female. You say something that makes

absolutely no sense, then expect me to either interpret it or ignore it."

"What a surprise. You actually see something female in me. Even if it is negative." She stretched slightly, bracing her back to loosen muscles that hadn't appreciated sitting on rocks.

Devin felt his mouth drop open. From the shock, of course. Not from the hunger generated when she ran her hands over her hips and down her legs, dislodging leaves that were lucky enough to be close to her. Controlling his need to attack her body, he thought about what she'd just said, and how she'd said it. As though she'd been hurt, not helped, by the night before.

"You're the one with a problem seeing yourself as a female."

"More cowboy philosophy?" Sydney asked idly, choosing the easiest path down the rocks.

A feral growl was her only warning. Devin was off his horse and by her side in one flowing motion. "That mouth of yours is going to get you in real trouble one day."

⌘

His hands curled around her rib cage. She let him lift her down from the rocks, let him pull her closer as he set her feet on the ground. When she felt the tense hunger in his body, she pushed away.

"I'm sure you have better things to do than waste time chatting with me, Devin. I won't cut any further into your social life. You obviously need to visit your woman."

"That does it." Devin reached for the zipper on her jacket. One fierce tug opened it, with an ominous tearing sound at the bottom. Before she could pull away, his large hands were inside the jacket, easing it off of her, then holding her steady, thumbs just below her breasts. "My woman is right here, dammit. It's time she realized that."

Sydney stood very still between his hands. Wanting, but afraid to want too much. His face lowered, blocking out the sun. Warm breath flowed across her face, caressing her mouth before his lips could, melting the icy wall around her heart.

It was a surprisingly gentle kiss. His lips pressed and lifted, tasted and left, then settled in for a long joining. When she slid her arms around his waist, seeking more, he cradled her against him, his arm firm around her back.

"Yeah. Like that, babe. Get closer," he murmured against her lips, tasting her in tiny licks.

Sydney felt his fingers at the front of her shirt, felt buttons being pushed through holes, felt the first touch of his long, hard fingers on her skin. She had no time to feel fear, only impatience. Rising on her toes, she completed the union of their mouths as she put her hands to work on his shirt.

Snaps were better than buttons. It required only a sharp tug to open his shirt and give her clear access to the warm strength of his chest. She'd made only a brief, unsatisfying acquaintance with this part of him the night before, and she wanted so much more.

Before she could feel embarrassed because her breasts were barely large enough to need a bra, the fastening was undone and Devin was cherishing her with his hands, rubbing his thumbs over her tender nipples, pulling her close until she felt the rough heat of his chest against hers.

This time his kiss pillaged, stealing her breath as he gave her his own. Sydney wasn't worried about breathing. Something wonderful was happening, and she didn't want to risk missing any of it. When his big hands cupped her bottom, pulling her closer, she coiled her arms around his neck, pressing her breasts against his body, pulling at his head to take more and more of him.

"Sydney," Devin said, gasping against her neck. "I want you."

She froze in his arms. "Not here. Not now."

"Yes. Here. Now. Where I can see all of you." He slid his hands down her arms, pushing her shirt off, exposing her to his hungry gaze.

The sun bathed her body, caressing the promise of taut nipples and highlighting the delicate strength of her arms, the ivory beauty of her pale skin. Devin retained enough sense to move them away from the rocks, to find a spot in the high meadow grass that was more protected, to lay their jackets down as a partial bed. Once their bodies touched in a yearning stroke, he lost what little sense he still had.

Clothes were pulled, yanked and slithered out of. Her shoes were a nuisance but nothing could stop the force of their desire, their passion. Devin shrugged off his shirt, and attacked his belt, hindered by small, eager, trembling hands. He pushed down his jeans and briefs. It would have to be enough.

They fell against each other, both groaning as they felt the bliss of the contact.

"Sydney. Babe, my timing stinks, but I don't have—"

"Now, Devin. Please." Her small hands tugged with amazing strength, pulling him over onto her. In the full light of the sun, she opened herself to him.

Devin sank into her, covering her, taking her mouth as he took her body, damning the consequences, claiming her as his mate, his woman. Reality slipped away.

It lasted forever. It was over too soon. Devin came back to himself, to the delightful feeling of her body under his. So fragile. So strong. He remembered how, at the height of his attack, her legs had wound around his waist, urging him on.

Now she lay very still, her eyes closed as though shutting out the world for just a little longer. A tiny smile lifted the corners of her generous mouth. As he eased away from her, a frown shadowed her face.

"I hurt you."

Sydney reached out to hold him before he could pull away. "No, Devin." She murmured, as she lifted a slender leg over his hips. "Having you inside me made me feel complete, for the first time. I just felt so empty when you left."

He thought he'd appeased his hunger, but at her honest words, it began all over again. Impossible. Maybe when he was a kid, but not now.

Quelling the shocking reaction, he turned to cuddle her closely against his side, sliding his leg between hers and wishing he had taken the time to remove his jeans so he could enjoy the feel of her all over his body. "Don't go to sleep, babe. You'll have a sunburn in some pretty strange places."

"You're big enough to shade me."

The rumble of his uninhibited laughter filled the mountain meadow. His arms swept her close as he rolled onto his back, arranging her along his body.

"Now who's getting shade?"

Sydney squirmed, actually giggling. Then she lay absolutely still against him and her bottomless gray eyes grew large. "Devin," she said, a note of awe in her voice.

"I told you, you make me hard. You think I'd be used to it by now. No, Sydney. Don't." Suddenly firm hands held her when she would have sat up to explore what was happening. "Once I could almost excuse. But not a second time. Not without protection."

Sydney knew her chances of conception were slim. It was one of the side effects to the intense training she put her body through. But there would be no arguing with him. For now, she could draw comfort from the feeling of his body against hers, and from knowing he was in no hurry to leave her.

So this was what it was like to feel beautiful. The strength and toughness of his large body made her feel dainty and feminine for the first time in her life.

His care for her, never getting rough even when he'd been aroused, protecting her from his weight, made her feel precious, and more of a woman than ever before.

ﻌﻌﻌ

"I told you you'd get a sunburn."

"You're one of those people who can't resist a chance to rub it in, aren't you?"

"None of that sexy talk, lady. Not when I'm being noble."

As he spoke, Devin helped her ease into the loose blue shirt and fasten what buttons were left. They'd only dozed for a brief time, but Sydney was already a delicate pink in some very fragile areas. Since he had plans for those areas, Devin had forced himself to shake her out of the satiated sprawl that made him feel like the greatest lover on ten continents.

"My bra..." She looked around for it then saw part of it protruding from Devin's jacket pocket.

"You're gonna hurt too much to have it on pretty soon. Besides, I want to feel you, behind me."

The drawling anticipation in his voice stilled any comment on her part about there not being enough to feel. Instead, she accepted the rest of her clothing as he found it and tossed it to her. It wasn't as much fun to pull clothing onto her lethargic body as it had been to remove it with Devin's help. Every button and zipper seemed to be in collusion, and nothing wanted to slide on as easily as it had come off.

"If you don't want a repeat of what just happened, you'll stop that right now."

She looked up from struggling into her jeans, to find Devin watching her with the meager patience of a predator. Never losing eye contact, she closed the zipper, fastened the button, then buckled the belt with excruciating care. Rising to her feet, she smoothed the wrinkles out of her jeans and casually looked around for her socks and shoes.

"Witch." Laughter took away the bite in his voice as he scooped her up and deposited her on the saddle of the patiently waiting bay horse. Both feet dangled on one side and he brushed her soles before producing her thick socks. "You have sexy toes, lady." He fingered her fuchsia colored toenails, in contrast to the sophisticated mauve which decorated her fingers. "You're a sexy lady from head to toe."

Sydney managed a bittersweet smile. For now, she would let herself believe it. For now, she would forget how much it could hurt, and would hurt, when he tired of her. For now, she would let herself think she deserved him and could be woman enough to hold him. For now.

❦❦❦

She was still asleep on his couch. Swathed in his favorite old dark blue wool shirt, she nestled against tapestry pillows, a hand-loomed blanket across her legs. He'd put the blanket over her himself when he returned to the house half an hour before. It was meant as a deterrent to the erotic images trying to control his thoughts and had helped while he showered and dressed in the other room. He doubted it would work any longer.

She looked good in his shirt. She looked good in his house. In spite of what had happened in the meadow, he knew she had no idea how vibrantly lovely her sleek elegance was to him. The world was overloaded with tall, bosomy predators. There was only one Sydney.

And she was his, dammit. No matter what ridiculous feminist crap she could come up with, she'd been created to stand at his side and fill the void in his soul. This he knew as surely as he knew the approach of a storm or the scent of danger.

She stirred, as though sensing his presence though he'd made no sound crossing the room to stand behind the couch. Her awareness of the world around her was amazing for a woman who had spent her life in civilization. Slowly, her lashes lifted and tired gray eyes peered up at him.

"Ty expects us for dinner," Devin said, grinning at the size of the yawn she couldn't control.

"How does he expect us to dress?"

Devin leaned over the back of the couch. "Not like that." She smelled of hot showers and high meadows and he didn't know how he was going to keep his hands off her long enough to eat dinner.

Sydney watched his face harden as he looked down at her without speaking again. One large hand raised, reached for her, then fell onto the back of the sofa.

"Devin?" What was probably meant to be a self-confident tone came out as something of a croak. "I—we never got any of the rest of my clothes, and I needed something to wear. Do you mind?"

"Mind? The only thing I mind is that any part of you is covered up." Giving up his quest for restraint, he vaulted over the back of the couch, landing lightly beside her. "It's too bad dinner is early here. But that means we can go to bed earlier."

He touched the shirt, running his fingers down the buttons, trying to decide if it would be worth the time to unbutton or if he should trash the shirt and get to the good stuff. The only thing stopping him was the hesitant look in her eyes. Sydney could save a failing company or take on an unruly stallion single handed, but still had no confidence in herself as a woman.

"You thought I'd dropped you off here and forgotten you, didn't you?"

"I'm sure you had more important things to take care of." She worked very hard to not expose the insecurity of being made love to so fiercely then deposited like a used video.

"I had something to take care of I couldn't ignore any longer. All I could think about while I was gone was how you looked up in that meadow."

"Desperate?"

"Incredibly, mind-bogglingly, sexy."

"That's me, Syd, the sex goddess."

"You aren't just sexy, Sydney." He cupped her face between his hands. "You're funny and smart and you care. In my book, that makes you beautiful all the way to your bones." He forced her to meet his probing gaze. "You have no idea how sexy you are like this. Your eyes are barely open, your face is all soft from sleeping, your hair is begging me to feel it." He allowed himself to look down her body, enjoying every subtle sign of her growing awareness. "Did you know your nipples show through this shirt? No you don't." He captured her hands as she sought to cover the telltale peaks. The ensuing struggle pulled the wool material back and forth across her breasts, increasing the friction.

With a barely suppressed groan of expectation, Devin brought her across his lap and sat back on the couch. He entrusted both of her delicate wrists to one large hand, keeping her his sensual prisoner by holding her hands in the small of her back. This arched her gracefully, lifting her breasts even more under the loose shirt.

Holding her gaze with his own, Devin reached for the buttons of the shirt she wore. He had the control now to release them one at a time. Neither of them looked down, but carried on an in-depth conversation with their eyes. When the shirt hung open, he lifted his hand to her hair, running his fingers through the tousled strands, cupping the delicate heat at the nape of her neck as he pulled her forward.

"I went wild in that meadow, and I didn't take the time you deserve." He kissed her mouth in passing, sliding his tongue along the smooth ridges of her teeth, sucking on her lower lip. When she stirred, seeking a closer union with his mouth and body, he lifted her to straddle his lap.

With his free hand, he pushed open the shirt and framed her body in dark blue. As the woven material slid across her nipples Sydney quivered, biting back a whimper

He trailed a long finger around her breast, stroking up to, but not quite touching, the peak. Pulling against the gentle restraint, Sydney tried to arch into his touch.

"Gently, babe. You're so delicate, so sensitive."

"I'm not. It's never—" She gasped as his large hand cradled one breast, pressing the peak into his palm. "Rick didn't like to—"

"We don't need to talk about that inconsiderate bastard," he said roughly, but his touch on her body was gentle. Cupping her breast, he leaned down to press delicate kisses on her soft skin, never changing his rhythm no matter how strongly she squirmed to free herself. Her struggles only arched her more toward him and got him even harder.

Finally, he touched her nipple with tiny, cherishing strokes of his tongue. Closing his eyes, he concentrated on the taste of her, the musky aroused female scent of her, the passion dewing her skin. He released her wrists, slid his hand down to cup her bottom and pulled her more firmly against him. It eased his own aching flesh for a brief second.

She grabbed at his shoulders, digging into the taut muscles, not sure if she should push or pull. "Devin, please."

He took hold of her knees, spreading them even wider before his hands slipped up her thighs. His thumbs met at her center, pressing lightly against the soft damp cotton of her panties. Slowly, as his mouth traveled leisurely across her chest to her other breast, he slid his thumbs under the elastic.

"So hot. So wet." His thumbs zeroed in on the tiny pulsating nub as he opened his mouth over her nipple and sucked gently.

Sydney gave herself over to his care. His lips were pursed around her breast, his eyes squeezed shut, and his face showed equal amounts of pleasure and pain. Every touch of his fingers, every pull of his mouth and tongue, was controlled, gentle, aimed solely at giving her pleasure. She clutched at his hair as she felt the shock race through every nerve in her body. A wild, keening cry burst from her throat.

When it was past, she sat limply on his thighs, supported by his arm, her cheek against his hair. His large hand was inside her panties, nestled in the thatch of damp hair, seeking the last faint tremors. He comforted her with soft kisses that wandered across the valleys and aching peaks of her chest. She stirred, pressed against his hand and shivered.

"Devin, what about you?"

"Turning you on turns me on."

"But—" One small hand traveled down his chest to the evidence of his aching need. She touched him hesitantly.

"Babe, don't." When she would have pulled her hand away he abandoned his warm moist nest and grabbed her wrist, holding her against him without moving. "I was going to wake you up for dinner. Then I just wanted to pet you a little. I was on you like a starving beast out there."

"I wasn't complaining," she said. Turning her hand under the restraint, she slid his button free of the hole and reached for the zipper. The sound of the zipper being released tooth by tooth was a counterpoint to their uneven breaths.

Amused, intrigued by her new boldness, he leaned back to watch her, offering silent encouragement. In this area she was so unsure of herself. He could tolerate a little torture for her sake.

It was a blissful torture. Her small cool hands slid around his pulsing heat, exploring tentatively. Patiently, he guided her in the ways of pleasing him, and nearly lost it all in the process. He slid trembling fingers into his shirt pocket, bringing out the ubiquitous foil packet.

While she opened the packet, frowning in concentration, and sheathed his eager hardness, he lifted her, sliding her panties off. Holding her hips steady, he eased slowly into her moist heat, completing them both. He closed his eyes and held her, savoring the moment, the rightness of their union and the utter trust in how she gave her body.

"Devin," she whispered, squirming to free her hips from his restraint. "I'm awake." She proved it by flexing her lower muscles.

When his eyes flew open she smiled and repeated the exercise. Then she watched the cords in his neck tense as he leaned his head back, clenching his jaw. Even so, the groan came out and she felt the pulse of his life deep within her. She savored the moment, storing his absorbed expression in a secret place. Then the blinding shock overtook her again, and she forgot rational thought.

Chapter 7

Glad you could find time to join us." Ty's voice held a gentle teasing note, but there was no doubt of his approval.

Devin managed a non-committal grunt, his attention on the woman across from him. Of course, tonight of all nights Maria would fix chicken. Sydney had been cutting dainty bites out of the thigh she'd served herself, and now she lifted the piece to her mouth, intent on not missing a drop of Maria's barbecue sauce.

"Did Jamie track down those strays?" Ty asked, hiding his smile by taking a large gulp of coffee.

"He hadn't gotten in when I was at the barn."

The end of the bone disappeared in her mouth and slipped out again. There was a touch of sauce on the corner of her mouth. Her tongue took care of that while she listened.

"If we can get enough ahead this year," Ty said,

realizing how little attention was being paid to his words, "I'd like to try some new bloodlines. There's always a good market for ranch raised horses, especially for endurance riders and rodeo horses."

"Might be," said his partner.

Ty looked up from his own dinner to see Devin's plate still half full. It was easy to see the focus of his partner's attention.

"You're a dangerous lady, Sydney Castleton," Ty said, laughing. "It's lucky you're Devin's woman, or we'd never get any work done here."

Sydney almost believed the note of sincerity in his voice. Almost. But Ty had shown himself to be good at finding the right thing to say to make someone feel good about themselves. She smiled briefly then decided to turn the conversation to less personal matters.

"With all the interest in back-to-nature and experiencing life first hand, why don't you try for some income outside of ranching?"

"Like taking in boarders and 'dudes'?" Ty asked, gallantly going along with her change of subject.

"Maybe not in a formal sense. You have a lot of beautiful country around here. Maybe one or two select groups a year, if someone would like to guide them." She paused, taking a sip of the water that was almost as good as wine. "If you could control the people who came."

"We don't encourage sport hunting here," Devin said, turning to his meal as though the food angered him.

"I can certainly agree with that, but have you ever thought of an exclusive fishing camp? It could be a good source of extra income. Fishermen usually just need to be pointed in the right direction and left alone."

"Some of the spreads up here have tried that," Ty said, his brow furrowing as he considered the possibilities.

"It wouldn't work here," Devin said flatly. It was obvious he didn't intend to elaborate on his statement. "You want to go into Taos tomorrow, Sydney?"

As a conversation stopper, it was ideal. She lifted her chin, straightening her back. "I'm not some child you can reprimand then placate with the offer of a trip to the fair if I mind my own business. Since this seems to have become a private conversation, I'll finish getting my things together." She rose gracefully, taking her plate into the kitchen, leaving an uncomfortable silence behind her.

෬෨෬

"Sydney, I asked you to come to Taos with me because I want to take you there. I didn't mean to cut you off about the fishing camps. Having a lot of strangers around just wouldn't work here." Devin's voice pierced the dark coldness that had settled between them, on either side of the oversized bed. "I want to spend some time alone with you."

"If you want, I'll go with you." Sydney's voice showed none of the control she'd been forcing upon herself.

"What I want," he said, reaching across the bed, "is for you to be closer to me." He pulled her gently toward him while he moved across the bed, meeting her in the middle. "We need to show you more of New Mexico than just Stormhaven. You'll think it's nothing but rocks and cows and hard-headed men."

"That would be a logical conclusion." She tried to resist him. There was no hope. Even with the hurt of his careless words, she couldn't deny her need for this man's touch and the comforting warmth of his big body. If he wanted only this much of her, at least he wanted her.

"That's better," he whispered against her scalp as his hands roved over her slender body, encouraging her to relax further. So small, but so strong. So sweet. "I want to see if it would be different in a bed." He slid his hands under her prim cotton nightgown, as though hungry for the feel of her skin, the thrill of her reaction to his need.

Sydney arched into his touch, giving up any further thought of resisting. They would have so little time together. It was foolish to waste it trying to remake him into something he could never be. As she felt the completion, the joining of their bodies that had become so crucial so quickly, she decided to take and give what she could. It would be a small warmth in the ever-spreading coldness of her life.

❧❧❧

Devin was waiting for the words. The words always came, the questions about "forever," plans for the future. Sometimes the conversation would be subtle, a discussion about changing the paint, maybe buying something for the house. Sometimes it was an outright question. "What about us, what about tomorrow?" All women asked. What kind of a future did he have planned, would he be on the ranch for the rest of his life?

In the past, when he'd heard the words, it was a sign things were getting too deep. Hearing the words in whatever form was a signal for him to be on his way. Now he was edgy, waiting for them, telling himself he didn't care if he never heard them.

They spent as much time together as possible. They'd visited Taos, wandered through the pueblo ruins. She'd gone riding with him and some of the men. Every night, she shared her emerging passion with an enchanting trust. Sharing her body, never herself. Never her thoughts, her past, their future. Never the words.

လာလ

Sydney could feel his eyes on her when they were together. Devin was waiting for her to say something, to do something. He'd never tell her what. Whenever they were together, he was touching her, holding her hand, slipping an arm around her, making her feel wanted. He made love to her with exquisite care, treating her always like a fragile, precious treasure. It was special. It was frustrating as hell.

She knew he wanted her to say something. Many times, he left the conversation open to questions about the future, their future. She wanted to ask these questions, but how could she? There was no future for them. Whatever she was at this moment, at one time she'd been anything but the delicate, feminine woman she knew he wanted in his life. So she took whatever ease and pleasure she could, and felt a little emptier every day.

☙☙☙

Sydney cradled her cell phone, staring at the faded wallpaper pattern, her mind racing in circles. Time had run out. She heard the dining room door open behind her.

"Problems?" Devin leaned against the entrance to the dining room, where they'd been lingering over coffee with Ty.

"That was Brian. He needs me back in LA. One of his biggest accounts has an emergency. They asked for me."

"You coming back?" he asked casually. *I need you here,* he thought. The pain he swore he wouldn't feel waited to attack.

"He'll need me in Europe by the end of the month." *Ask me to stay,* she pleaded mentally.

"After that?"

Sydney turned away from the glacial coldness that had taken over his face and voice. "I'd better pack. Brian made reservations. I'll need someone to take me to the airport."

"I'll take care of it, Sydney." Ty's quiet words dropped into the absolute silence that had taken over the hall. When she nodded agreement, he turned back to the dining room.

"Wait a damned minute," said Devin. "You can't just up and leave like this. What about us?"

"What about us, Devin?"

"That's what I've been trying to find out. Every time I try to pin you down, you clam up. What about the future?"

"We can't have a future. Be happy with what we had. It's more than I ever had with my husband."

"So this is it? You got your vacation fling? A little R and R with the cowboy stud?"

"If that's how you want to see it, believe what you want. You will anyway."

The dead tone of her voice and droop of her erect carriage drew his attention, but she was turning away. Devin saw ahead to the days without her. He wheeled away, slamming the door decisively behind him.

∽∾∽

She was going to miss this. The ranch could never be a permanent solution for her future but it had been healing. She would miss the quiet, the pine-scented clean air, the reality of heat and sweat and an honest day's work, the sense of completion that pervaded every task. She would miss the cats and Mosby and people who were finding their peace. She would miss Devin.

"Babe, I'm sorry."

She should have known he would find her sitting on the rock that had become her favorite thinking spot. Keeping her attention on the horizon, she shrugged. "It doesn't matter. You were expressing your opinion."

"You acted so casual about leaving, I lost it." He reached out to pull her off the rock and into his arms.

"Devin, I'm not the woman you think I am," she began bravely, attempting to push away from him, but he wouldn't let her go on.

"You don't know what I'm thinking." His cheek rested against her hair. "And now's not the time to discuss this. I'll come visit."

"You hate airplanes."

"I'll get over it. Maybe I'll take a train."

He held her inside his jacket, against his steady heartbeat, while darkness covered the ranch. She felt warm and safe, until Ty called from the house.

"Let me take you to the airport."

"No." She was barely holding on. If he went to the airport with her, she'd fall apart and beg him to come with her, or let her come back. He had to be ready to see her for what she was, not what he wanted her to be. "You go up in the mountains. I want to think of you up there while I'm in the city."

"Think of this, too." His mouth covered hers and he kissed her with desperate passion. She responded freely, not cautious now of where it would lead. "Whatever damn-fool ideas you may have in that head of yours, you do belong to me. Remember that."

ↄ৴৩ↄ৴

She remembered. In the airport, on the plane, she remembered everything about that magical interlude in the mountains. When the cabin crew admitted in Phoenix to over booking the next leg of the flight, she came out of her fog long enough to give up her seat to a family. She would land at Burbank instead of Ontario, but her luggage would transfer with her. Since she was in another part of Los Angeles, she would take a room in a different motel of the same chain.

LA was, as always, noisy, hot, and smoggy. Brian hadn't heard any more from his client by the time she checked in with him. Knowing she wouldn't sleep, she rented a car, deciding to go to an antique flea market in Long Beach. It was crowded, and the constant noise battered ears accustomed to the mountain stillness. In one small booth, she found a chunk of high quality Baltic amber, with darker streaks inside, proof of ancient life, almost as beautiful as Devin's eyes. The fine gold chain held it against her heart.

Sydney searched for a place that was quiet and cool, but everywhere there were even more people than she remembered. At the arboretum, her favorite quiet spot, she found herself dodging wedding parties and photo sessions. Finally, she gave up in favor of an early dinner. At least Los Angeles had a lot to offer food-wise.

She didn't recognize this restlessness in herself. It wasn't like she wasn't used to spending a lot of time alone. It was just that she had become accustomed to spending so much time with someone very special. During her solitary Japanese dinner, she studied the amber, and tried to ignore her memories. If this was what being lonely was all about, no wonder people wrote so many songs about it.

Still deep in thought and mentally miles away, she returned to her motel room as the setting sun was making silhouettes of the palm trees and power lines. Her normal cautious nature had been softened by the time spent in New Mexico.

That was the only excuse she could come up with for not noticing something wasn't quite right until after she stepped into her room.

∽∾∽

Devin turned his lathered horse over to Jamie and strode to Ty's house. Something wasn't right. He had no idea what, but it had bothered him enough to bring him out of the mountains.

Ty was working on the books, a cup of after dinner coffee at his elbow, when Devin burst into his office.

"Have you heard from her yet?"

"Good evening to you too, Dev. What in hell's wrong with you? Did you find Charlie?"

"Have you heard from Sydney?"

Something in Devin's face and the tone of his voice set off long buried alarms in Ty's head. It had been many years since he'd heard so much icy tension in his partner's rough voice.

"Not a word. Let me get you a cup of coffee."

"She was supposed to call as soon as she got to LA."

"Something must have come up. Maybe she had to go to work right away. Want a brandy?"

"Don't you have the number of that damned agency somewhere?" He stepped toward the desk, but Ty blocked his progress.

"Sit down, before you fall down. Now, dammit."

Pulling himself together with an effort, Devin threw himself into a chair and accepted the snifter of brandy. He drank it in one gulp, hesitating slightly as the fumes rushed back up into his mouth.

Using this break to his own advantage, Ty moved back behind the desk and reached for his card file.

"Stay there. There's an emergency number here that has an answering machine on it. You don't move."

Devin held himself very still while his friend called the number and left a brief message for someone to return the call at once.

Control had never been such a problem. Something was wrong. It had come over him a few hours before, and he'd almost pointed the big bay gelding directly down the mountain to get back. He'd experienced premonitions in his past, before a battle or a critical assignment. But he had never felt this sense of wrongness.

Maria, with the sixth sense developed by years of working with active men, came in with a tray of sandwiches, a coffee pot, and an extra mug. Devin wanted nothing, but he knew his body would need the fuel. He just didn't know why.

Ty picked the phone up in the middle of the first ring, before Devin could rise from his chair.

"Stormhaven. Yes, I am. Yes, he's here. Oh, my God!"

Devin wrenched the telephone away from Ty's nerveless fingers and shoved the ashen-faced man into a chair. "Who the hell is this?"

"This is Brian Alder. Are you Devin Starke?"

"Yeah. What's going on?"

"There's no time to be tactful. Sydney was attacked in her motel room. She's in the hospital. She's been asking for you."

Chapter 8

There might have been a fountain in the middle of the circular driveway and a fancy pipe sculpture between the buildings, but it was still a hospital. Hospitals were right up there on his list, along with airports and hotels. As he'd been instructed, Devin parked in the empty handicapped lot. This time of night there was no one in the spacious lobby.

Sydney was hurt and asking for him. He'd been running on automatic since those words had come across the telephone line, delivered by an exhausted voice. Brian hadn't had the ranch phone number with him and hadn't wanted to leave her long enough to go back to the office.

Devin had refused to think about why Brian could not have gotten the number from Sydney. Instead, he snapped out orders as though he were back in the field. Ty called the Bar-J for a lift to Albuquerque by plane. Reservations had been made on every flight departing to the Los

Angeles area. Devin took the first one out after he reached the airport. Once on the plane, he forced himself to sleep. This was no time for flight nerves.

The elevator was empty, and fast. New carpeting and paint almost overcame the normal hospital stench. He didn't notice the decor, beyond the fact that mauve walls and carpet were not as jarring to his senses as stark white walls and slick tile floors. Devin ignored the nurses talking quietly in a pool of light at the central desk, looking instead for the large white board on the wall.

Sydney's name was there, along with a doctor's name and some notations that made no sense. He looked quickly at the numbers on the walls and strode down the darkened hall. The nurses called after him, and one slipped out to follow him. He lengthened his stride. Short of breaking into a run, she wouldn't catch up to him. If she did, and tried to stop him—he'd never before hurt a woman who wasn't trying to kill him.

The door was half-closed and the curtain pulled around the bed, as though they wanted the maximum privacy possible without jeopardizing her care. Drawing a deep breath, bracing himself for whatever her condition might be, he slipped around the curtain.

It was at once better and worse than he'd been imagining. She lay very still and very white against the bleached bedding. A network of tubes snaked from under the sheet to more machines than he had ever seen outside of a cockpit.

A needle was taped to the back of her hand, attached to more tubes and running up to an assortment of bags on a metal pole. The covers seemed to be arranged over her body rather than laying directly on her.

Her thick, normally fresh-smelling, chestnut hair lay in sweaty clumps against her head. Bruises darkened her closed eyes and shadowed the uncompromising line of her cheek bones. Her nose was intact but the mouth that had kissed his so sweetly was swollen and broken. At the base of her neck, a red line had gouged deeply. As he watched, her eyes squeezed slightly and her lips parted, allowing a tiny sound, not quite a whimper, to escape. The lines alongside her mouth deepened.

Devin found himself by her bed without remembering when he'd moved. He lifted a hand and hesitated. Where could he touch her without causing more pain? Carefully, he stroked the bridge of her nose. Her nostrils flared and she lifted her head slightly. The brackets alongside her mouth seemed to ease as her chest rose on a deeply drawn breath.

"You must be Devin."

The quiet voice came from the other side of the bed. Devin tensed, amazed that anyone could have approached without his awareness. The tall man was lean to the point of gauntness and his body slumped in exhaustion that was mirrored in his lined face. The blue scrubs were as badly rumpled as his bright red hair. Steady hazel eyes and consciously relaxed posture spoke of more.

He stood very still, away from the bed, his hands in his pockets until Devin eased his own stance. Then he stepped forward, one large hand outstretched. "Dr. Erik McFarley."

McFarley shook hands with the same calculated ease with which he stood—as though he realized his right to be in the room was not yet confirmed in Devin's mind, as though he was familiar with rough, battle-weary men who weren't quite sure they had the right to be there themselves.

Devin relaxed completely, only then realizing how close to full alert he'd been the last six hours. A memory of the sight of his fingers against Sydney's face came back to him and, for the first time, he noticed how disreputable he looked. His hands were still stained with the mud outside Charlie's cave, and his clothes were probably all that was holding him up.

"You can clean up in the staff washroom later if you want."

Devin knew he should express some appreciation for the offer, but there wasn't time yet. "How bad is she?"

"Not as bad as she seems. A lot of bruising, some scalp wounds, and hair loss. Nothing permanent, just painful. We have her on pain medication until her body adjusts to the shock." He was calm and clinical, the perfect professional. But there was an underlying horror in his eyes that Devin recognized intimately. Then McFarley looked straight at him. "Was there any possibility of pregnancy?"

Outrage swept through Devin. What right did he have? The import of the words sank in, and he turned back to the still body on the bed.

Finally, he understood the significance of how the covers were arranged. Before he could give in to the cowardice draining his strength, he took hold of the sheet.

A framework wrapped in foam and soft flannel supported the covers. The body he had stroked and worshiped and made exquisite love to was a mass of red abrasions surrounded by bruises in varying degrees of darkness. The delicate breasts she'd been so ashamed of had the marks of what he knew to be fingernail gouges.

He surveyed the damage grimly. There were minor marks along her ribs, but no indication of any breakage. The desecration resumed farther down her body. Here the bruising was darkest, above a thick white bandage that he knew was for more than protection of her modesty.

"It's not as bad as it seems. There's been some bleeding but no indication of permanent injury. Our top gynecologist will check her out once the initial pain lessens."

"Who did it?"

McFarley eased the bedding from Devin's clenched hands and covered Sydney's battered body. "We won't know for sure until she wakes up. The other guests reported a disturbance. By the time the police got there, she was alone. Fortunately, when she checked in she listed her agency as a contact so there was no delay in reaching me." He automatically checked the needles, the bags of fluid and the gauges as he talked.

"You said you 'won't know for sure.' You have some ideas?"

"Not any reasonable ones."

McFarley rearranged the blanket to cover her hand, but not before Devin had a chance to take a closer look at her fingers. Folding back the blanket on his side, he saw the same thing. Two of Sydney's fingers still ended in elegant pink ovals. The rest were raw skin. Devin eased his fingers underneath hers, supporting her small, cool hand.

"What the hell happened to you, little one?"

He spoke more to himself than anyone else, but McFarley answered. "You knew she had overlays, of course. The police found tissue samples on the ones that came off." He looked down at the slender woman and stroked the hair back from her face in a very unprofessional manner. "It looks like, this time, she fought back."

☙☙☙

Sydney was calling for him, somewhere on the other side of the fog surrounding the jungle. He couldn't see her, couldn't tell exactly what direction her voice came from, but she was calling for him. The ugly little men with dead eyes and large, lethal knives would hurt her, and he couldn't get to her in time.

"Mr. Starke?"

Devin jerked awake, his body protesting the sudden movement after the night of abuse it had already experienced. A nurse waited patiently at the foot of the bed, holding a covered tray. "Miss Castleton's not up to solid food yet, but Doctor thought you might need something."

He remembered to thank her as he moved his feet from the chair facing him to make room for her to set the tray there. He would have taken the tray from her, but his arm was wound through the bed rails and his hand supported Sydney's cool fingers. Smiling slightly, the nurse pushed the chair closer for him then looked over Sydney's tubes and monitors.

"She's doing much better than I expected." She looked up as she spoke, and her expression was not quite as remote. "I volunteer two nights a week at a battered woman's clinic. The first night always seems bad but the really rough times come later."

દ્વઃ

Pain. So much pain, in so many places, threatening to overcome the barriers she'd erected. She could not give in to the pain. If she did, if she lost control to that extent, the yawning abyss of dark loneliness would swallow her for good.

Then a beam of light, dim but familiar, reached her from the other side of the abyss. It warmed her, comforted her, helped her hold the pain at bay. She reached for the light, drew strength from the warmth, until she could cross the abyss. She rested, sheltered in its glow.

The black eased to a gray fog, shot with lighter areas. Now there were sounds, voices, intruding on the bleakness of the gray. She knew she needed to wake, to speak to the people around her about…something. She didn't want to. As long as she was in the shadow world, protected within the beam of light, she could pretend she wasn't alone.

"I know you're awake, Sydney. You have too many monitors on you to fake it."

The voice was quiet and known to her, one she normally liked hearing. It just wasn't the right voice. She eased her eyelids apart, wincing at the pain she could almost feel under a layer of something not natural.

"Dr. Erik. What'd you hit me with?" Her voice sounded rusty and appallingly weak.

"Whatever it took to get you a good night's sleep. Don't worry, I'll back off the meds soon and let you be an Amazon."

She dared a smile then wished she hadn't. Something pulled then gave when her lips moved too far. "Was I in an accident?"

Erik's hazel eyes narrowed suddenly. "You don't know? What do you remember?"

She concentrated, reaching inside her personal library. Memories began to flow in to fill the empty shelves in her conscious mind, and she suddenly remembered too much. There had been the trip, the loneliness. Devin. She put that volume away without looking into it. "Someone was in my motel room."

"Someone? Anyone in particular, or just someone?"

She stared up at the man who'd been her closest friend for years, and her first crush. If anyone could help her make sense of it, Erik could. He would also keep it to himself. She opened her mouth then caught movement out of the corner of her eye.

He stood very still, silhouetted against the soft early morning light, with the air of having been there for a very long time. The embodiment of her dreams, but all too real.

This time she managed a smile no matter how much it

pulled. "I thought it was a dream," she whispered, trying to reach a hand to him but only managing to lift a few fingers.

He was at her side in a single gliding step, and his large hand slid under hers, cradling her fingers, completing the union that lent warmth and strength. The lines on his face were more deeply drawn than ever, emphasizing the tiny scars. She tried to lift her other hand to his face, but it was held down by the needles and tubes.

"Dr. Erik, would you get this thing off me?" There was no one to hear the command.

Devin set his hand on her wrist above the needle, pinning down her arm. "Be still. You need to rest."

"I need to get up. I feel like I've been run over by a steam roller."

There was no mistaking the flash of killing rage that overtook his face for one crucial second. Then one corner of his tightly held mouth relaxed into a smile. "You look like a morning after picture. No." He grasped the hand that tried to fly up to her hair. "It's nothing a shower won't fix. Your doctor friend said none of the injuries were serious, only painful."

"He was right, there." She shifted, trying to ease a stray twinge. "I think he used something stronger for the pain than he let on. That would be like him."

"Have you known him for long?"

"For years. He worked with my father." She felt the lassitude returning and fought against it. "He always thinks he knows better than I do about what I want. Dammit, I hate to be doped up!"

Devin laid gentle hands on her shoulders. The rough

warmth was soothing and familiar. She felt the tension ease in her battered body.

"Devin?" she whispered as the insidious drug slid through her system.

He rubbed her arms gently. "Right here, babe."

"You won't disappear, will you? You'll still be here later?"

"I'll be here as long as you need me, Sydney," he promised harshly, holding his fingers against the pulse beating in her throat. "Probably long after that as well."

ఆఌఌ

The next time Sydney woke, it was in reaction to a movement at the side of her bed. Distracted by the drugs in her system, for a moment she thought it was someone leaning over her, trying to sabotage the bags sustaining her health. Emitting a choked cry, she tensed, ready for the pain she would feel when she struck out to defend herself.

Then a hand rested on her chest, holding her down gently as a shadow rose past her. Before the nurse could react to Sydney's muted cry, her wrist was grasped by a hand that could break her arm without effort.

The attractive blonde's face appeared ashen in the dim light, but she didn't pull away from Devin's hold. "Excuse me. I was just doing a quick check."

"I don't recognize you." Moving his hand from Sydney's chest, Devin found the call button in the bed rail and stabbed at it in a pre-decided pattern.

Within seconds, the room was lighted and filled with

people, including the charge nurse, a floor guard, and, a minute later, Erik McFarley.

The yawn that split Erik's face stopped abruptly when he saw the group by the bed.

No one said anything to the hard-faced, rumpled man leaning protectively over the hospital bed. They all stood very still, including the nurse he restrained in an unbreakable hold that was not painful—yet. When Erik walked into the room, the watchers turned to him, their relief obvious.

"What's going on?" Erik asked Devin, ignoring the rest of the group.

"I didn't recognize this nurse. Usually they introduce themselves when they come on shift."

Erik looked at the blonde carefully then turned to the charge nurse. "I don't recognize her either. Who is this, Ruth?"

"She's from the temporary service. Alice came down with the stomach flu, so we had to call someone in to finish her shift. But she wasn't supposed to come into this room."

"I was just doing night checks, getting to know the patients in case someone called," the nurse finally said, a tremor in her voice. "No one said this room was off limits." Although she was still held in an unbreakable grip, there was more professional outrage than actual fear in her demeanor.

"You're pretty cool, considering the fact I could dislocate your arm without trying."

"I took most of my training at County, just up the hill.

If a patient doesn't have a gun or a knife, I figure they're just joking."

Her wry statement helped ease the tension in the room considerably. Devin released his hold and stepped back, his hand resting lightly on Sydney's shoulder. His attention didn't relax.

"This patient is under private care and is not to be disturbed," Erik said. "You don't need to concern yourself about her."

"Yes, Doctor." The nurse left without further comment. The rest of the group followed, apologizing to Erik for the disturbance.

"Do you believe her?" Devin asked, seating himself once more. His fingers stayed on the racing pulse in Sydney's neck.

"I want to," Erik said, his eyes on the monitors. "Sydney, if you don't relax, I'll have to give you something. Breathe."

She nodded then took as deep a breath as she could manage. This was followed by more, all slow, all regular. After a minute Erik nodded and touched her shoulder lightly.

"Good. Now stay relaxed." He frowned, leaning a hip against the back of a chair. "We use nursing services when we need them. I'll check on it in the morning. Just as a precaution, we'll move Sydney. I can have Ruth keep everyone busy for a couple minutes."

Devin must have felt Sydney's tension, though she tried to show nothing but polite interest. "It's okay, babe. I'm sure it's no big deal, but it's better to be safe."

"Until you are able to walk across the room unaided and do ten sit-ups, you will let someone else take care of you," Erik said in a stern voice.

Then he smiled when Sydney wrinkled her nose at him. Since Devin's attention was on Sydney's face, only Erik saw the brief flicker of a universal finger signal from under the sheet.

ↃↄↃↄↃ

Sydney marveled at the pleasure to be found in something as simple as waking up clear-headed. The pain was still there, but it was no longer a ravenous monster ripping at her nerve endings. Nor was it being kept at bay by chemical forces. For the first time in two days, she woke up feeling like herself. Alone.

Devin had been there every time she woke. He never said much, but his touch had brought her out of more than one nightmare. He'd been beside her when they moved her into another part of the large hospital, had slept in the chair next to her bed, and held the glass whenever she needed water. He'd been at her side every time the police came to question her.

It had been like having her own personal guard lion. Finally, Dr. Erik had been able to convince him to go out for a while and reacquaint himself with a shower and a real bed.

As though conjured up by her thoughts, the lean, red-haired doctor eased around the curtains, his hands deep in the pockets of his hospital smock.

"At last. Bright eyes and a glimmering of intelligence."

"As much as ever, Dr. Erik."

"Have I ever told you how old it makes me feel when you call me that?"

"I've called you that since the first day I met you."

"Precisely." He examined the monitor readouts and charts automatically before coming to stand by the bed. "Do you realize how long ago that was? I was wet-behind-the-ears medic."

"And I was a brat who resented the time her father spent with anyone else." She sighed then put aside the memories. "Are you going to play the heavy-handed father image here?"

"Is it needed?"

Shrugging was still uncomfortable and looking away would have been dishonest. "I don't know. I—this has never happened before. It's..."

"Frightening? Exhilarating?"

"Different."

"Always so cautious. Syd, what does Starke know about you?"

"He knows I'm Lana's sister. He knows I'm a materials expert, and that I work wherever the jobs are."

"And the rest?" Erik rested one hip on the bed, bracing himself by extending one long leg.

"There is no rest. Not anymore."

After a long pause, he sighed and looked away. He would know from experience there was no arguing when she didn't want to talk. He pulled his hands out of his pockets, looking down at what he held rather than at the stubborn woman in the bed.

"We'll shelve that for now. What happened in your motel room?"

"He was in there when I opened the door and jumped me from behind."

"You still have no idea who it was?" He looked up abruptly.

As before, she turned her head from side to side, hiding her answers behind her gray eyes.

"I find it hard to believe you weren't aware of someone else being in the room, Syd."

"Believe it. I've felt the same way. I was...thinking about something else."

"That I can believe." Whatever else he meant to say was cut off by the new expression in her face. No sound had come from the other side of the curtain, but she looked in that direction, a glow he'd never seen before lighting her face.

e⁄ɔe⁄ɔ

Devin hesitated for another instant behind the curtain. He should have felt sneaky listening in on Sydney's conversations, but information was impossible to get directly from her.

Not that he heard all that much. Just further reinforcement of his realization that there was far more to her than she ever let anyone know. She would tell him one day, he vowed fiercely. Of her own free will, she would trust him enough to tell him what lay behind the shadows in her eyes and in her dreams.

When there was a convenient lull in the low-voiced conversation he stepped around the curtain, reaching inside his jacket. "I found this downstairs," he said with a small smile. "He needed a new home." He proffered the stuffed cat, not much smaller than Sydney's feral kitties, on his outstretched hand.

Wincing at the pain in her lower body, she sat upright, reaching for the tiny toy balanced on his palm. When she got a look at her own hands she automatically curled her fingers into a fist. Since she could not have new nails put on until her fingers had healed, one of the nurses had helped her remove the few remaining overlays.

Devin grabbed one wrist before she could slip her hands below the covers. He turned her hand over and gently massaged until the pressure opened her fingers against his palm. The stuffed cat was deposited in her hand, and his fingers closed over hers until she took full possession. Only then did he release her, with one final, hidden caress.

"We need to talk," Erik began, rising casually from the bed. "As much as I enjoy having Sydney around, she can't stay here forever, and I don't think it's a good idea for her to stay in Los Angeles."

"Muggings can happen anywhere," Sydney reminded him. She didn't look up from the toy on her lap as she spoke.

"Save the fantasies for someone who'll believe you." Devin helped her shift over in the bed then sat next to her, leaning his weight on one hand braced against the wall. "If this were the only incident, I might agree with you. There've been too many random attacks."

"You said something happened on the trip to New Mexico?" Erik asked as he lowered himself into a chair. His hand clenched around something, distracting Sydney's attention.

"Some kids started beating on the trailer," Devin said. "At the time, I thought it was just some punks. After I thought about it, I began to wonder."

"Brian told me yesterday his office has been getting calls for her, from someone who won't identify himself. You know the assignment Sydney came back for was phony."

They'd decided it would be easier to hide her if Brian stayed away from the hospital.

All messages were relayed through Erik, with Brian using pay phones. Maybe the deception wasn't necessary, but no one wanted to take any more chances.

"You're both making too big a deal out of nothing," Sydney said carefully through her swollen lips.

Devin pulled her hand off the toy cat, laying it out on his palm. "You call this nothing?"

He smoothed his finger along the top of hers, not quite touching the ends where nails had been ripped out during a fight for survival.

"I call it ugly."

"Don't have a 'stupid' attack now." He curled his fingers around her hand, pressing her palm against his thigh. "I'm taking you back to Stormhaven."

"I was about to suggest that," Erik said before she could explode. "It's the only solution, Syd, at least until you can move around better."

Sydney didn't like it, but she was in no shape to argue with two overbearing males at the same time, especially when they were agreeing with each other. "Fine, so how do I leave your lovely city?"

"Driving is out of the question, unless you can go in an ambulance or a motor home. Maybe a van, if it had a big enough bed. It's too long a trip for you to sit up."

"Not a lot of chances to hide if someone does get an idea which way we went," Devin mused.

"I was thinking about that. I have a friend with a Medevac flying business. The usual charges for that trip would be four to five grand. He would do it for a couple grand."

"No planes," said Sydney firmly.

"Babe, it would be the fastest way," Devin said. His voice was almost calm, but she could feel the tension in his body.

"If it's a matter of money, I could cover the fee," Erik offered.

"No planes."

Erik shrugged then accepted her decision. "Whatever you decide, do it soon. You'll be ready to go in a couple days." He pushed himself out of the chair then hesitated. "Have you spoken with the police lately?"

"Just briefly, a couple days ago. When I couldn't give any definite identification, they left me with a number to call. Why?"

"They didn't want to tell you until you were better. It wasn't a random attack, Sydney. Apparently whoever attacked you was in your room for a while. Your clothes were trashed. This is about all they found that was really worth saving."

Erik held out his hand over the stuffed kitten, dropping something into her opened palm and closing his fingers over hers in brief support. Patiently, he waited for the effect his words would have to have on her.

At first, Sydney sat, stunned. Then she began to shake. Her fingers clenched around the support of the two men's hands. She could not control the shudders racing through her body. Devin slid his arm around her shoulders, holding her firmly. After a moment, Erik released her and she raised her clenched hand to cover Devin's. A fragile gold chain dangled from her fingers.

"What do you have there?" Devin asked softly, trying to distract her. He cradled her hand, encouraging her to open her fingers and reveal a chunk of golden amber, on a broken chain of the same fineness as the mark around her neck. Catching his breath against a sudden tightness in his chest, he dropped his cheek against her head.

"We're getting you out of LA as soon as you get hospital clearance," Devin said grimly. "I have a surprise for you."

Devin's surprise started with a collection of soft, bright-colored exercise outfits. The oversized sweat pants and tops would cover her fading bruises while not pressing against any tender spots. To go with them were frivolous leather tennis shoes in coordinating colors. One of the bags contained camisoles, cotton panties, and fuzzy socks.

Sydney was charmed with the gift, although it seemed rather pragmatic for a man to buy a woman he'd made love with. A frilly nightgown or two would have been nice. She wondered if that was all in the past. He'd been with her constantly for almost a week now and had done no more than hold her hand.

It wasn't surprising. All her little feminine features had been lost in the attack. Although her hair had been washed, it no longer fell around her shoulders in shiny, fresh-smelling waves, and her nails were a total write-off. Why shouldn't Devin want to cover her up from head to toe? There was nothing dainty about bruises.

It was one more score to be settled in an endless game. The settling would remove any last vestiges of her feminine façade. She had to believe it would be worth the loss.

രൗരൗ

Devin could feel Sydney slipping into a dark hole, where she wouldn't let him follow. When he questioned her, she would manage a tiny smile then change the subject. The bruises on her skin would fade in time. But how long before she would have back her "conquer-the-world attitude"?

He wanted to grab her up and give her his own strength. But that was impractical for so many reasons. Her body was still far too frail to be held closely right now, and he was afraid he wouldn't have the control to stop once he *could* hold her. So he concentrated on sharing all the lessons of self-worth he'd learned in a lifetime of survival, and hoped it would be enough.

Chapter 9

The early morning air held a definite chill and a whiff of what would be a first-stage smog alert later in the day. A few other travelers straggled toward the small brick building.

Devin and Erik had maintained an air of mystery, like two small boys who wanted to give sis the best present ever. Devin had wakened her in the pre-dawn darkness, offering his support while the nurse helped her dress. Contrary to hospital policy, Sydney walked out of her room, leaving by a service elevator and getting into Erik's car in the employee garage.

The silence was maintained through a long drive along nearly empty freeways, traveling at first against the growing commuter traffic. Sydney recognized the major intersections and was more baffled than ever when they turned east along the San Bernardino freeway, then south along the Orange freeway. A short drive along tree-lined streets in the college community of Fullerton and they were stopping in front of a red brick building, set in front of train tracks.

"AMTRAK?" She glanced over at Devin. "Why didn't we just use the main station? You could practically see it from the hospital."

"Which would make it the most obvious departure terminal for someone to watch," Erik reminded her. "Now pay attention. You two are about to leave on a fun-packed two week vacation. Your plans are to hike and camp out in the mountains around Taos. Attempt an air of enjoyment."

Sydney briefly managed the act of a carefree vacationer about to set out on a journey. By the time they were approaching their departure point, she could feel the weakness spreading throughout her body.

"Just a little farther," Devin whispered in her ear. He slid his arm around her waist, letting her lean unobtrusively against him.

Erik carried the brightly colored luggage and backpacks that fit in well with the image they wanted to project. His attention was split between Sydney and the few milling passengers on the platform. When he saw the perspiration begin to bead on her forehead, he stopped near a pillar, setting down his burdens. "We've got time. Let her rest a minute. It would be natural to say our good-byes here."

"Sorry," she gasped, letting Devin take more of her weight. "I didn't think such a short walk would take so much out of me."

"Make haste slowly and follow the doctor's orders."

Eric handed Devin a small brown bottle. "You'd better take charge of these. She'll just flush them."

"What are you pushing on me now?"

"Better living through chemical intervention, brat. They're for the times when the people around you are tired of listening to you bitch about your puny aches."

"I don't remember that brown leather piece," Devin said, looking at the luggage at their feet.

Sydney lifted her head, studying the battered backpack. Frowning, she looked at Erik then tried to pull away from Devin and lean down for a closer look.

"Don't try that just yet. Yes, it's yours, Sydney. Remember that last time you flew out, when your dad and I took you to the airport? You accidentally picked up this backpack instead of your other one."

Sydney nodded. "I was so excited about the job, I grabbed my old backpack automatically instead of the new one Dad had bought me. He had to ship it to me. But how—"

"Since I didn't want to carry it through the airport, I decided to take it back to my car and meet you at the gate. My beeper went off while I was in the parking garage, and I never made it back."

"You called on the courtesy phone," she remembered, her voice softening.

"I was in surgery for eight hours. By the time I got out, I'd forgotten all about the backpack. When I remembered, your dad told me to hold on it until we could get together again. That was the last time I talked to him."

"The accident was about a month after I reached Singapore."

"Sydney and her father shared a house," Erik began to explain to Devin when it was obvious Sydney couldn't.

"I know. She told me."

"I see." Erik smiled, and held out his arms. "Come say a proper good-bye, Sydney, so I can get back to work."

"Dr. Erik." She whispered into his hug. "When will I see you again?"

"You never know." He bent to place a chaste kiss on her cheek. When he spoke, his voice carried no farther than her ear. "You'll have to learn to trust enough to let someone help you. Maybe this is the someone."

Eric straightened and held out a hand to the tough-looking man who was not trying to hide his glower. "There's a lot more to Sydney than you know. Take care of her."

With an eerie moan and a rush of displaced air, the train pulled up to the platform and paused—a creature of motion, only temporarily held still by the needs of the travelers.

c⁄ɔc⁄ɔ

"Where are you sleeping?" Sydney asked muzzily, fighting the effects of the pills Devin had forced on her.

"Don't worry about me."

"There's plenty of room here."

Right. There was just enough room to drive him crazy. He'd been an idiot to set this up. Not only was she

within touching distance from anywhere in the compartment, the rhythm of the train itself set up a sensual beat in
his blood.

Even worse, Sydney didn't seem to enjoy the ride as
much as he'd expected. In the dim light, he could see that
even with extra padding and pillows, she was straining to
brace herself on the rocking bed. It would do her no good
if she started to tense up, worrying about him as well.

"Well, move over and stop hogging it all." What the
hell—he couldn't get much more frustrated than he
already was.

He slid cautiously in behind her, letting her find the
most comfortable arrangement for herself. Once her back
rested against his chest and her head tucked under his chin,
all the stiffness seeped out of her. When he felt her melt
against him, he wondered what else Purgatory would have
to offer.

"Thank you, Devin," she said through a tiny yawn.

He made a questioning little non-sound in his throat.

She lifted a hand to stroke his fingers, fisted at her
waistline. "The train. You remembered. Thank you."

He covered her hand with his own, reminding himself
that they would be confined in this damnably tiny
compartment for twenty hours, and Sydney was not
recovered. This was not the time to be anything but a
cheerful companion. Still, he cherished the feeling of her
fingers curling around his palm. "It was only fair, since
you kept me out of another airplane."

"I have to admit, even I dislike the tiny ones." She
shifted, pretending not to wince. "I wish I could see more.

But it feels good." Snuggling closer to him, she finally gave herself over to his care and slipped into sleep.

c/ɔc/ɔ

This hadn't been one of his brighter ideas, Devin decided several hours later. The plane would have been nerve-wracking, but nothing could equal the pain of her body rocking against his. Erik had been adamant about avoiding arousal until she was more fully healed. He'd had no wonder drugs or words of advice concerning Devin's problems.

Devin felt his much vaunted control fly out the window. It took no great imagination to think of pulling Sydney over on top of him, sliding into her heat and letting the motion of the train do the rest. If they concentrated, they would be able to make it last longer than ever before. Rocking, rocking, until the explosion, and the endless sweet nothingness of their union.

Light filtered around the window covering, exposing the darkened bruises on her face. Whatever arousal his fantasies and the feel of her body had created, the thought of her current condition deflated it immediately. Cautiously, he slid a little closer to her, not worried now about the pressure of her sweet rear against his vulnerable groin. There would be time in the future to satisfy his needs. For now, he simply held her safely against his body and joined her in sleep.

c/ɔc/ɔ

Sydney felt good, finally waking clear headed and much closer to her old self. She felt even better waking up hungry and able to do something about it herself, instead of having to wait for someone to come take care of her. It was much saner relishing the little joys of life than bemoaning the large miseries. Dr. Erik's pills always did make a wretched philosopher out of her.

She'd slept through dinner, having gotten up for a late lunch and a walk around the house with Maria. Someone had looked in on her earlier, probably Ty. As before, Devin was scarce although she almost caught a whiff of his body scent as she was waking. Delusions, no doubt, the same as her memories of her bed rocking in a soothing rhythm, with her wrapped in comfort.

By the clock, it was just after nine. Late hours on some ranches perhaps, but it was not unlike the men here to talk well into the night. Maria would have left for her apartment off the kitchen by now. If Sydney was very quiet, she could manage a snack without bringing any of the watchdogs down on her.

✷✷✷

"I'm glad Charlie's doing better. I tried to get up to see him, but he's kept himself hidden too well. Guess he's not ready for company just yet." Ty poured himself a small amount of brandy into a snifter and lifted the bottle in a silent question to his partner.

"He seems to be keeping himself happy there. Don't know what he'll do once the snow comes. We'll have to deal with that when it happens. Thanks." Devin accepted the brandy and held it between his hands, absorbing the aroma as it warmed. "Too bad we haven't had luck finding any family. He mentioned feeling alone since his wife left." Devin understood more about loneliness lately than he ever had before.

"Jamie asked about Sydney today." Ty took a small sip of the brandy. "He offered to bring one of the kitties up to the house if she needed company."

"He seems to be taking a lot of interest in her." Devin tilted back in his chair, wondering whether or not he dared look in on Sydney again before he went to his house. Wondering how soon she would be healed enough to take home. It had only been two days since he'd carried her into the bedroom. It seemed like two years.

"Don't be ridiculous. Jamie's a good kid. I think he wanted to talk with her about some man who's been asking questions in Willow Springs about you."

"The hell you say!" Devin let the front legs of his chair drop. "What are you talking about?"

"Some city guy's been showing around an old picture of Sydney and asking about a big dark-haired man with a limp."

"When did you hear about all this?"

"Just this evening. I sent Jamie back into town to pick up anything else he could."

"When were you planning to tell me?"

"When I had enough information to give you a complete rundown and not just rumors. I've already alerted Morgan."

"Damn. We'll have to pull some men off hunting strays and have them watch the perimeters. Maybe set up some long range recon posts."

"It won't do much good," said a quiet, frighteningly calm voice from the doorway. "Unless you can post full perimeter guards and have them armed with state-of-the-art weaponry, you might as well keep looking for cattle and putting up hay."

The men twisted in their chairs.

Sydney stood in the doorway, but it was a Sydney they'd never seen before. She wore a soft pink sweat suit that should have made her look sweet and cuddly. It was like putting a velvet bow on a machete.

There was a fine-edged quality to her as she stepped soundlessly into the room that had both of them sitting on the edges of their seats, watching for her next move.

"Sydney, you're up!"

"Ty, you're so observant," she said lightly, belying the tension in her body as she glanced toward Devin. "What's this about someone asking questions?"

"You shouldn't be up this late, Sydney," Devin said, rising to pull out the chair next to him.

She sat instead at the end of the table, cradling the mug of tea she'd brought in with her. "I appreciate your concern, but I've been hurt far worse than this before and not rested half as long. Tell me about this city guy."

"Sydney, we can handle it," Ty began.

"If he's asking about me, I have a right to know. Especially if he's planning to harm someone from the ranch when he can't get any information."

"You don't understand, Sydney. We're very capable of taking care of you here."

"Are you capable of avoiding sniper fire while you feed the stock? How about a long-range missile? Your barn would be a bonfire and Mosby would be a crispy critter while you were still trying to figure out where the shot came from."

Devin wondered if his dreams had taken on a new twist. The woman sitting at the end of the table was Sydney, but she wasn't. What he'd seen in small flashes before, hints of extraordinary intelligence and a grasp far beyond the average of the darker side of life was now very evident in the way she sat so still, yet so ready to move.

He realized that she'd not once met his eyes since she had entered the room.

"Do you know who it is, Sydney?" he asked quietly.

Now she did look at him, and he wished she hadn't. Her eyes were frozen barricades to what lay behind. For just a moment, he saw a wasteland of lost dreams and forgotten promises, a place of loneliness and horror. She looked away.

"Rick Wallace. My ex-husband."

"I thought he was dead," Ty said, frowning.

"So did I. I need a car, Ty. Something innocuous, with a good engine and tires. If I get moving soon enough, I can be well past Willow Springs by morning. Once he sees me, he won't be interested in the ranch."

"Honey, we can take care of you." Ty reached out a hand to cover hers. She pulled away before he could make contact.

"I can take care of myself, without endangering anyone here."

"You don't seem to understand what I'm saying. We—"

"I understand that only about fifty percent of the men who work here were originally cowboys. I understand that you and the other fifty percent have a military background in infiltration, unarmed combat, and various other useful talents. Some of the men aren't ready to make it yet in the world, and this has become a sort of halfway point for them. Once in a while, they aren't even ready to be here, and you get one of them hiding out in the mountains, not quite sure where they are or who's around them.

"Devin," she continued, staring at her tea, "has a more complex background. He probably continued on after the military. From what I've seen of him in action, I've met most of the people who taught him how to fight and I know at least one of his trainers personally. You're a credit to them."

Devin nodded, leaning forward to try to catch her attention, make her look at him again. She had to see but did not turn her head—as if she were afraid of her reaction.

"Who are you, that you know all this?" Ty was quickly losing the habitual good-humor he used as a shield.

"Have you ever heard of 'the Rook'?"

⌘⌘⌘

Devin leaned forward, his eyes narrowing. Ty was a

little slower placing the name, then he nodded. "He was a Ranger, wasn't he?" Ty asked.

"For a while. When his wife divorced him and left him with a kid to raise, he retired and went into business for himself." She was fairly sure they understood what she was saying, but it was best to make herself perfectly clear. "He was my father. Later, he was my boss."

Sydney sat very still, letting the reactions at the table wash through her. Then she rose, very carefully, and set her mug down. Not daring to look at either man, she stepped away.

"So, you see, I'm more than capable taking care of myself. Since it's my ex-husband causing the trouble, it's best that I handle this alone. If you don't have a vehicle here, perhaps you can call a rental agency in town? It'll only take me a minute to pack."

☙❧☙

She'd hoped for a little longer. Even one more day of peace, the chance to see Devin one more time, even if he didn't really see her anymore. But it was time to move on. At least she had a little notice and was in better shape than the week before. She pushed the last of the sweat suits into her traveling bag and refused to think about where they had come from.

Later, when she was far away and feeling lonely, she would bring out the bright memories of her interlude here and examine them. She added the stuffed kitten, fastened the bag, and headed for the door. Along the way, she picked up the battered leather knapsack that had been dropped behind a chair. Time to put fantasy behind her and get on with the job.

Devin leaned against the wall opposite her door, one foot propped on the wall, his arms crossed—the picture of a man with endless patience, as long as you didn't look close enough to see the tension tightening his mouth, the barely restrained power in his arms and legs.

"I'm disappointed in you," he said, not bothering to move away from the wall.

"You're not the first man I've disappointed. I'm sure you won't be the last." She turned toward the front door.

She'd seen him in action. She knew how fast he was. Still, it was a shock when he'd gotten hold of her arm in one hand, her bags with the other, and turned her, before she even sensed his movement.

"You're not going any farther than my house."

"Look, I'm sorry you lost your lady executive play toy before you were tired of her. I don't have time for any more games." She tried briefly to free herself.

Without hurting her, he kept her still until she relented, staring toward the door.

"It's not a game, Sydney. It never was."

"Give it up, Devin. You're just not used to being the one who's being told it's over. We're even. I've never been in the position of deciding when to end a relationship. It's kind of a high. I might try it more often."

"Enough, dammit. You're coming to my place tonight. We'll make plans in the morning."

That was all it took to set her off. Oblivious to the

pain, she jerked her arm free and spun away from him. He dropped the bags and reached for her with both hands.

"I will be far away from here by morning. It's over, Devin. You said it yourself. You're disappointed in me. Let me go now, before it turns to outright disgust."

"I'm not disappointed in you as a woman. I'm disappointed you didn't have enough trust in me to tell me who you were."

"When was I supposed to tell you? When you took the feed bags away from me because you thought I was too frail to carry them? When you tucked me into bed like something fragile and precious and watched over me all night long? When you took over all the physical work and driving?" She gulped, refusing to look at him, not wanting to see the condemnation in his eyes. "Maybe I should have waited until I got here and told you after you expounded on your theory that a woman's only function is taking care of the men who save the world.

"Devin, no one has ever cared for me, cared about me the way you have. I knew, as soon as you knew about me, you'd treat me either like a pariah or one of the guys. Was it so wrong to want someone for once, for just a few days, to see me as a woman?"

Devin took it all unflinchingly, his hands resting on her shoulders, his narrowed gaze never leaving her face. She was too tense to listen to him until she'd had her say. "What about after we made love?" he demanded.

"That would've really worked." She nodded, as if contemplating the scene. "For the first time in my life I felt as though a man was interested just in me. It would have done wonders for the mood for me to start discussing the best method to field strip an Uzi. Would've really geared up the old sex appeal."

"Are you going to start on that sex appeal crap again? I told you before, you're the sexiest woman I've ever known."

"Don't humor me. My experience may be limited, but I know all too well how a man's body feels when he's lost interest. I was drugged on the train, I wasn't unconscious."

In another of his lightning moves she wasn't quite ready for, he pinned her body against the wall with his own. He grabbed her hands, countering her resistance with his hard body.

"You were drugged. You were also covered from head to toe with bruises and I had just endured a ten minute lecture from your doctor friend on being sure you were healed before we made love." He used his body against hers, blatantly letting her feel his arousal. Gathering her hands into one of his behind her back, he slid a finger under the neck of her sweat suit and lifted the mended chain. In his palm, the amber glowed with its own life.

A strained smile pulled at the corners of his mouth. "All I could do for twenty long hours was hold you and fantasize about all the things we could have been doing. That train ride was one of the most miserable, frustrating experiences of my life."

Sydney felt the hope build deep within herself. Even now, she sensed twinges from healing body parts. She also felt totally, blissfully, alive for the first time in days. Still, she had to question, had to wonder. "What about after we got here?"

"We didn't know who had attacked you, but we knew it hadn't been a random attack. I had to go up in the mountains to check on something, and we didn't want to leave you alone. It worked out better that way. I'm afraid my nobility could only stretch so far if I had you alone in my house at night."

Something hurtfully tight let go deep inside her, and she relaxed, just a little. Feeling the easing of her tension, Devin slid his hands around her back, holding her close. The peace grew within each of them and between them.

"If you two are done tearing into each other, we need to talk," Ty said from where he leaned against the doorway, watching with great interest.

They turned, but Devin would not allow her to step away from the shelter of his arm. "Just for a little while. We can't really make plans until after we hear from Jamie, and Sydney shouldn't be out of bed for too long." Leaving the cases in the hallway, he guided her toward Ty's office.

"If nothing else, she shouldn't be out of your bed any longer," Ty said as he passed around coffee.

The fireplace offered warmth and a light, with just the right amount of rustic ambience for the room. None of the furniture was new, except for a computer stand tucked discreetly behind Ty's desk. All of the chairs and couches were covered in soft leather and were sized to fit large men. Ty settled in his favorite armchair, leaving the couch for the two of them.

Sydney gave up maintaining a physical distance

between her and Devin. She also gave up holding herself erect. Releasing a tired sigh, she settled on the comfortable old leather couch, leaning her weight, just a bit, against Devin. It wouldn't last, but for now it felt so good to share his warmth and strength.

"I heard of your father," Ty said, cradling his coffee mug. "I don't think I ever met him. How long did you work together?"

"Two or three years. When I left Rick, I went back to live with Dad while I finished college. By then, Dad had changed from active work to mostly consulting on security systems. He did some hostage negotiations, and sometimes an old client would contact him to clean up someone else's mess."

"So you didn't really work a lot of jobs with him." Devin's voice was a comfortable rumble against her shoulder, but he couldn't disguise his concern.

"Of course I did. I coordinated supplies and took charge of logistics so the operations would run more smoothly. Since I minored in applied psychology, I helped with some of the human details of the clean-up operations. That was how I met Jamie."

She could feel them exchange glances over her head but concentrated on her coffee. It would be foolish to hide anything else from them, but it would be even more foolish to give them more information than they were ready to digest. A fine line.

"Would Jamie know Dr. Erik?" Devin asked, pretending to be casual.

"Possibly, but that's Jamie's story to tell. Dr. Erik

started out as a medic in Dad's unit. When Dad changed jobs, so did Erik. Eventually, Erik made enough to go to medical school and intern at some of the best trauma units in the country. Wherever he was, he always kept in touch. After Dad retired, he and I had a small house near Dana Point, between LA and San Diego."

"Erik said your dad died?" Devin asked, quietly.

She hesitated, wondering if she had the energy for this. Best get it over with. "Our house blew up. I was in Singapore. Erik called to tell me to about it. The police said it was an accident. I doubted them, but I had no way to investigate."

Ty looked directly at her. "Do you think your ex-husband did it?"

"Rick had been reported dead by then but I always wondered. Then again, Dad made as many enemies as friends, maybe more." She shrugged, feeling the exhaustion start to take her over. "Rick is a sociopath, totally without conscience. I don't know if he actually enjoys hurting and killing as much as he enjoys the power it gives him over the rest of the world. He measures his own worth against the people he hurts."

Having delivered this profundity, she turned to the man who was holding her up in so many ways. "If I promise not to seduce you, will you take me home, Devin?"

She could almost think there was a flush of red below his tan. No, it must be a trick of the light, and her tired eyes. But there was no mistaking Ty's laughter, nor the glare of retribution Devin offered before he rose, pulling her up with him.

"That's definitely enough for you tonight. Let's go, Sydney. Tomorrow," he said to Ty. "Once Jamie gets back, we need to figure out what we're going to do."

"No cops," Sydney said through a yawn. "They won't be able to do much until it's all over, and you wouldn't want them nosing around the place anyway."

Ty rose as they did, not bothering to hide his smirk. "Sleep well, you two."

Chapter 10

Once they were in his bed, under the covers, their bodies touching as many places as possible, exhaustion seemed a distant problem. Sydney moved closer, trying to draw her thigh up across Devin's. She couldn't quite hide a wince.

"Easy, hon. Not just yet." Devin dropped an almost-chaste kiss on her forehead, trying to hide the tension in his body. He cradled her against himself, supporting as much of her weight as he could. "I can't believe you really did that kind of work. You feel too small, too delicate to have done everything you said."

"You make me feel that way, Devin." Sydney hesitated, sorting through various possible retorts, then settled on the truth. She was too tired to hide much anyway. "I don't do that work now, but don't ever doubt I did it in the past."

He soothed her with strokes of his large hands down

her back. Through the nightshirt she could feel the tension of his body. "I believe you, hon. I'm sure you were very—"

"Don't you dare say I was 'cute' in fatigues."

"Never crossed my mind. I was going to say you were very efficient and a big help to your father."

"You're patronizing me."

"You're being a grouch. Probably because you're tired."

She was tired. She was aware of the hard body she lay against. She was also smart enough to know she wasn't up to doing anything about the arousal that was attempting to migrate to the outer edges of her nerve endings. Knowing how much both of them were going to need their rest, she allowed herself to be petted into a state near relaxation. Devin seemed to be accepting her past. At least, what he knew of it so far.

As she felt the sleep wash over her, she raised a hand to cradle the hard edge of his jaw. "No night creatures tonight."

"No, babe." He kissed her temple softly. "Not to-night."

❦❦❦

Sydney breathed deeply then raised her arms above her body, continuing the ancient stretching exercises that had started her days for so many years. She took her body to its limit then pushed beyond, testing her healing strength. There was a slight sound behind her that she automatically classified as Devin, who'd been gone from the bed when she woke. She began the kicks that would limber her lower body.

"Warn a man what you're doing, woman!"

Devin barely missed intimate contact of his chin against a dainty foot. Sydney continued the movement smoothly, balancing with a kick to the other direction before testing her body with increasingly difficult stretches. She concentrated on the movement, on the feeling of the blood running ever stronger in her body.

Flowing through a final, slowing series, Sydney brought the session to a graceful close. She stood for a moment, drawing deep breaths into her body while she eased herself back into a normal metabolism. Perspiration held her hair tightly against her skull and created darker spots on her T-shirt.

"Aren't you pushing it just a bit?"

She shrugged, picking up a towel hanging on the doorknob. "I don't think there's a lot of free time left."

Devin tilted his head to the side, studying her. "You're upset about something, aren't you?"

Sydney slung the towel around her neck, holding both ends and leaning back against the pull. "Yes...no ...maybe."

"Just what I always liked, a clear answer."

"If you wanted a clear answer, you should have taken up with a reporter." Sydney held the towel up to her face, hiding the sudden blush. She was appalled at the nasty words that had tumbled out of her mouth. Mounting adrenaline and frustration ate at her but it wasn't fair to take it out on him.

Then Devin was at her side, sliding his arm around her, pulling at the towel, putting a hand under her chin to tilt her face up to his gaze. "You sure woke in a hell of a mood this morning," he teased gently. "What's wrong?"

"You weren't here when I woke up." She knew she sounded weak but her time with Devin would be too limited to waste on games.

"I was afraid to be," he admitted, pushing the damp hair back from her face. "As sweet as you look in the morning, if I hadn't gotten out of bed before you, we wouldn't have gotten out of bed for days."

"Days?" she teased, suddenly feeling more confident. Even if he was only saying this to make her feel better, it was working. She wanted to believe him. "Isn't that a slight exaggeration?"

His face hardened into full awareness as his warm golden gaze poured over her face then dropped to her mouth. Giving in at last to the temptation, he lowered his head.

Careful of her sensitive lips, he joined their mouths, angling his head for the perfect fit. Then Sydney's tongue eased out to shyly trace his lips and then retreat. Growling in the back of his throat, he slid his hands down and cupped her bottom, pulling her against him as the kiss took root and grew.

She locked her hands behind his neck, rising on her toes to perfect the fit of their bodies. As her tender nipples rubbed across his chest she whimpered, suppressing a small shudder.

Devin pulled back, taking hold of her hips to move her away from his body. For a moment she resisted, seeking his hardness growing against her stomach. Then she relented, sliding her hands slowly, reluctantly, down his arms.

Before she could move completely out of his reach, he pulled her back, cradling her against his side while he brushed his knuckles against the nipple beginning to peak under the loose T-shirt. "God, Sydney. If you have a cast iron brassiere with a padlock, you'd better put it on."

He bent his head, leaning down, bracing her across his arm. Ever so slowly, he extended his tongue, depressing the tip of her nipple like a push-button. When he raised his head, he covered the damp nipple with his palm, keeping it warm while he kissed her trembling mouth once more.

"Get your shower, babe." His voice was husky. "Ty wants to brainstorm over breakfast in his office."

෴

Early morning sun bathed the room in soft golden light. The elegant old office offered an appropriate setting for their gathering. The smell of fresh, strong coffee mingled with leather, wood smoke, and other timeless masculine smells. There was even a hint of fine cigars from a dusty humidor on the shelf. Ty and Jamie were deep in conversation when Sydney came into the room, followed closely by Devin.

"You look pretty bad, Syd." Jamie spoke with the brutal frankness of youth and friendship.

"So kind of you to notice. Actually, I'm feeling much better." Drawing her legs underneath her, she sat tailor fashion on the couch, her back perfectly straight. "It's not as though this was the first time I was ever hurt."

"Remember that time your fingers were messed up?" Jamie nodded at her hands, which she tried to keep out of sight while she drank her coffee. "It was when I first met Syd and her dad," Jamie told Ty and Devin, in spite of Sydney's scowl. "I took a job, that I knew going in wasn't a good idea, in one of the Central American countries. When things went to—when they went sour, I figured I might as well hang it up. It was like a troop of marines when The Rook showed up."

"You have a flair for the dramatic, Jamie. Ever think of writing men's adventure novels?" Sydney's voice was repressive but Jamie merely grinned.

"They convinced me, and a couple of the others, to get away from group. It wasn't too hard. Our leader was dead and the guys left weren't too sane. Unfortunately, someone had booby-trapped almost everything. Syd and I were in a small shed when it came down on us. I couldn't get her to leave even though she got herself free pretty fast. She knew her father would search harder with her in there.

"The damned place was on fire, and I was pinned down by a column. Syd almost got it off me once, but it slipped and came down on her hands. Fortunately, her dad got there about then and got us both out."

"You could have been killed," Devin said, his voice flat with suppressed emotion.

"I was in far more danger from Dad than any building. If I'd been a few years younger, he would have blistered my bottom for sure. As it was, he nagged at me all the way home."

"He also changed the dressing on your hands three times a day," Jamie reminded her. "Did your nails ever grow back?"

"More or less."

Devin took hold of one of her hands, smoothing her fingers over his palm and gently touching the ends. The raw spots were healed over, and new nail tissue was forming to protect the tips of her fingers. He cradled her hand in his, as if comparing it to his work roughened palm, and traced the ridges formed by calluses obtained in training for combat. He also touched the faint scars of old injuries on some of her fingers, extending into the nail areas.

"You've lived an exciting life, little one." His voice was low, matter-of-fact. But there was a fine trembling in the hand cradling hers.

"Her dad would have agreed with you. Sometimes he couldn't keep her still long enough to eat."

"I really think that's enough, Jamie."

Either the menace in her voice finally got through, or he was finished baiting her. Jamie reached for a muffin, stuffing it into his mouth with a huge grin. Sydney sipped at her coffee and ignored the undercurrents.

"I had Jamie wait until we were all together before he

told me about last night. No need to go over it more than once," Ty said, re-filling the coffee mugs before settling into his chair.

Before Jamie could swallow the muffin in his mouth, they were interrupted by the brash ring of the telephone. Ty looked at the clock as he leaned back in his chair, reaching across his desk for the receiver.

"It's awful damned early to be getting calls here," he muttered. "Stormhaven," he announced into the receiver. He listened a moment, frowning.

"Wait a minute, Kyle." Ty moved around his desk as he spoke. "This is something we all need to hear." Punching buttons on the telephone, he cradled the receiver.

"As I was saying, Ty, I had a visitor here last night." Kyle's tone was brisk, that of a corporate executive. "Some blond California type told me he was looking for a woman by the name of Sydney Wallace."

Sydney's coffee sloshed dangerously near the top of her mug as she sat straighter on the couch. Devin took the mug out of her clenching fingers then once more cradled her hand in his. When she attempted to pull away, his fingers closed around hers firmly.

"I told the guy I'd never met anyone named Sydney Wallace," Kyle continued smoothly. "Then he said she might be using the name Sydney Castleton." There was a pause, obviously for effect, on the other end of the telephone connection.

"And…"

Kyle continued when prompted by Ty. "I had to say I didn't recall anyone of that name, either."

There was an immediate easing of the tension in the room. Devin did not relax. He'd known Kyle for too long. There was still a punch line to this story.

"We appreciate you telling him that," Ty said cautiously. It was obvious he also was waiting for the next shoe to drop.

"You know I have a problem with names sometimes. Now, if he had asked me about a sexy little morsel with shiny chestnut hair and eyes like a mountain pond in the moonlight—"

"That's enough, Jorden," Devin said, keeping his hold on Sydney. She had obviously not gotten over blushing at odd times.

"Good morning, Devin," Kyle said, momentarily cheerful. Then the amusement faded from his voice. "You guys have any trouble over there you need some help with?"

"Nothing we can't handle right now," Ty said.

"Let me know, okay? I'm not scheduled to leave for a couple weeks. Of course, if you would move into the twentieth century and put in an airstrip, it would be easier to help you."

It was obviously a long-standing discussion, and Ty made the several rude remarks about people who were so unorganized they had to fly everywhere to have time to get things done. Sydney stopped trying to pull her hand away from Devin's and sat very still, a frown forming between her brows.

"She's thought of something," Jamie said in an undertone to Devin, as though bragging on a favorite pet's trick.

"Kyle, where do the private planes land if the owners don't have their own airstrip?" she asked, cutting through the friendly banter.

"Hel—lo there, Sydney." Kyle's voice dropped into practiced intimacy. "I knew you were where you belonged. If you ever feel a need for a change of scenery..." He let his voice trail off suggestively then went on, once more brisk. "There's a field in Willow Springs most of the pilots use. I know the people who run it."

"Could you find out if anyone new has flown in recently, like the man who came by your place?" She stared at the cold fireplace, planning as she spoke. "If he did fly in there, is there any way you could be alerted when someone else comes in?"

"For you, honey, anything. Who are they supposed to be watching out for?"

"I don't know what name he's using. He's about five-ten, slender build, fair complexion, wavy light brown hair. He's an All-American type, could be mistaken for the coach of the Little League baseball team at first glance. If anyone has the opportunity to see him with his sleeves rolled up, he has an old scar on his right forearm. There should also be some healing scratches, maybe bruises, on his face." She didn't look at Devin as she spoke, but she could feel his struggle to remain calm.

"Sounds like a real appealing fellow. I went to school

with some of the guys in the Sheriff's department. Want me to talk to them for you?"

"No." Now Sydney made her voice as firm as possible. "Just get a message to one of us. Do not say or do anything to this person."

Ty lifted the receiver, pushing the button that would take the telephone off speaker, to enforce the warning and hold a short, private discussion with his friend. No one else noticed. Jamie stared at Sydney, shaking his head in denial. Devin merely sat, but it was the motionless posture of a hunting cat watching for its prey.

"But—he's dead, Syd," Jamie muttered. "I saw the reports."

"So did a lot of people. No one ever saw the body." She raised a hand to run her fingers through her hair, then grimaced when she remembered she didn't have nails that would scratch her scalp satisfactorily.

"Is this her ex-husband you're talking about?" Devin asked, his voice devoid of emotion.

"Rick Wallace was the leader of the group that hung us out to dry when I first met Syd and her dad," Jamie explained. "When we heard he was dead, everything went to pieces."

Sydney could feel the shaking deep in her body, but worked to hide it. She couldn't let them know how scared she was or they'd never let her out of the house, especially Devin. The large hand he kept around hers relaxed, twisting to link his fingers with her, tightening slightly as though seeking reassurance. She returned the subtle pressure.

"Rick won't show until he's positive I'm here. We'll need to let them know where to find me without realizing they're being set up."

"No," Ty said, hanging up the telephone and joining the conversation in the middle. "You're safe as long as they don't know where you are."

"Safe is a relative term and a temporary condition. As long as they don't realize we're on to them, we hold the upper hand. Since they'll have the superior firepower, we'll need all the advantage we can steal."

She stared at her nails, seeing plans and plots instead of stubs. Devin and Ty waited.

"Jamie, we'll need to know all you can remember about the men looking for me. Particularly where they seemed to hang out. I need to go into town, anyway. The nail shop will be a good place to start."

"Sydney," Devin began, a warning obviously ready to be administered.

"He was never really happy roughing it," she went on relentlessly. "We have to get him away from town and into the mountains. It'll be the only way to retain our advantage."

"I'm going into town with you," Devin said, accepting no argument.

"If you want. You can get your nails done, too."

❦❦❦

"You really want to get your nails done again??

Sydney smiled at him. It had taken some coaxing to

get them to go along with her plan, but eventually even he had to admit they wouldn't get anything done until they brought Rick and his flunkies out into the open.

"I've gotten used to them by now." She held a hand up to the sunlight streaming through the truck window. It was going to be a beautiful day. "Actually, the final product is much nicer than I could ever grow on my own."

Devin glanced over at the small hand lit by morning sun. Most of the bruises had faded, and it was only the lack of nails now that gave any evidence to her ordeal over a week before. That, and an occasional stiffness she tried to not let him see.

Petite warrior. The image of a gun-toting Sydney dressed for deadly combat was difficult to conjure. In spite of her story, he still saw her as she'd been in Los Angeles, a driven, independent, very feminine businesswoman. Maybe because he still got chills thinking about some of the stories Jamie shared so eagerly.

"Won't you run a risk of getting them caught on things?"

"They can be made any length, and they protect my fingers better than my own nails."

Devin gave his attention to the morning traffic as he eased onto the state highway. A comfortably intimate silence filled the truck cab until he reached highway speed.

"While we're in town, don't go anywhere without me," he said abruptly. "I won't be far away from you at any time."

"How romantic," Sydney murmured, turning to stare out the window at the late spring flowers along the side of the road. She wasn't sure why, but she wanted to egg him into some other reaction besides a professional concern.

"Sydney, I'm trying to keep you safe."

"I'm trying to get this over and done with so I can get on with my life." She knew she sounded perverse, but Devin's automatic assumption of masculine superiority was as hard to take as him realizing she made a more convincing man than a woman. Not that he had said that. Not yet, anyway.

"All ready for that job in Europe?"

"Sure. It pays well, and they need my particular expertise. It'll be a great boost to my career."

Devin slammed on the brakes, wrenching the truck to the shoulder of the road. He stopped, both hands tight on the wheel, staring at the road in front of them and the traffic going past.

"Let's make a little deal, okay? Until this is over with, let's not talk about your career. Especially not while we're in town."

He wouldn't look at her, and she refused to answer until he did. When he finally turned to her for an answer, she wished he hadn't. There was no emotion in his amber eyes.

"You're not making a lot of sense, Devin."

He reached out to her finally, one gentle stroke along her cheekbone with his calloused finger. His hand rested briefly on her shoulder.

"Bodyguards don't have to make sense. They just guard."

His hand wandered across her neck, then traced along

the shoulder strap of the seat belt. He followed the strap to the closure at her hip. For a moment it seemed as if he would release the latch, giving her freedom to move in the truck cab and a subtle invitation to come closer to him. Then he let his hand drop to the truck seat.

"Sydney, I know you've taken care of yourself very well in the past, and you think you have a handle on this situation. No matter how much experience you have, I have more. Would you let me take care of you?"

"If it means that much to you—"

"I can't concentrate on watching over you if I never know where you'll be next."

Confused by the emotion he showed in his voice and actions while his expression remained remote, Sydney reached out a hand to touch him as he had touched her. His chin was freshly shaved that morning, and a warm pulse beat at the base of his neck. Rigid muscles under his denim work shirt held him ready to react at a moment's notice.

She reached the taut cords on the back of his hand, where it lay clenched on the seat. After a moment he relaxed, turning his hand to take hers in a firm, gentle grasp.

"Okay, Devin. I'll refrain from discussing Europe, and I'll let you play bodyguard. Good enough?"

Chapter 11

Through the front window of the parked pickup truck, Devin could see all the entrances to the small strip mall. Sydney had chosen well. All the stores she needed were in one location, with adequate parking and few places for anyone to hide.

He'd gone in with her at first, risking noxious acrylic fumes and the amusement of the manicurists. Once it was obvious nothing could happen to her in the shop, and knowing he could breathe far better outside, he retreated to the truck. She waved as she came out, indicating another shop with nothing but feminine apparel in the window. Devin followed, hesitating in the doorway. The blue-haired clerk probably wore the last steel corset in the continental United States, and did not seem to think he would be able to help Sydney shop.

This time, he waited on a bench in the shade, his back against a stone wall. In a surprisingly short time, she came out laden with packages she handled carefully, guarding her nails.

"All done. What's for lunch?"

A smile the likes of which he'd never seen before widened her mouth, adding a new sparkle to her eyes. Desire, never far from him these days, returned with a vengeance. Devin took the packages under one arm, placing his hand against the small of her back to guide her toward the truck. "It's your operation. What do you want?"

"I want something from some national chain that has to manipulate figures to make up a nutritional chart. I've been eating healthy meals for way too long."

Devin laughed as he put her and her packages into the truck. Who would have thought the daughter of a famous soldier, a sophisticated world traveler in her own right, was a junk food junkie? How could he deny her the treat? They could look for bad guys later.

✂✂✂

Sydney slid the last French fry into her mouth, following it with a noisy slurp from her milk shake. It was like playing hooky to be enjoying depraved food while they were supposed to be making plans to locate and deal with someone who wanted to kill her. She wanted to keep the fantasy alive as long as possible.

The restaurant was nearly empty, plastic seats taken up by midweek shoppers and mothers with very young children. She could almost believe she and Devin had stopped off for a quick snack before going to pick their own children up at nursery school. Almost. In that direction lay more misery than she had ever experienced. She had to change the images in her mind quickly before she lost all her self-preservation and discretion.

"Tell me about Charlie, Devin," she asked quietly, crumpling the hamburger wrapper and stuffing it into the French fry bag.

It was fortunate he'd already swallowed his coffee, or he would have ended up sputtering hot liquid all over both of them. Devin set the Styrofoam cup down, automatically looking around to be sure no one could have overheard. He'd chosen well, a table in the corner with full view of the restaurant and no one nearby.

"Where did you hear about—Jamie," he said slowly, answering his own question.

"I knew something was going on. If there had been cattle missing, Ty wouldn't have been around so much, and you wouldn't have ridden out alone. Jamie just hinted me in the right direction." She sipped at a cup of water, helping to wash down the rich thickness of the milk shake. "How long has he been hiding out?"

He actually looked like he was going to tell her. Then a habitual glance around the room and into the parking lot took his attention away from their conversation.

"Let's continue this conversation outside, shall we?" he asked casually, sliding out of the booth and reaching for the tray of litter in one smooth move.

Sydney responded without question. A quick look, as she rose with him, showed her two men in casual dress with a far from casual demeanor getting out of an innocuous rental car. The men glanced around the parking lot, noticing everything while pretending not to. Kyle Jorden and Jamie had described them perfectly as California beach types with death on their minds.

"Bingo," she breathed, feeling her instincts begin to go on alert.

Devin took a firm hold of her elbow.

"Remember, these are only flunkies. We want them to see you and report back, that's all."

Her nod indicated that she did hear and was willing, for now, to go along with the plan as outlined at the ranch. She felt a centered energy in the way she walked and kept herself at a perfect distance from him. Some old habits never died.

In the end, it was a prosaic encounter. They slipped through a side door that only served as an exit while the men entered through the main doors. After a moment, Sydney walked past the windows, appearing absorbed in something across the street.

The men stiffened like pointers on a scent when the sun glinted off Sydney's hair. It only took a casual glance on her part at the children playing in a nearby park for them to confirm the identification. Unfortunately, by the time the men were out the door, intending to follow the truck sedately merging with traffic, all the air had leaked from both of the car's rear tires.

Sharp objects tended to have that effect on rubber, particularly when the objects were inserted with some force.

ↄↄↄↄ

As the pick-up truck sped down the interstate, heading west and south, away from Stormhaven, Sydney started displaying an unusual giddiness. After the second or third giggle escaped her control, Devin looked over, trying to control the smile on his face.

"Do you always act silly when you're on a job?"

"Not at all." She managed perfect sobriety for a few seconds, then her composure crumpled again, and she hid her face in her hands. The new nails, a muted shade of copper, were thrust into her hair as she tried to pull herself together. "I've always been accused of being far too intense. Particularly at the beginning of a job. I usually don't relax until after everything is done."

"You must be making up for a lost childhood."

"Mmmm, perhaps. Maybe it's the company."

Devin didn't know how to respond to that. Sydney had never been easy for him to understand. The revelations about her upbringing only confused him more. She'd sounded so accepting of her father's work, even somewhat proud. How would she accept another battle scarred ex-warrior? He was not helped by the continuous demands of his body. Now that her injuries were healing, there was no reason to avoid resuming intimacy. Except for the uncertainty he felt at this new side of her.

"You're doing it again," he said, studying the traffic in the rear-view mirrors.

"Doing what?"

"Judging me against people you've known in the past.

Throwing out mixed signals. Confusing me." He signaled for the next exit, heading for the county road that would take them around Willow Springs, back to Stormhaven. "Changing. Any minute now, I expect to see you wearing a business suit, with your hair back in that God-awful knot."

At this she turned to face him, easing the shoulder belt and raising her left leg onto the seat. With the switch off the freeway, they weren't driving as fast, but the route required more concentration. Devin frowned beneath his hat, his concentration seeming to be fully on the road.

"I don't have any business suits, remember?"

"You went shopping. You could have gotten some."

"Are you trying to pick a fight with me for some reason? Maybe to show I don't have enough control to be trusted on this job?"

"Don't be ridiculous. You're in on this because you know one of the people involved."

"I'm 'in on this,' Devin, because it's something I should have taken care of long ago, instead of letting other people do it for me. Rick should never have been allowed to get away with what he did."

"You're not Superwoman, Sydney. Nor are you responsible for righting all the wrongs in the world. If you make this personal, you'll blow your concentration."

"Am I the only one taking this personally?"

"I'm dealing in the here and now, not trying to atone for something I couldn't do anything about before. No matter how well you were trained, you're still only one person."

"And a female. Don't forget to add that," she said, jerking back around to glare out the window.

"That's one thing I'll never forget, Sydney."

His voice was a warm caress, easing into her confused mind. Sydney caught her breath, letting herself let go, just a bit—just for now, while they were ahead of the bad guys and the sun was shining. She could pretend, for a while, that she was out for a drive with her guy, and her greatest worry was what to fix for dinner.

"I didn't," she said, stifling another, softer, giggle.

"Could you be just a bit more specific?" Devin attempted to growl, but he was trying too hard to suppress a chuckle at the sudden mischievous tone in her voice.

"I didn't buy a business suit. I hate the damned things. That's why I store them at a dry cleaner in between jobs."

"What did you buy?"

The smile she gave him was another new one, this time filled with the timeless mystery of all females.

✃✃✃

Jamie met them at Devin's house, with the message that Ty wanted to see them as soon as they were back. On the way out, Sydney picked up her old leather knapsack.

"In the office," Ty called out to them as they entered his house. "How'd it go in town?"

"Not bad," Sydney slung her knapsack onto a chair as she came over to Ty's desk. "I got some new nails, new clothes, and a positive ID by Rick's goons."

This brought Ty around from behind his desk. His

concern was relieved when Devin came in behind Sydney, shaking his head.

"You're gonna turn his hair white, Sydney. Ty's not up to shocks like that."

"Sit down, you two, and tell me what happened."

They arranged themselves in chairs while Devin went over the day with a minimum of embellishment. Sydney added comments from time to time, but mostly stayed quiet, her feet tucked under her while she relaxed in the large chair.

"You're sure they were the same guys Jamie saw?"

"No doubt about it. They definitely recognized Sydney, and I made sure they got a good look at the plates."

They had used a truck registered to a cattle company in Las Cruces. The man who loaned it to them was up to have a look at Mosby before the formal showing scheduled for the next month. He hadn't asked why they needed to borrow it, hoping his generosity would give him easier access to stud rights.

"That should slow them down a bit."

"Someone will call that company and find out Harris was up here. You might have gained a couple hours, if they don't get an answer back on the plates immediately," Sydney pointed out.

"You sound like you've done this before," Ty said, turning to her with a slight frown.

"Contingency planning was my specialty. Dad used to have me come up with every possible glitch in a plan, and two ways to get out of it."

"Was that when you were working with him?" Devin

shifted on the couch. It wasn't as comfortable without her pressed against his side.

"It started when I was in middle school. Dad used to go over battle strategy as a study exercise. I suppose it helped, I always had high marks in history and math."

The two men could only look at each other, then at her. There wasn't much that could be said. Sydney caught the glance, and some of the animation went out of her face.

"I know it wasn't an ordinary upbringing for a girl, but it was the only thing Dad could share with me. He didn't know about much else but fighting and strategy."

"He knew about raising a daughter to be decent and honest, Sydney," Devin said quietly. "He must have known something, or you wouldn't have turned out the way you did."

Sydney looked up, meeting the warm gold of his eyes. Her lower lip slid in between her teeth. She'd never seen him so open, with no remote shield on his expression. Then Ty cleared his throat and reached for a paper on the desk, and the moment was gone.

"Your Doctor Erik called while you two were playing *Mission Impossible* in town," Ty said, finally managing to get hold of the paper without getting up. "Seems he had a call from Rick Wallace. Wanted you to know—as he put it—'The slime has come out of the swamp.' Wallace was trying to find out where you were."

"I forgot to call Erik and warn him Rick was still alive."

"He didn't seem too surprised. Said he knew you weren't telling him everything, but you never had.

Anyway, Wallace was still playing good guy so he didn't try any threats. Just asked where in New Mexico you were staying."

"If he did have us followed here, it wasn't past that truck stop." She pulled her legs up against her body and rested her chin on her knees. "That's been bothering me for a while. How would he know to have men ask about me in Willow Springs? It's not a major stopping off point. I don't think I had anything identifying the ranch in my luggage."

"It's one of those things we'll have to worry about later," Ty said, standing up from his chair and moving again behind the desk. "In the meantime," he went on, his voice muffled as he searched for something in a lower drawer. "We might as well get ourselves ready."

Clutching something in his hand, Ty moved over to a row of file cabinets. Unlocking the cabinet on the end, he reached in to the back of the drawer, and they heard a faint click. A powerful shove moved the cabinet away from the wall, obviously on hidden wheels. This revealed a door in the wall, with a recessed lock.

"I must admit, I am impressed," said Sydney, the mischief back in her voice. "Do you have a secret passage to your getaway jet mobile?"

"My grandfather always liked to have someplace only he and the family knew about. When I took over the ranch I upgraded his system."

With a conjurer's flair, he swung open a heavy door, stepping back with a wave of his hand.

"I like to call it the Equalizer room."

"Good grief, are you planning a war any time soon?" Sydney said, rising gracefully to her feet.

The open door revealed a small, shallow chamber, lit from within and filled with classic weapons of all descriptions. From the condition of the gun barrels and sword blades, it was obvious the chamber was protected from dust and moisture. Sydney approached, her attention riveted on the display.

"My many-times-removed great-grandfather started collecting before he ever came to New Mexico, and we've kept up with the habit," Ty said, reaching out to the corner of one of the walls. "All of these were personally collected by the family. Nothing was bought. Not with cash, anyway." Releasing the lever, he swung the wall out, revealing a more modern array.

Sydney showed some interest in the shotguns and machine pistols, but soon went back to the original display. Flintlock pistols were set next to Samurai swords and, below them, ancient crossbows. There were knives of finest Damascus steel with hand-carved bone handles, and roughly fashioned primitive knives with wickedly sharp edges. Early horse pistols made matched dueling weapons look exquisitely deadly, and slender swords seemed incongruous next to battle axes.

"My family has always accepted the call to fight," Ty said quietly. "As rational human beings, they saw the need to protect what was theirs."

Sydney carefully fingered the deadly edge of a broadsword. "It's a fabulously valuable collection. No wonder you keep it locked up."

"That used to be habit. Now it's a necessity. No one brings weapons to Stormhaven beyond this house. Devin and I have weapons locked up in our houses. No one else is allowed to keep a weapon. It was for safety, when some men showed up who weren't real tightly wound."

"It's the best way we could come up with to help men make the adjustment," Devin explained. "The hardest thing to learn is that you no longer have to be responsible for your own hide."

"If that's the case," Sydney said, her smile growing as she walked back into the room, "I'd better give you this."

She reached for the knapsack, transferring it to a chair near Ty's desk before unzipping it. Jungle fatigues, dark T-shirts, dark bandannas, and a small mess kit were set to one side. Then she reached back in, pulling out cloth wrapped packages and placing each one on the desk.

"That's the bag Erik gave you at the train station, isn't it?" Devin asked, drawing closer to the desk.

Sydney nodded, her attention on the items she was now unwrapping, using the cloth as protection. Memories flooded through her as she touched each item. Protective oil soiled her fingers, but she ignored it, concentrating instead on what she uncovered.

"This was my work bag, when I was with Dad. I could get a minimum of food and a maximum of weapons in here, mostly knives. It held enough to last a month if I could find somewhere to wash up." She laughed, but it was not a cheerful sound. "No perfume, as you can see, and I kept my hair almost as short as Devin's. Not exactly Mata Hari, but I got the job done."

After looking at Sydney for her approval, Devin reached out to pick up a small, intricately carved knife in a worn leather sheath. When he pulled out the knife, he found the blade was razor sharp. Against his dark hand the knife looked exceptionally delicate, an elegant instrument of death.

"That was my first knife. Dad brought it back with him when I was in grade school. I think that's when my mother decided to leave."

"Was she afraid of him?" Ty asked, quick interest on his face.

"Not at first," Sydney chose her words carefully. She didn't often speak about her life, but Ty had the right to know why Lana would never have been able to live here. "I think she was fascinated by his aura of power and danger. She had an interesting career, so she didn't even mind the long absences. Then I think she began to realize that sometimes he couldn't leave the battles behind."

"Did your father ever get…rough with her?" Devin asked.

"Never. Dad was very gallant and old-fashioned about a lot of things. We used to argue about it." She smiled at a long-buried memory. "No, Dad would come back from some of his assignments and he would need time to himself. Culture shock, I guess. Toward the end of his military career, I know he had lost a lot of faith in his superiors.

"Anyway," she continued, reaching for another bundle. "He started talking about getting out and spending more time at home with all of us. My mother didn't like that idea at all. Looking back, she probably had a boyfriend, and she didn't want the arrangement upset. At the time, all I knew is that they argued a lot, then she left, and Lana went with her."

Before either man could react, before any of them could continue on this sensitive subject, Sydney finished unrolling the bundle in her hands.

"Here they are," she said with a laugh. "My little 'balis.'" She sorted through the collection of folding butterfly knives, ranging from totally functional to extremely ornate. Then she reached out and chose two knives, manipulating them in flashing patterns that seemed to be random but were the result of hours of intensive practice. She finished with a satisfied smile, the blades concealed, the knives in her pockets.

"It's amazing, the things they teach girls now in school, isn't it, Ty?" Devin sounded almost...proud.

"Utterly fascinating," Ty said, sorting through the collection of weapons. "My sister's going to love meeting you. What's this?"

"Um...That looks like a pistol to me, Ty," Sydney said, gravely, barely suppressing her amusement. "Standard military issue. It was Dad's."

"I'd have thought you'd have something high-powered and exotic, that couldn't be seen on an airport's X-ray."

Sydney's hands stilled, and she raised her eyes to meet Ty's. His grin faded when he saw the expression on her face. Devin stepped forward, raising a hand to her.

"Sydney," Ty said quickly, "It was a joke. Not a good joke, but it was still a joke."

"Of course." She smiled as she turned back to her inspection. "We never…Dad was involved in stupid wars in countries that only existed for a few years at a time. It wasn't the best vocation, but it was what he did best. He considered terrorism a game for cowards and fools."

Ty was for once without a reply or a smile, and an uncomfortable silence dampened the spirits of the group. Then Devin picked up a folded knife, extended the blade and studied the workmanship somberly.

"I have one a lot like this."

"Only yours is longer?" Sydney ventured.

"You two aren't going to get into a 'mine is better than yours,' are you?" Ty's humor was a bit forced, until Sydney and Devin both chuckled, and he could join in.

Ty turned back to the storage room, once more studying the available weapons with an eye for choosing the most appropriate for the up-coming trip. Behind his back, Devin reached out to stroke the back of his hand gently along Sydney's cheek. After a moment she offered him a small smile of reassurance, rubbing her cheek against his fingers. When the telephone rang, he let Ty answer it, since he was too busy at more important things.

"Stormhaven. Yes, Kyle. Hold on a minute." Ty twisted around, pushing various buttons until the neighboring rancher's voice came in perfectly clear.

"—and she told me they were due in sometime to-night."

"Back up a minute, Kyle," Devin said, stepping closer

to the speaker. "We missed the first part of that. Who's coming?"

"Not sure who, but he must be important. The same plane that brought in the goons called for airport clearance. No way to know who's on the plane yet, but the two surfer boys are already there, wearing a hole in the floor."

"You didn't tell anyone anything," Sydney said. It was a statement, not a question. She rose fluidly to begin pacing around the room.

"Hey there, sweetcakes." Kyle's greeting sounded as eager as ever, but there was a note of exhaustion in his voice. "You see, there's this luscious little red-head over there, name's Holly. She just naturally likes to talk to me, so when I asked them to keep me informed—"

"We need to get them up in the mountains, away from the ranch," Sydney mused, holding the back of her neck as she paced.

Devin slipped an arm around her waist, stopping her restless movements by pulling her against his side. "You're making me dizzy, babe," he murmured, holding her still when she would have pulled away. There was a fine trembling in the body he held, a new tension. "Kyle," Devin said, raising his voice slightly to be heard on the speaker phone. "How long before the plane is scheduled to land? Enough time for someone to get over there?"

"Not for your antiquated transportation. I'd take you over there with me, but you'd have to get your own way home."

"You can't go over there," Sydney protested.

"Holly's expecting dinner in Santa Fe. I can't disappoint the ladies."

Kyle's disembodied voice sounded breezy, but there was a power to him unlike any Sydney had heard so far. This was the man who controlled international corporations. She doubted he could be dissuaded by anything she said. Turning in Devin's hold, she lifted her face and he leaned over to her.

"Don't let him do it," she said in an undertone. "Rick's too dangerous for Kyle to handle."

"I've never known anyone who could tell Kyle what to do," he murmured back, taking advantage of her worry to hold her closer, stroking his hand along her back. "The man can take care of himself."

"Sydney's worried about you, Kyle," Ty said loudly, leaning back in his chair. "I'm not too thrilled about this myself."

"If I promise to be a good boy and not talk to strangers, will you let me go, Mommy?"

"It's not a joking matter, Kyle. If the man flying in is who we think, he's extremely dangerous." The concern in Sydney's voice intensified.

"Let's cool down a minute," Ty said, over the indignant spluttering from the telephone speaker. "Sydney knows more about this guy than anyone, Kyle. If she says he's dangerous, you should listen to her. However," he went on, still ignoring the noises. "We do need someone to get a message to the man, so we can send him where we want him to go."

"I should be capable of that," Kyle said, still sounding

indignant, but calmer. "What do you want to tell him?"

"We need to get him to follow us into the mountains," Devin said, holding a finger over Sydney's mouth. "Hush a minute, babe," he said softly.

"You sweet-talking that little cutie?"

"The man's insatiable," Sydney muttered, moving Devin's hand off her face. "Kyle, do you think the men you talked to before will remember you?"

"Should be able to. I can certainly remember them. Why?"

"It would be natural for you to talk to them if you were going into the airport to pick up your date. They're going to be grasping for information, so they'll have something to give their boss when he gets in from LA."

"Utah. Holly said the plane's coming in from Salt Lake City."

"Damn," she muttered. "That makes them closer than I thought. Why Utah?" She shook her head, deciding to shelve that puzzle for now. "Tell the men you remembered seeing me, but you never heard my name. Give them the general direction of the ranch, and tell them I'm not here any longer."

"You're not leaving," Devin's suddenly possessive hold was as strong as the note in his voice.

"You know I can't stay here. Rick has to be lured away from the ranch to someplace he can be handled."

"Tell them she's gone off into the mountains," Ty suggested. "With another man. From the sound of things, that'll get his attention. She'll be gone a couple of days."

"Make it a week at least," Sydney said. "Any less and

he might be willing to wait. He never much cared for roughing it."

"Want me to tell him you're on a pleasure trip?" asked Kyle, interest easing into his voice.

"No, tell him they're looking for sites for hunting camps. We need to start taking on tourists for extra cash," Ty said, warming to the story.

"Not hunting," Sydney corrected. "Someone at the airport is bound to know you don't hunt here. Fishing camps. Remote ones, where planes can't land, for executive types who really want to rough it."

"Good idea," Devin gave her a quick squeeze. "There are places up there so rough, you couldn't find a spot to set down a chopper."

"Got it." Kyle sounded impatient to get on with his task. "Anything else?"

"Yeah," Ty said. "Be careful, buddy."

"Always. I owe it to a lot of young ladies to take care of this body."

He hung up amid the general groans of his listeners. The humor soon faded, and the three of them looked at each other gravely.

"There's still time for me to be out of here," Sydney offered. "I can lay a trail to a city somewhere else, away from the ranch."

"You'll do anything to get out of roughing it, won't you?" Devin didn't sound angry over her continued attempt to leave the ranch, only slightly preoccupied. "We'll need to get going as soon as possible. If you pack up what you need, I'll call down to the barn and have them get a couple horses ready."

"Three," she said, stowing wrapped weapons back into her knapsack. "We're supposed to be taking a long trip, remember?"

"You never stop planning do you?" Devin smiled quickly. "Okay, three. Now, get going. We'll get things set up here and I'll be right behind you." He looked her over somberly. "Hope you're up to some serious riding, babe. I want to be up to the tree line before it gets dark."

Chapter 12

The gray mare snorted softly, clearing her nostrils of dust picked up on their swift ride across the ranch to the trees. The setting sun made stark silhouettes of the mountains, set off by a golden red sky. Sydney shifted in the saddle, wondering if this was really a good idea. She didn't want Rick near the ranch, but how long could she keep up with Devin on horseback, particularly on the rugged trails he chose.

"Doing okay back there?" he asked, looking back over his shoulder. The wide brim of his hat concealed his eyes, but Sydney had no doubt he was enjoying himself. It was evident in the relaxed way he sat his horse and the tone of his voice. Once they'd begun climbing, he'd removed the pack horse's leading rein, leaving only a very short rope.

"No problem," she assured him. This had been her idea after all, and there was no other way to handle the situation. It would do no good to mention she was fairly sure her backside was permanently numb.

It looked like she would be experiencing another unnerving scramble up loose rock, between the pine trees, to a higher level of non-trail.

Devin eased his horse up the slope, making it look easy, and the pack horse scuttled blithely up behind. Allowing a moment for the dust to settle, Sydney leaned forward, taking a strong hold on some mane and giving the gray mare her head.

Once the horses were grouped together on a small ledge, Devin didn't immediately head in a new direction, as he had for the last three hours.

Instead, he nudged his bay over near Sydney, bending in the saddle slightly to get a closer look at her face under the borrowed hat. She lifted her chin, offering him a bright smile.

"Can you hold on just a little longer?" he asked, obviously not fooled by her attempted bravado. "It'll start getting rough now, but it's not much farther to a good camping spot."

"Getting rough?" She gulped. "No problem, fearless leader. We Castletons are in for the long haul."

Now he did smile, one side of his mouth tilting up while he reached over to push a stray lock of hair behind her ear. A quick tug pulled the collar of her coat, actually one of Ty's sister's, farther up on her neck.

"Remember that later," he said with an enigmatic twist to his smile. At the press of a heel, the gelding turned away, taking the lead again in a series of uphill lunges.

ღღღ

Sydney eased herself down onto the bedrolls Devin had arranged for her use, letting her eyes slide shut. He was tending to the horses and building a fire, although it seemed much warmer at the campsite than she would have thought. Her job, he had said, was to rest. She hoped she had enough energy left for the job.

The sun finally deserted their side of the world, leaving a night sky that was intensely black, a perfect backdrop for the shawl of stars flung across the horizon. By ranch standards it was still early, but here in the mountains it was time for bed. She only wished she could have a shower to wash off the aftereffects of their mad dash up the mountainside.

"Tired?" a soft voice asked near her ear. If she could be bothered to open her eyes, she was sure he would be wearing that funny grin he'd found on the trail. It was almost worth the effort.

"I don't know if I'm tired as much as totally bone-less," she admitted, finally easing her eyes open. Yep, he had that smile on, and a warm glow in his predator's eyes. Maybe that was just the fire's reflection.

"Could you find your bones long enough to wash up and eat?" he asked, an oddly disappointed note in his voice.

"What is it?" she asked, stiffening her spine and pushing herself into a semi-erect position.

"Nothing, babe. You need your rest."

"We need to call Ty," she reminded him, accepting

the warm damp towel he'd carried over to her. It felt heavenly against her hands and face.

"I called him just before we turned into this valley. Otherwise the mountains block reception."

"When were you planning to tell me?"

"When you were on the ground and relaxed, your majesty," he teased, setting out sandwiches Maria had packed for them. Coffee was already made and staying warm by the fire. "Kyle dropped your little bombshell and is now on his way to Santa Fe with Holly. He only talked to the goons, but he saw a man who fit your description getting out of the Learjet as he was leaving. Apparently the news did not make Wallace happy."

"Too bad." Sydney bit into the thick beef sandwich, enjoying the taste treat of imported mustard and homemade bread. "If Rick follows his normal routine, he'll be on the move at first light. He'll probably try to spot us from the air and hope to land nearby. When he finds out he can't, he'll get as close as possible. I doubt he'll bring many men with him. He'll want to take care of this personally."

"Why did you ever marry him?" Devin asked, looking away from her, his pose anything but casual. He drank the steaming coffee in small sips, having devoured two sandwiches already.

"I was lonely, I guess. Dad was gone all the time and I was off at college, cramming as many courses as I could, to get done earlier. Rick came by to visit. I'd known him before, and it was like holding on to my youth for a couple more years, to go out with him." She hesitated, staring at the cheerful fire. "He convinced me that he'd always cared about me and had just been waiting for me to grow up. It seemed…I don't know, romantic or something. When he found out I was still a virgin, he even wanted to wait until we were married." She drew her knees up to her body, hugging herself into a small ball, and continued in a tired voice.

"When I told Dad, he didn't say much. He'd never told me what to do with my life, and since his own marriage was such a disaster, he didn't feel he had the right to tell me who to marry. He did ask, a couple of times, if I was very sure, and if this was really what I wanted." She paused, gulping. "God help me, I said yes."

She didn't go on, for which Devin was profoundly thankful. Knowing what he did about Wallace's type of man, he didn't need her to fill in the details about her wedding night, and her subsequent marriage. No wonder she'd had little use for intimacy. It was a miracle she'd allowed him as close as she had. He eased his arm around her shoulders, offering silent comfort.

"When I left Rick, Dad still didn't say much. He didn't ask why I had come home, but he apparently saw or sensed something. I heard later that Rick was in the hospital for about a month. Word was he got mugged."

"I wish I'd met your father."

"He would have liked you, and what you and Ty are doing at Stormhaven." She allowed herself to relax, drawing strength from his nearness and warmth.

"We haven't done all that much. Just hired some guys who were looking for jobs."

"You've tried to make a difference. You've succeeded too, for the most part."

"Not always. Every time we think we're doing good, something like Charlie happens." He eased her closer then pulled her onto his lap, cradling her between his legs, her back against his chest. After a moment she relaxed, trusting him to take her whole weight. Wrapping his arms around her, he offered the coffee then rested his cheek against the cool silk of her hair.

"I don't think Charlie ever really came back from his last mission," he said, watching the mug held between their hands. "It was in Rhodesia and ended up pretty ugly. No one ever got all the details, but only a couple guys out of his unit made it back. Charlie was one of the leaders, and I understand some of the wives and families blamed him. That was all it took to push him over the edge."

"It's harder, sometimes, when you do it for pay," she said quietly. At the questioning tone from deep in his throat, she went on. "When you're in the midst of atrocities and senseless deaths during a military maneuver, you can always claim that you do it for the greater good. If you need a scapegoat, you can say that anything you did was done under orders.

"Most of the men I knew fought because that was what they thought they did best. Some of them had been trained to kill by their government and found out they had a certain knack for it. A few actually enjoyed it, but most of them were convinced they couldn't make money any other way."

"What about you?" He rested his face in the curve of

her neck, letting himself get drunk on the warmth and smell of her. When she tilted her head, allowing him free access, he felt every nerve ending in his body come to life.

"I enjoyed solving the logistics problems. By the time Dad would let me work with him, he was more likely to avoid a fight if he could. He made sure I knew how to defend myself then made very sure I never got a chance to do more than practice."

A tiny moan escaped her as she felt the edges of his teeth close, ever so gently, on the sensitive skin above her collarbone.

When his tongue eased away the sting of the tiny sensual wound, she shifted restlessly, trying to turn in his arms, trying to get closer to him than two jackets and other layers of warm clothing would allow.

"Devin, what are you doing to me?"

"What I've always wanted to do and never had the chance. I was so worried about hurting you the way Wallace did."

"You could never hurt me the way he did," she assured him. "Rick claimed he loved me."

"Babe," Devin whispered, his voice strained. "I—"

"It's all right, Devin. You want me with a blazing honesty. I've learned honest lust is far better than love that can only be a lie."

Devin swallowed past a knot in his throat. He sensed something wrong in her soft words but couldn't track down the thought. He tossed the rest of the coffee into the fire and set the mug out of the way.

Shifting, he stretched both of them out on the bedrolls,

holding her still with the weight of his leg thrown across hers.

"How tired are you, honestly?" He rose over her to see the firelight reflected in the darkening silver of her eyes. The fire would paint all of her creamy skin golden.

"I seem to be less and less tired every second." She arched against his leg and the hard warmth of his body. "Maria must have put extra vitamins in the sandwiches."

"It's the fresh mountain air." He eased the buttons of her suede jacket open, while she worked on his. "Revitalizes you." He laid back the edges of the jacket, framing her in creamy fleece lining, revealing what she wore underneath. He stopped, holding himself very still, looking at her in the firelight, trying to hold in his reaction.

The air was chilly, but heat rose around them in great waves. Sydney felt blissfully lethargic, and was content to lie back, allowing Devin to do whatever he wanted. Once she had his jacket opened and could rest her hands in the warmth trapped by the heavy shearling, she was happy. For the moment.

Devin opened her coat as though he anticipated uncovering a treasure of great worth. Then his hands stilled on her body and he raised his head. Reflected fire danced a pagan ritual in his eyes. A great tension took over his body, and he began to tremble against her hands. Sydney lay very still, not wanting to jeopardize the moment.

The trembling deep within finally made its way to the surface and Devin was overcome with laughter. It started as a chuckle, then a full booming roar of delight. At first Sydney was intrigued by his obvious pleasure. When he fell back against the bedrolls, his forearm covering his eyes in a vain attempt at control, she decided it had gone far enough. Pulling the jacket closed around her suddenly chilled body, she turned away, facing the fire grimly.

A gentle, firm hand on her shoulder turned her back. Warm palms covered her fingers, releasing her grip on the jacket, and she was once more exposed to his gaze. Amusement still lurked on his rough, scarred face but it was a warm glow now.

"I thought we dispensed with these problems."

"You laughed at me."

"Look at yourself!"

The opened jacket framed an incongruous picture. Sydney had splurged on pretty cotton sweaters in town. The aqua one she wore now had a lace trim and dainty bows decorating the scooped collar. Over the sweater she wore her heavy old fatigue shirt, clean but stained, marked with roughly patched tears. The contrast was amusing, she admitted to herself after a moment.

"That's better," Devin whispered, as he bent over to taste her growing smile.

What had been intended as a tiny kiss became a deepening embrace. Once his mouth brushed hers, and her tongue slipped out to delicately trace his lower lip, Devin had to press closer, trying once again for the bliss of near perfect union. By the time he forcibly raised his head they were both breathing raggedly.

Devin rested his forehead against hers, wondering if it would always be like this with her, so hot and wild, fulfilling on all levels. They were fully clothed and had done no more than exchange a kiss. He was painfully aroused already, and Sydney's breath came in short gasps that heated his cheek.

He opened his eyes enough to look down their bodies. Yep, there was the bulge in his jeans that had been making life interesting for a long time. Under the ridiculous fatigue shirt, even through the sweater, he could see the rise of Sydney's sensitive nipples. He had touched and held and tasted those delicate nubs, entirely too long ago.

Raising his head enough to look into her slumberous silver eyes, he began to work on the buttons of her over-shirt.

"I didn't mean to laugh at you, babe. It just struck me funny to see you in lace and jungle gear. Like garters and gun belts. Kind of makes me hot, now that I think about it."

"Give it up, Starke. You had an attack of the sillies. Happens to girls all the time." She tried to sound nonchalant, to banter with him archly as an experienced, sophisticated woman would be able to. Her effort failed as he pushed open her fatigue shirt, sliding the thick cotton across her aching nipples. It went through her like the jolt of an electrically charged fence.

She arched up, twisting in an instinctive effort to find some kind of release from the torment he caused. This was ridiculous. It wasn't as though they'd never touched. Devin had shown her many ways men and women could love each other and they had shared passion that was frightening in its intensity. This was different.

She didn't realize she had spoken until Devin raised

his attention from the soft aqua sweater that did so little to hide her body's reaction. He smiled, that twisted little grin she'd just recently seen on his face. His rough fingers stroked her cheek then traced a path down her body to press lightly against a demanding nipple.

"I feel it too, babe. Like it's all new again. More than just stored up frustration. It's like I only saw part of you before when I looked, just the lovely, stubborn witch who enjoyed tormenting me with every breath she drew." He ran the tips of his fingers around and across her nipples, weaving a design of frustration along her body. "I still don't see all of you now, but so much more is clear..."

His voice trailed off. Once more, he lowered his mouth to feast on hers, to plunder and tease and arouse until she writhed against him. All the while, he was inching the sweater up her undulating torso, feeling the hot silk of her skin against his rough hand. When her hands slid under his jacket and she raised herself so he could ease the sweater up her body, he felt the laughter welling inside him again.

It was a different laughter, gentle and healing. There had never been enough laughter in his life. It was odd that this small woman, whose own life had been frighteningly grim, could bring him so much joy. All rational thought fled from his fevered brain when his fingertips felt the rise of her delicate breasts through what could only be a covering of fine silk.

"I told you I got a couple of things in town," she breathed, trying to push her breast more completely into his hand.

Devin preferred teasing, until one of her small hands deserted the warm cocoon of his back and slid down his body. She cupped and stroked, measuring him with devilish delight, enjoying the shudders that wracked his big body.

"I thought more than a handful was wasted," she observed, trying for a scholarly tone.

The effort was ruined by the tiny moan that escaped her lips when Devin plucked, ever so gently, at the silk-covered nipple he held between his fingers. He shifted, pulling her across his left arm, into the curve of his body, leaving both hands free to pillage. While his left hand investigated under the sweater, exploring with all the bravado of a high school jock, his right hand slid down her body, reaching for the webbed belt that secured her fatigue pants. All the while, he arched into her delicate touch, retaining his control with a grim desperation.

The trouser buttons yielded eventually, revealing silk, again, beneath his hand. He delved further, venturing into a treasure of damp warmth. In spite of her tightening thighs he pressed his palm against her mound, massaging her sensitive nub with a large knuckle. Her body pulsed against his fingers and she clenched her hand, stroking him in a mindless frenzy.

"Wait a minute, babe," he gasped, reluctantly pulling his hand away from the warm nest and grabbing her wrist. "I've got plans for that particular part of me that don't include being rubbed into madness."

He kissed the hand he held, pausing to touch his tongue to her palm and in between her fingers. Then he sought out her other hand, securing both of them above her head in a strong, painless grip she couldn't break. She tried, straining against his hold and the leg he had thrown across her thighs, her mouth set in a grim line.

"Devin, let me go," she warned. "You won't like how I get even."

"You'd be surprised what I like. Hell, sometimes I'm surprised myself."

Once she stopped struggling and lay under him, quietly panting, he eased his hold slightly but didn't release her. The view was too good, peach silk peeking out from below her aqua sweater and in the opening of her olive drab pants. A heady aroma rose from her body, the fragrance of an aroused female in the vicinity of her mate. Not that she was going to docilely let him have his way. Sydney would fight him from now on. He wouldn't have it any other way.

Devin realized she'd gone very still against his body, and he flexed his hips, letting her feel the enormity of his need. Tiny tremors rippled under her skin, matching the erratic shaking he felt in his hands and chest. The firelight bathed her in a golden glow and gave enough illumination for him to be able to see what else Sydney had bought in town.

"Pretty, pretty," he whispered, easing the sweater up above her breasts. The peach silk enhanced rather than concealed, and a front fastening was decorated with a frivolous satin bow. "Clever people, these lingerie designers."

He bent his head, licking at each nipple in turn,

sucking and gently tugging while he released the fastening with a deft twist of his hand. When he raised his head, her damp nipples stood up dark and proud, holding onto the opened bra in spite of her continued writhing.

"More, babe?"

"I won't beg, Devin."

He gently pinched an upraised nipple, laughing beneath his breath when she came up off the ground, not trying to hide the whimper that came out of her throat. Then he stroked her, passing his hand along her body, pushing back the opened bra, sliding under the loose trousers. When her hips raised, begging soundlessly for his help, he pushed the trousers down, bringing his hand back up to trace a lacy heart inset in the front of peach silk panties.

Sydney felt as though she were being stretched on a rack of sexual desire. Devin's mouth once again tormented her increasingly sensitive breasts, his tongue lapping and holding while his lips sucked. A large warm hand marauded between her thighs and she could do nothing but twist under his touch. Her lowered pants kept her from wantonly spreading her knees the way she wanted to, and the hold on her hands was unbreakable. Somehow the helplessness of her situation added to the excitement, as though she were a favored slave girl, being taught the pleasures of her own body.

His hand pressed and stroked her through the panties. The silk enhanced his touch and increased the frustration. With a final tug, his mouth left her breasts, and he rained tiny, biting kisses along her torso. His tongue touched, ever-so-gently, along the slight discoloration still under her skin. Then warm moisture covered her navel, and a clever tongue pushed into the depression as though tasting every body opening.

The night air was cold against her damp nipples, tightening them to near pain. She heard another of the edgy whimpers slip from the back of her throat and felt a rush of warm breath against her quivering stomach. The rat was enjoying this! Plans for revenge took on an erotic aura that did nothing to diminish her current excitement.

Hot breath and a moist tongue traveled across her belly and over her panties, teasing at the increasingly damp area between her legs. Then, finally, he was pushing down her panties. She raised her hips, wriggling and writhing, trying to encourage him to hurry, dammit.

The panties went no farther than her thighs. With a muffled groan that could have been a curse, Devin nuzzled into the curls at the juncture of her legs. One hand slid under her, easing into her heated opening from behind while he leisurely savored the taste of her. His other hand covered her breasts, rubbing and massaging, returning the warmth stolen by the cool air.

It took Sydney's passion-fogged mind a minute to realize her hands were free. By the time she did, she couldn't remember how she intended to get even. She could only clench at his hair, his shoulder, his arm, straining for an end to his sensual torment. Still his tongue stroked, sliding along the rioting nerves at the edge of her woman's secrets, dipping in to taste and sliding back. His fingers spread, stretching her opening from a totally new angle, showing her things about her body's pleasure potential she would never have believed.

Devin felt the dig of her nails in his back and pushed his face harder into her fragrant curls. He knew she wanted him to get rid of their damned clothes and mount her. His aching member was threatening to dig a hole in the ground. There was something satisfying on a completely new level about teasing and tormenting and tasting her that he wanted to explore fully. Later, he would satisfy the dictator in his pants. Now, he wanted to impress himself permanently on her body's memory.

She whimpered, her scent making him drunk as she convulsed against him. His fingers felt the tightening, the erotic tremors as she trapped him in a sensual web he had no desire to escape.

ↄ৴ↄↄ

Sydney drifted in a mist of contentment, curled around Devin, the fire warm against her back. Then Devin eased her onto her back and began sliding her disheveled clothes off her body. She felt too blissfully sated to do much but straighten or pull back a limb at his low-voiced, half-laughing requests.

Soon she felt the slightly chilly sleeping bag along her bare back, and the comforting warmth of the fire on one side of her. She stretched, experimenting with the different sensations on various parts of her body. A low growl prefaced the dropping of a covering over her.

"Wench!" Devin wasn't sure where he had dredged

up the word. It was not one he'd used in the past but it perfectly described her sensuous squirming against the fabric of the bags. He tossed a bath sheet over her, reluctant to cover her but knowing he would never finish undressing, much less anything else he had planned, if he watched her much longer.

Shucking his coat and shirt, he toed off his boots and pulled his belt loose from the loops. He left his jeans on. At the moment, he wasn't sure they could be unzipped without some permanent damage done to an important part of his body.

He bent down to lift her, sheet and all, high against his chest. She stirred in his arms, slowly opening eyes misty with desire. The fire in his belly began to take on frightening potential.

"What—Devin, what are you doing?"

"Carrying you off to my secret lair where I can have my wicked way with you."

"Oh, that's all right, then. Where is you secret lair, by the way?"

"Around the bend a bit, my dear."

"That's not all that's around the bend. I can walk, you know."

"Yes, but it's more fun when I carry you." He lifted her in his arms, bestowing a chaste kiss on her brow and laughing at her impatient squirm.

"Gently, babe. You'll understand in a minute."

He carried her around a large rock that had been reflecting the heat of their small fire. If anything, it was a few degrees warmer on the other side of the rock, but the only light was from the stars. A light mist rose around them, overcoming the natural dryness of the mountain night.

Sydney eased her eyes open, looking down from her comfortable position high against Devin's chest. Stars danced at his feet, a slight distortion giving an impression of distance.

She twisted to get a better look and was distracted by the sensation of chest hair against her over-sensitive nipple. Turning back, she reached around his wide shoulders with both arms, pressing as much of her chest against his as she could. His neck was a tempting target for her teeth, and she greedily tasted the film of perspiration along his collarbone.

Devin growled at her, a laughing, deep warning that only served to encourage her. Finally, in self-defense, he released her legs, dropping the bath sheet to the ground and letting her slide down his body. He cradled her, pressing against her heat while he stroked her back and buttocks, trying to touch as much of her at one time as he could.

"You feel better and better every time I touch you, babe."

"I've missed this so much," she whispered, standing on tiptoe to hug around his neck. "It's been so lonely by myself." She cuddled against him, feeling the erotic contrast of sleek muscled skin, coarse hair, and rough denim against her bareness. His arousal was impossible to conceal, and she rubbed against him wantonly. Eyes closed, she sought out his nipple amongst the chest hair and touched it delicately with the tip of her tongue.

"I think I may have created a monster," he groaned, trying in vain to hold her away from his desperate body. "Babe, don't."

"It's about time you stopped giving me so many orders, Devin." She reinforced her command with a delicate nip at his chest as her hands slid down to the waistband of his jeans.

Working carefully, she eased open the button and edged the zipper down. Without touching the part of him that leapt out to greet her she slid the jeans and briefs off his lean hips. When she reached the long scar that marred his thigh, she paused long enough to touch it gently then continued to push the jeans downward.

To finish the disrobing, she sank to her knees on the crumpled bath sheet, nuzzling against his groin while she pushed the denim off his hard legs. A touch on his ankle, and he stepped out of the confining material, shoving it away with the side of his foot.

Always a creature of control and restraint, Sydney had never felt so free in her actions. At first he tried to push her away, then long fingers threaded into her hair and he pressed against her, uttering a groan of pure bliss. She reveled in his musky scent, exploring his different textures with her tongue as she nuzzled from springy hair up hot smoothness to the rounded tip. Daring greatly, she opened her mouth to take him in, sliding her hands around his hips to clench his hard buttocks.

Looking down at the sprite kneeling in front of him, Devin stood stock still as the most excruciating bliss imaginable flooded his body. Sydney's eyes were closed, but the expression on her face was one of total involvement. The faint light outlined her sleek body in silver, casting the secret parts of her in deep shadow. Realizing how close he was to total loss of control, he leaned over, sliding his hands out of her hair and down her neck.

When she protested his interruption, taking a firmer hold of his hips, what little mastery he had over himself was gone. His hands slid quickly down her front, briefly cupping her breasts before settling at her waist. Their relative strengths became obvious when she was easily lifted, her hold on him broken as though she were a delicate child.

Devin raised her above his head, bringing her sweet breasts on the level with his mouth where he feasted greedily on her swollen nipples. Then one arm slid around her thighs, one at her shoulders, and he pulled her against him. Her legs parted, wrapping around his waist as she yearned toward him and finally, at last, he buried his aching flesh in the damp warmth waiting for him.

With a last conscious thought before his legs collapsed under both of them, he stepped into the hot pond. Taking one unsteady step, he sank onto the ledge that jutted out at the end.

"Oh." Sydney uttered a brief exclamation of surprise when the warm water surrounded the two of them, then her thighs tightened and she flung back her head, face up to the stars. It was a moment of ecstasy, when life pulsed between them and the rest of the world, for now, ceased to exist.

Chapter 13

Sydney woke slowly, fighting to experience one second longer of the warm comfort flavoring her sleep. She stretched, her leg sliding between two longer, harder, legs, rough with hair. It had been no dream.

In the shadowed pre-dawn, Devin was as much a presence she could feel as a shape she could actually see. His chest rose and fell easily against her shoulder, and his arms encircled her in a sensuous confinement she didn't resist. It was difficult to judge if he was any more awake than she was, although only someone unconscious would be less awake. Knowing what could lay ahead that day, she held onto the solace of near-sleep for a moment longer.

A tightening of the arms around her presaged the movement of one of his hands across her body to her breast. As his strong fingers stroked her nipple, his head moved just enough to join their mouths in a deep, lazy kiss. Within moments, she was once again overcome by the hunger for a more intimate contact.

Growling against her lips, Devin shifted, pulling her more completely underneath him. The combined sleeping bags didn't allow her to do much more than lift her legs around his thighs, but it was enough. With a grunt of masculine satisfaction he sheathed himself within her. A powerful rocking echoed the thrusting of his tongue within her mouth. She was quickly overwhelmed by the combined sensual assault and tensed, stifling her cry against his mouth, absorbing his yell within her own.

✧✧✧

"It's nearly dawn," he said when they were breathing more normally.

"Do your finely honed instincts tell you that?"

"No, I set my watch to wake us."

"Ah, the technological warrior." She felt him shifting, as though to pull away, and tightened her hold to keep him there just a moment longer.

"Sydney, we have to get up."

"I thought you just did that."

"A comedian at dawn. What more could a man ask for?" Giving in to her, he resettled himself against her body, shifting to support some of his weight on his elbows. His chest brushed against her erect nipples with every stroke of his body.

What followed was slow, leisurely, erotic, and continued as the air around them lightened. This time release snuck up, washing over them in a consuming wave. When it passed, Sydney felt herself slipping back into a blissfully sated sleep.

He was reluctant to wake her, to remind her why they'd raced up the side of a mountain the day before. In the increasing light she looked completely loved. Her mouth was swollen from his kisses the night before, damp from that morning. The sleeping bag held the scent of their lovemaking, a heady perfume that could almost distract him from the purpose of the trip. Almost.

Setting his mind against the erotic temptation, he separated their bodies, lowering the zipper on the sleeping bag and sliding out in one determined movement. He could let her sleep until the horses were ready. It was the only comfort he could offer.

Ↄↄ

She was so quiet behind him. Even when he spoke briefly with Ty, confirming that Wallace's plane had taken off before dawn, she said nothing. Only the occasional scrape of the mare's shod hooves told him she was still there. The early morning had become chilly once they were out of the secluded hollow, and the sun only now was taking away the fog of their breath from in front of their faces.

He urged his gelding through the trees, growing almost too close together to allow passage, and heard the pack horse close behind. When no third set of hooves scrambled along the hard granite path, he pulled up at the next wide spot in the trail and encouraged the lightly laden pack horse past. Once free of this stand of trees, the horse would head for the small grassy clearing just beyond while Devin turned back down the trail.

Sydney had stopped at a turn in the trail. From there, she looked across the gorge to the mountain face a half mile distant. The sun spread golden light across the bare rock face, softening the granite into a wilderness castle.

Saddle leather creaked as she shifted, obviously trying to find some position less wearing on her backside. He could have told her it was impossible. Only many years in the saddle could accustom the human body to the unrelenting pressure of reinforced leather against soft tissue. The fact that she'd spent more of the night before riding him than sleeping could not be helping. The memory certainly wasn't helping the fit of his jeans.

"Hey, lady," he said as gruffly as he could, trying not to react to the sight of her silhouetted against the golden light. "You think this is some kind of a sightseeing tour?"

She turned to him without concealing any of her awe at the immense majesty and beauty of the area around them. Under the felt hat her silver eyes glowed with the discovery of life and beauty and the purity of a new day. Some of her hair had escaped the confining scarf and was dancing around her face, crackling with its own energy.

"It's so beautiful, so peaceful. No wonder you don't want to leave it."

"At one time, these mountains were all that stood between my memories and my sanity." Devin spoke quietly, felt the peace of the morning deep in the same bones that had once been overloaded with pain. "My

Cherokee ancestors knew about these mountains while my European ancestors were still wasting time on foolish royal wars."

"At one time?" she asked, tilting her head sideways and squinting to evade a sudden glare.

The sun shouldn't be glaring from that direction. Acting instinctively, Devin yelled and flattened along his gelding's neck, offering as small a target as possible. Sydney followed suit, digging her heels into the gray mare's sides and heading for the dubious protection of the closely growing trees.

Air displaced past their heads, and a lighter streak appeared in the rock next to her. The report followed seconds later, echoing lethally on the peaceful morning. Bullets at that speed tended to sound like angry oversized bees, ripping into the bark and needles of the protective trees. The shooting continued until they were well under cover.

Only when they had put a piece of the mountain behind them did Devin call a halt. The horses snorted, their breath still steamy on the air as they danced a bit, affected by the excitement. Sydney's mare settled first, being an old hunting mount and accustomed to strange noises in the woods.

"That came a little too damned close for comfort," Devin said, sliding off his mount for a closer inspection of the horses. He contemplated going back on foot, then dismissed the idea. It was too early in the game, and there would be no point in it.

"It was as close as he wanted it to be," Sydney said,

almost tonelessly. "Rick's one of the best shots with a rifle I've ever seen. He doesn't want to hurt us yet, just let us know he's here."

"He's going to do more than that, if we don't get farther away from here. Any more of your ex-husband's talents you'd like to tell me about while we're at it?"

She flushed, looking absurdly young, while she stared at their back trail. The peace of the morning was gone, and with it the lingering beauty of the night before. Now she reacted to every sound, evaluating, cataloging. She was changing before his eyes into a wary, lonely stranger. One more sin to lay on Rick Wallace's black soul.

"From past experience, he'll try to set up some sort of ambush. He won't waste any more ammunition right now, unless we make ourselves too easy a target for him."

"No problem. We'll go a little farther today, then ditch the saddles and turn the horses loose tomorrow. We should be able to keep him on the move too much to set up a decent ambush before we can set one up of our own. From the sound of it, he's closer to Charlie's area than we wanted."

"Will that be a problem?"

"Hard to say. Charlie hasn't been too keen about rifle fire lately." Satisfied with the horses, he swung back into the saddle and settled his hat. "Ty should be right behind Wallace with enough men to take care of that bunch. With any luck, we'll be back at the ranch tomorrow night, at the latest."

എൻ

There were surfaces that felt worse against your backside than a saddle. The unpadded boulder beneath her seat proved that. It was a close call, though, and not much comfort when there was no other choice.

Sydney considered taking off her jacket and folding it beneath her abused bottom. Rapidly cooling air did not encourage that idea. Devin had put her on the rock and placed the horses' reins in her safekeeping so she couldn't even get up and move around. It was an obvious ploy to keep her out of the line of fire but she was too tired to argue at this point.

There had once been a time when she could have kept up with the best of warriors, recent injuries or not. Five years of desk work did nothing for stamina, no matter how many hours were spent in aerobic effort. Nothing could prepare for day-long treks except for day-long treks.

The situation was not eased by the feeling that they were the primary attraction at a county fair shooting gallery. Rifle fire came from too many places on the other side of the gorge to be the work of only one shooter, no matter how good. Only Devin's experience under fire had kept them from harm.

Permanent soreness of the backside was not considered a life-threatening condition, although the possibility of another long hospital stay seemed greater every minute. More irritating than the chafe spot developing on the back of her thigh was Devin's seeming imperviousness to any discomfort. There was a job to do, and he was doing the job to the best of his abilities.

He'd started to change. As they led the horses out of

the small canyon and mounted in the early morning mist, Devin began to evolve. The loving, laughing man of the night before, even of this morning, disappeared beneath the grim visage of a warrior. This was a man who had lived for years on the fringe of society, giving up civilization—and all that most men took for granted—to complete his mission.

Drawing her feet onto the rock with a supreme effort, Sydney folded her arms across her knees, resting her chin on her forearms. Was any of this worth the price Devin was paying? She'd called this side of him forth from where he'd successfully hidden it. Would he ever forgive her? Would she ever forgive herself?

If seeing Devin revert bothered her, how much worse would it be when they actually confronted the slime who was her ex-husband in person? She was sure Devin had killed, efficiently and well, and doubted he was reluctant to kill again. She thought she could accept this. Could he accept her own willingness to do whatever was needed?

"Babe? Can you come up here a minute? Tie the horses down there somewhere."

Responding to the low voiced request, Sydney anchored the reins in a notch of stone and scrambled up the path Devin had taken. It was even steeper than it had looked, not at all the best thing for rapidly tightening tendons. Fortunately, the last few feet she had a large hand to clasp. Once out of the hollow, she stood in the shelter of his body, braced by a solid arm behind her back. A cellular phone rested in his free hand.

"Reception's fading in and out," he explained, his

deep voice pitched low. "It sounds like he may have some problems with outsiders."

The small cellular crackled and voice-like sounds began to emerge.

"Sorry I cut you off," crackled Ty's voice. "We've had an invasion here."

"What's happening?" Sydney spoke directly into the phone, pitching her voice so that it would only carry to the person on the other end. Devin held the phone so they could both hear.

"Right after Dev called this morning, rental cars started pulling in. Weird guys in three piece suits spouted all sorts of letters at me and demanded to know what we were doing with Rick Monroe."

"His step-father's name," Sydney inserted.

"Yeah. They finally explained that. I gave them the best example of ignorant I could do, but I don't think they were buying it. They know about you, Sydney."

"What do they know?" Devin growled, tightening his hold on her waist with enough force to bruise. She merely moved closer, a source of warmth that reached under his skin.

"Her current name, her marriage to Wallace, her occupation. Her father's name and method of death. One of them tried to pin his death on her, but that didn't get very far." Even over the miles his satisfaction was obvious.

"Don't get on their bad side, Ty," Sydney warned.

"Kiddo, they don't have a good side. Turns out they need Wallace in one piece and happy, so they can go after his bosses. We couldn't move beyond the barn this morning." His voice dropped even lower, and he rushed the rest of his message. "We'll try something tonight, after they shut down. Just don't—" He hesitated then raised his voice to a normal level. "Don't let Sydney get a chill, dammit. You know she's just out of the hospital. Why you thought she was up to a trip in the mountains is beyond—"

There were some indistinct noises, as though a scuffle ensued. Ty came through clearly, cursing the officious attitude of government ignoramuses. He was silenced by an authoritative sharp voice.

"Ms. Castleton, are you there?" the voice asked, pretending to be polite. Sydney decided to play along.

"Who's this, please?"

"Ms. Castleton, I must demand you cease immediately and return to the ranch. Mr. Monroe is a valued contact and we cannot risk losing his services."

"Rick Wallace is an amoral low-rent dope dealer. The fact that you are willing to talk to him is a miscarriage of justice and a waste of taxpayer's money. If there were an official who could be trusted I'd turn you in for dereliction of duty. Since you refuse to identify yourself, and you consort with known drug offenders, I'm forced to believe you're attempting to protect him to hide your own incompetence."

Before she could say anything more, the phone was pulled away from her grasp and moved far out of her reach. The arm behind her back shifted and she was held against a body quaking with suppressed laughter.

"Are you trying to make him pop a blood vessel?"

Devin managed between gasps for control.

"If I can convince him I'm a flaming liberal, they won't be as worried about us not coming in. As far as they're concerned, your average rabble-rousing former hippie has trouble balancing a checkbook, much less taking down a government informant."

Once more, Devin was impressed by her cool ability to evaluate the situation and come up with the best solution. Not the easiest, or the most obvious. Just the best. When the sounds emanating from the phone settled into word patterns, he brought the phone back to his mouth.

"Ty?" he called into the receiver. "You there, buddy?"

"Your partner is here, Mr. Starke, but we are controlling all outside communication. You will not speak with Randolph until you return, which I strongly urge you to do at once. Your companion may not be aware of the gravity of this matter, but I assure you—"

He seemed ready to carry on a lengthy lecture. Devin tapped the receiver with his palm then blew into the lower section, whistling slightly. "What's that you say? You're breaking up, must be atmospheric." He scraped a nail across the transmitter section then tapped. "Nope, can't hear you. I'll try you back a little later."

Spluttering could once more be clearly heard until Devin flipped the off switch.

"Well, babe," he murmured, pocketing the phone and sliding his other arm around her. "Looks like it's just the two of us."

His chest felt so good, the heartbeat strong against her

cheek, Sydney dared to circle her arms around his waist and lean, just a little. Just enough to share his strength for a few minutes. Just enough to be able to store this perfect moment up for later, when she was alone with her memories.

എൻഐൻ

The fire was beginning to die back as shadows grew around their encampment. Sydney shifted on the sleeping bags, trying to find a comfortable part of her backside to sit on. They'd stopped early enough to give the horses a chance to rest and for Devin to build a fire before it would be too obvious.

Plain hot coffee had become one of life's true luxuries, she decided as Devin split the last of the pot between their mugs. Once they were off the mountain she might prefer over-priced, richly brewed *caffes*. She would never lose her respect for the comfort of strong, boiled coffee. Even if she did have to spit out grounds from time to time.

"Sorry we couldn't make it to a hot spring," Devin said with a muffled groan as he settled next to her.

"That's all right. I'm afraid I'd fall asleep and slide under tonight."

"I'd hold you up."

"Who would hold you up, oh fearless leader?"

They chuckled, a tired sound that quickly died out. Sydney finished what was still liquid in her mug and tossed the rest onto the dying fire, where it sizzled in rich coffee scents.

The shadowed forest around them was alive with the subtle sounds of predator and prey, gearing up for another deadly game of life. She heard them on the edge of her quickly dimming consciousness, but couldn't manage more than a casual interest. Devin would take care of it. This relying on a man was an odd way to approach life, but it was somehow very right.

"Why don't you crawl into that sleeping bag before you pass out on top of it?"

Devin's voice was tender with soft laughter. It was really too bad she didn't have a tape recorder. Voices had never been one of her strengths. Faces were another matter. She could easily picture the faces of people she had only seen once, many years ago. There was that radio specialist in Bolivia—his bright red hair danced in front of her eyes—

"Sydney!"

Her eyes flew open and she jerked awake, far closer to the fire than she remembered. Devin's arm was across her chest, holding her back from pitching face first into the smoldering embers.

"That's it. Bed for you."

"What about you?" she mumbled as she let him remove her boots and slide her legs into the cozy warmth of the sleeping bag. Somehow, tonight it seemed too big and cold.

"I'll keep watch for a while at least. You need your rest."

"You promise to wake me when it's my turn to watch?"

"Of course."

Her eyes were already shut, her body falling bone-lessly into the sleep of total exhaustion. If they were marginally lucky, she would be able to get at least enough sleep to make it through the next day.

Devin moved away from the temptation of Sydney and the sleeping bag. It would be so good to just be able to hold her while she slept, offering his warmth in exchange for the pleasure of her trust. But until he was sure Ty could get to Wallace, he didn't dare let down his guard.

After that? He wondered. In spite of the closeness developing between them, he knew Sydney wasn't completely candid with him. She still hid little bits of information, dispensing them only when necessary. It was the first time he'd ever experienced "need to know" as applied to someone's personal history.

There was every possibility she'd leave once the danger had been taken away from Stormhaven. For too long, Sydney had considered the whole world as her personal playground. It was too much to ask her to stop now, while she was just beginning to enjoy herself. He knew she'd found pleasure in her stay at the ranch, but doubted she would remain permanently.

Nor did he want to, he admitted to himself as he moved around the camp, banking the fire and checking the horses. Stormhaven had helped him re-find the young man who'd once traveled forth, thinking he could cure the world's problems.

Ty had offered him a place to invest money earned in ways that didn't bear close inspection. At the same time, he offered Devin a way to atone personally for what he'd done. Now, it was time to move on, to make room for the next warrior who wasn't quite ready to rejoin what passed for humanity these days.

A low, cynical laugh eased from between his tightly held lips, not traveling beyond his own ears. There was nothing like late night guard duty to bring out the philosopher inside him. Truth was, he'd been slowing down, had lost the fighting edge it took to dodge bullets and anticipate ambushes. If he hadn't taken himself out of the business, it would've taken him out.

He settled into a notch in the rock, the phone placed next to him for maximum range, automatic weapon snug against the small of his back. A contemporary knight, with modern weapons, keeping watch over his lady. Under the limitless canopy of the New Mexico sky, it all fit.

℘℘℘

Sydney stirred, struggling against the narcotic effect of sleep on an exhausted system. There were noises on the far edge of her conscience that should mean something to her. Then a few words were murmured, closer to her hard resting place. The voice was one that brought her an immediate impression of safety, and she let herself begin to drift back down into total sleep.

A cold draft touched her side. Before she could utter a protest, a large body aligned itself against hers. Murmuring unconsciously provocative sounds, she turned in the tight quarters. Strong arms encircled her, pulling her even closer, and she nestled happily. This was so right, she thought, giving in once more to sleep.

⟨✿⟩✿⟨✿⟩

"Good news/bad news, buddy." Ty's disembodied voice lacked the energy to project much beyond the cellular receiver.

"How so?" Devin asked, his attention on Sydney trying to brush out her hair by the morning fire. She was so grumpy when her wash water wasn't warm enough. It was hard to believe she'd spent years in the field. When he dared to mention that, she pointed out that her father always ensured she received the best of care.

"Wallace."

The laconic answer brought Devin's attention back to the conversation. He waited for further information, knowing Ty was not yet able to talk freely.

"We found the camp, two of them, in fact. Wallace had been at the second one, but he got away just before we moved in. The alphabet soups are pissed, of course." There was another static filled pause, before the low voice continued. "They had to take the guys into custody, or risk blowing Wallace's cover. Moving them out got rid of a few of the leeches, but not enough."

Devin cursed, loud enough this time to get Sydney's attention. Abandoning her brush, she came over to his side, her hair lifting away from her head in a static frenzy.

"Dry air," she explained as she approached. "That Ty?"

Devin gave a quick overview of the conversation so far, and she nodded. "I wouldn't be surprised if one of the goons told Rick. You don't know how far they'll go to protect a source."

"They're keeping a closer watch on us than before, and threatened to lock up the crew if we try anything else," Ty said, his frustration apparent even long distance. "Some of the guys are starting to get edgy. I'm tempted to push things a bit."

"Don't," Devin said, straightening away from the rock he had been leaning against. "You got the numbers down. We should be able to take care of the rest."

They signed off quickly, Ty asking to be kept informed and promising to help however he could. Devin closed the phone with a flip of his wrist, sliding it into the holder on his belt.

"You handle that like a six-shooter."

"Modern times, modern weapons," he reminded her. "Get your basics together. We'll stash the saddles here, and turn the horses loose. There's enough pasture to keep them for a while, and they know the way back. Wallace is on foot now, and alone. We don't need to be held back by anything."

Nodding curtly, she turned to obey like a highly trained soldier.

"Sydney," he called, grabbing her arm before she got out of reach. "You forgot something."

As though he had all the time in the world, Devin bent his head. When their lips met, parted, and melded, one of them moaned. It was a lover's kiss, slow and tender, and both of them were breathing too hard when it was reluctantly stopped. Devin held her a moment longer, cherishing the feminine feel of her against his body before he relaxed his hold.

"Ten minutes, Sydney, and we're out of here."

ఌఄఌఄ

Twelve hours before, Sydney would've sworn she'd do anything to not have to get on a horse's back again. After a couple of hours providing her own energy to follow in Devin's wake, she was longing for the hard saddle and bumpy gaits. Anything to relieve her feet.

"Some people are just never happy," she reminded herself.

"You say something?"

She shook her head, lacking the energy to speak out louder. Devin seemed disgustingly fresh. Life wasn't always fair.

The least fair part was that this interlude, comforting in spite of her aching feet, was almost over. Devin might be able to ride all one day, hike the next, and dodge bullets. He'd never dealt with the treachery of a snake like her ex-husband. Nor did she intend to permit the encounter.

It was past time. She'd been encouraging Devin to think she was even more tired than she really was. The next chance she got, probably that afternoon when he would stop to give her a longer rest, she would have to slip away. This was her fight now, and she fought her own battles.

Chapter 14

It was amazing how much bigger and emptier the mountains got when you were in them alone. Sydney had never been a devotee of mountaineering. Once she was out of here, she would never watch *Sound of Music* again.

It had been frighteningly easy to slip away from Devin. He'd left her to rest while he checked their trail from a higher point. Once he was well out of sight, it took only a few minutes to grab her backpack and head the other direction.

Before she left, she changed from hiking boots to the lighter weight running shoes she always kept with her. There would be no serious climbing on her path, and she needed as many energy advantages as possible. She left the boots in a convenient hollow at the camp.

Devin was not going to be happy with her. At best he'd be angry because she was putting herself in danger.

There was a good chance he would feel hurt and rejected by her going off alone. This would have to be faced later, when everything else was taken care of.

Letting Devin handle the hunt for Rick had been all right when they were only supposed to be the bait to lure him away from the ranch. She didn't want Devin to have to kill again. She'd taken away the peace Stormhaven had given him. Compared to what she'd done to Devin, she didn't care that much about what her own life could become.

☙❧☙

Sydney studied the thick stand of trees in front of and below her. Rick was around here somewhere. The sense of danger was too strong for him not to be. Her pathway down the mountain had been intentionally exposed. It had been risky, but not overly so. This had become a matter of revenge and ego for Rick. He would want to take care of her personally. Exposing herself ensured he would not continue to go after Devin.

All she had to do now was locate Rick, move in on him, and overpower him. Without him seeing her first, because she needed the element of surprise. Even though she'd fought him off in LA, Rick would not expect her to resist. He would remember her as the little girl who, in reaction to her father's profession, had disapproved of violence, and not the woman who had come to understand her father's philosophy. In Rick's mind, no female could accept the existence, and occasional necessity, of violence.

She'd already placed her knives in their usual positions on her body. Now the trusty .38 was slid into the back of her jeans, under her jacket. It wouldn't be available for a quick draw, but she'd never relied on cowboy stuff. The backpack strap across her chest was loosened, ready to release and drop whenever needed.

This time, she was ready. Nothing could stop her now.

"Stop, please stop. *Nooooo...*" Above the muted sounds of a mountain afternoon rose the scream of a woman in agony. Sydney tensed, reaching for the pistol. No one said anything about a hostage. The screams intensified, a woman calling on God to save her, coupled with a man's laughter.

The laughter she recognized, and with the recognition came understanding and anger. Rick had taped a woman screaming while he either beat her or watched her being beaten. The anguish in the woman's voice was too real to be even the greatest actress in the world. Once past her initial shock, Sydney could recognize the tonal quality and volume of a recording played full blast.

Closing her eyes, she drew a deep breath, trying to block out the sounds. Whoever the woman was, it was too late to help her now. It wasn't too late to punish Rick for this woman and however many others he had hurt. The punishment would fail if she let him ruin her emotional control.

❧❧❧

Devin heard the first scream while skidding down a

nearly vertical trail which was a short cut that might get him ahead of Sydney, as long as he didn't miss making all the turns. The woman's agony startled him, and he found himself clinging grimly to the edge of the trail while his heart beat too loudly in his ears to hear any more.

It wasn't Sydney. It couldn't be. Even if she'd raced straight down the mountain and immediately run into Wallace, she hadn't been gone long enough for him to bring her to the point of screaming. Not his little warrior princess.

Holding as firmly to this belief as he did to the corner of a boulder, Devin eased himself down another section of the trail. As carefully as he placed his feet, he forced himself to think logically. Ty had said nothing about a woman. If it wasn't Sydney, then who was being tortured to satisfy someone's amusement?

Whoever it was, Wallace was sure to be a part of it. Wherever Rick Wallace was, Devin was sure to find Sydney. When he found her, he debated between beating her and hugging her. Maybe he'd do both.

ဢ෮ဢ

"That's real class, Rick. It's nice to see some things never change, like your taste in entertainment."

The lean man whirled around, squinting against the late afternoon sun, peering into the darkening trees for the source of her smoothly taunting voice.

"You might as well come out where I can see you, bitch."

"I'd kind of like things to stay like this for a while," she whispered from another location, more to one side.

Rick whirled, bringing up a machine pistol and waving it slowly back and forth in the general direction of her voice. Moving swiftly, he took cover in the shadow of a large spruce, his gun at the ready. The tape finally stopped, and sounds in the clearing seemed amplified in the sudden silence.

"Just come on out, and I won't tell your friends about the 'woman' they've had visiting them." He used the word in a doubting, sneering way.

"Give it up, Rick. Just get out of here." Sydney turned her head as she spoke, projecting her voice into the clearing as she slid around a clump of saplings, heading for the more solid shelter of a boulder.

"You'd like that, wouldn't you? Then lover boy'd never find out about you. He must not care much about sex if he's kept you around. Or isn't he into that kind of thing?"

Rick had turned away from her, scanning the far edge of the clearing. The mountains facing him were backlit, black monoliths in a golden-red sky. This same light flooded the clearing he was in, making anything in the surrounding trees impossible for him to see, as Sydney had hoped.

"You haven't changed at all, have you? Still getting your kicks off other people's pain."

"At least I know how to get my kicks. Hey, remember how much you always wanted to be like your sister? She was always better than you, always prettier, always got what she wanted. She was a damned sight better than you in bed, but, hell, a corpse could be better than you." He laughed malevolently. "Now that bitch is just as cold as you are. She had herself a fatal accident after she told me where you might be." As he spoke, he edged around the spruce, keeping out of the direct light as much as possible.

Sydney fell against the boulder, clutching her revolver with shaking hands. No. Not Lana. Not now, when she finally understood how harmful, how foolish, their estrangement had become. Her first impulse was to charge into the clearing, then she stopped herself. That would play right into Rick's hands.

Putting the pain away where it wouldn't interfere, she stepped back. Rick would count on her being shocked for long enough to give him the advantage.

Neither one of them had dodged death for a while, but she was fairly sure Rick had been relying on other people to do his dirty work for him. If she could just keep her head she might win this one.

From above came the rattle of stones carelessly displaced on a mountain trail. Rick gave a triumphant cry, moving briefly into her sight as he dodged closer toward the bottom of the trail. "Time's up, bitch. Looks like lover boy thinks he can come to the rescue. This'll be even more fun than I thought it—"

His words were cut off with a grunt of pain. From the top of the rocks, Sydney launched herself into Rick's side, striking out at his pistol as they both fell to the ground.

⁓⤳⁓

After the tape stopped, Devin heard the man's taunting and Sydney's reply. For a moment, he hesitated on the trail, sending a message to whatever nebulous force watched over reckless Amazons. There was little need for caution, as the man seemed foolishly loud, but old habits died hard, and Devin flowed down the trail with no sound beneath his boots.

A cluster of boulders and bushes provided convenient cover above and to one side of the clearing. Wallace seemed more interested in mocking Sydney than hunting her, at least for the moment. It would give Devin more of a chance to set his own trap. Then he heard Wallace mention Lana, and he knew time had run out.

"Hang in there, babe. Don't let him get to you," he whispered, moving away from his hiding place. Setting his booted feet deliberately, he pushed a few pebbles down the rock face, following immediately.

He broke cover above the clearing as Wallace reached the bottom of the trail. Just in time to see a small shape launch into the man's side. Wallace's pistol went flying, and the two struck ground together, rolling on the rocky ground.

Both dusty figures rose with the automatic grace of trained fighters. Sydney was markedly smaller but there was no hesitation in her as she moved around the cursing man. It was like watching a terrier circle for advantage over a wolf. Valiant, but not necessarily bright.

"If you think you're going to take me down, I hope you're more of a man than you were before," Wallace rasped, eyes darting from side to side. "You're certainly not much more of a woman," He marked Devin's approach with a satisfied smirk.

As Wallace's attention was drawn briefly to one side, Sydney lashed out with her foot, following the blow in with a flowing attack that carried her past him before he could react. Wallace grunted then settled into a fighting crouch. What little humor had been on his face was gone, replaced by a deadly intent.

Devin saw no possibility of a shot that wouldn't endanger Sydney, and the fighters were too far away to risk closing in quickly. If her attention was distracted, she could be killed before Devin was in the battle. Not that he held much hope for her survival as it was. He could only ease closer, in hopes of stepping in at the first opportunity.

This time, Wallace didn't waste time or breath in taunting. As though he realized how brief the safe time was, he charged forward, feinting to one side then closing with a deadly intent. He snaked out a long arm and quickly drew it back, sporting a streak of red. Yelling his rage, he countered with a kick which caught Sydney on the upper arm, forcing her to drop her knife and step back.

Following up on this advantage, Wallace closed in, attempting to grab a handful of hair and a hold around her neck. Instead he received an elbow in his midsection and a glancing blow against his windpipe. He marked Devin's progress from the corner of his eye and changed tactics suddenly.

Shifting agilely to one side as he charged, Wallace grabbed at Sydney's hand, ignoring the flashing knife in her other hand while he pulled. At the same time, he kicked out at her legs, connecting solidly on one thigh. Her balance was thrown off long enough for him to pull her forward against his chest and wheel to face Devin.

"You should butt out of this, cowboy. You're way out of your league. Did you know your little play toy here once torched a village, complete with women and children?" He got the hold he'd been seeking in her hair and twisted brutally.

Sydney didn't waste time screaming in pain or denying his accusations. Her elbows flew back and she used a heel viciously in an attempt to throw Rick off balance. Drawing a breath in through clenched teeth, she ignored the burning in her scalp and concentrated on getting away from Rick before Devin closed in. There was deadly intent in Devin's fierce amber eyes, but Rick never went into a fight without hidden weapons.

Rick backed quickly before Devin's advance, giving a portion of his attention to his location on the mountain. This was obviously not turning out the way Rick had intended. He hadn't come this far without knowing when and how to cut his losses.

Yelling fiercely, Rick spun. Two quick steps brought him close to the edge of the clearing and the side of the mountain. He pivoted, holding Sydney brutally tight for a moment before releasing her. As she staggered, off balance, toward the sheer precipice, he lunged the other direction, away from Devin.

Sydney had known she was in trouble with the second charge. In spite of his years out of the field, Rick had lost little of his edge and none of his malice. She'd caught him off guard at first and landed a few lucky hits. Only Devin's approach gave her any hope of surviving the encounter.

When she was thrown to one side, instinct prompted her to go limp rather than resist the momentum. The leg she would have used to brake her speed was still numb from Rick's blow. There wasn't enough room to roll before flying off the edge of the mountain so she lunged, reaching for a bush and hoping it was well rooted in the dry soil.

The bush gave way, but not before she'd slowed enough to grasp a juniper clinging tenaciously to the mountainside. It was a good size for her. Before her legs slid out in mid-air, she had both arms securely around the trunk. From here she could get at least one foot back on solid ground and join Devin.

Hard hands grabbed at her waist, and she found herself flying away from the open air faster than she'd been thrown forward. There was no doubt whose hands were on her body. The air was livid with curses as a large body came down beside her, covering her before throwing her into a roll away from the edge.

Dust flew up around them in tiny spurts as bullets hit where they'd been only seconds before. Devin grunted once, but continued to roll and drag her until they were secure under an overhang. The gunfire stopped abruptly.

"Come get me, if you've got the guts, cowboy," Wallace yelled from the edge of the clearing. "Just be sure to watch your back. Sweet Sydney has a way of getting a man when he's looking the other way. Hope you don't need much sleep."

Footsteps rattled away. Quickly enough, but there was an unevenness to his stride that made it plain Wallace was not unmarked by combat.

⁊⁊⁊

Ragged breaths dragged into straining lungs punctuated the silence in the cool shadow of a protective rock overhang. Sydney could feel the tension in the large body holding hers down. This would not be a good time to point out he was crushing her. As soon as he was positive she was all right, he would probably strangle her.

"Just what the hell did you think you were doing?" She aimed the question directly in his ear and had the satisfaction of feeling him flinch.

"Me? Who was the one stupid enough to sneak off alone after a known killer? Were you trying to play Wonder Woman?"

She struggled futilely against his hold. "I was trying to wrap this up as fast as possible."

"I see you were doing a wonderful job of it. You were damned lucky I was close behind you."

"Fat lot of good that did," she muttered.

The brief shock of anger loosened his hold and she slid away, pushing herself as upright as possible in the confined space.

Devin raised himself on an elbow, his head nearly grazing the top of their shelter. "You seem to forget I just rescued your ungrateful fanny, woman!"

The roar would have done credit to a lion. Obviously,

it was intended to completely cow her. Sydney studied her palm, picking at a splinter that was beginning to sting.

"I was in no real danger, Devin. I had hold of the tree. You let him get away."

The silence that followed this calm statement was as deafening as his roar had been. Devin lay stunned, his large body shaking with suppressed rage. Glancing a look from the corner of her eyes, Sydney wondered if he would explode or simply self-immolate. She held her hand out to him, palm up.

"Do you have a tweezer? I can't seem to get at this thing."

The palm displayed under his nose was reddened from contact with the rough tree trunk. A darker streak showed the path of a long sliver of wood. Other than this, there was no indication this hand had just stopped her from plunging down the side of a mountain. Not even a tremor.

Disbelieving, Devin raised his head, trying to catch her eye, to evaluate her expression. Tangled chestnut hair had fallen forward and, from what little he could see, she seemed perfectly calm. Much like she had been after the encounter at the truck stop.

Understanding crashed upon him. The proffered hand was swallowed in a gentle grasp and he pulled, shifting himself backward as he did.

"Come here, Sydney."

She resisted at first. Her back stiffened and she braced her thighs against his pull. The lack of emotion in her gray eyes went with the thin line her mouth had established. Only the pulse throbbing against his palm and showing visibly in her delicate neck gave any indication she was reacting.

Still he pulled, gently, murmuring soft words that could coax a mustang or a frightened kitten. At first there was little reaction. Then his voice registered. With a suddenness that was almost frightening, Sydney fell forward against his chest.

"Dear God, woman, don't ever do that again. I think I lost a decade's growth chasing after you."

"I'm sorry." She quavered against his chest. He felt the shaking start, deep within her. "I really thought I could sneak up on him and get it all over with before you caught up with me."

"Since when did you become a super hero? You could've been killed. You damned near were."

A small shrug was her only answer. Devin forcefully restrained the shout that was growing in his throat. "Do you have so little respect for your life?"

Secure against the life-sustaining warmth of his body, Sydney nearly shrugged again then thought better of it. So far, Devin had only yelled, even though he was far angrier than—

She raised her head and eased away from the comfortable nest of his chest. She had to see. Yes. Devin's eyes glittered with the kind of rage berserkers used to overcome their enemies. Yet he held her with a gentleness that would have brought tears to her eyes if she'd had any tears to spare.

A small, grubby hand appeared near his cheek, and she felt the roughness of his beard against her sore palm.

His eyes closed briefly and he pressed lightly against her touch. The air flowed into his lungs in a ragged breath.

"I'm sorry," she repeated, this time softly, while she stroked his cheek, letting her fingers wander into his hair. "You lost your hat."

Warm gold poured over her as Devin's eyes drifted open. He even managed a slight grin, incredibly white in his filthy face.

"It casts too big a shadow. I took it off."

A last, shuddering breath slid between his lips and he loosened his hold. Releasing Sydney he rolled away, searching the surrounding area before moving cautiously out. The light had dimmed into heavy shadows. Evening birds had begun to chatter and squirrels danced along frail tree limbs.

"It looks like he's gone, babe."

"For now," she agreed, edging out to sit next to him. She wasn't totally sure she would have the energy to do much more than sit right now. With the adrenalin draining out of her body, she felt chilled and very weak.

Devin lifted an arm to pull her closer to his side. "What will he do next?"

"Most likely hole up for at least part of the night. I did manage to put a gash in his arm, so he'll have to treat that."

Devin felt the will she exerted to keep from falling apart, and he marveled again at her strength. He pulled her even closer, to share the warmth of his body. "You can let go now, babe."

"Not yet. It always takes me a while." She tried to concentrate on taking slow, deep breaths and to not allow herself to be overcome by the comfort he offered. At the moment, she wanted nothing more than to crawl into his lap and sleep for the next week. "No time," she whispered.

"There's always time. If Wallace is going to hole up, we should do the same. Are you up to a short hike?"

"Do I have a choice?" Her words were wry but the fleeting pain in Devin's face had her scrambling for a better answer. "I can if you can," she chirped brightly, jumping to her feet. Her knees buckled immediately.

Devin caught her on the way down. "Slow down. We already know you're Superwoman, but I'm getting too old for this stuff."

❦❦❦

Later that night, a small, cheery fire, concealed by an overhang of rock, offered enough warmth to finish the job started by instant stew and strong coffee. Sydney felt boneless and wondered how long it would take her to come back this time. Recovery seemed to be slower and slower, the older she got.

She thought of increasing her work outs, maybe throwing in some weight training. All thoughts fled when Devin settled next to her on the sleeping bag, a cup of hot coffee in his hand. It would be sweetened. Without asking, he'd fortified everything, even urging her to take extra vitamins to restore herself.

"We've eaten, had coffee, and made up a bed the likes of which you'll never see again on a trail. You even dug out that pestilence of a splinter. What's next, fearless leader?" Sydney allowed a tired chuckle to escape her as she sipped at the coffee. Yep, sugar. Lucky she didn't have problems that direction.

She'd been directly involved with the bed making. Massive armfuls of pine needles had been gathered and dropped into the simple frame he fashioned. The bed would offer extra warmth and protection from chilling. She doubted she needed the softness to encourage her to sleep. Not tonight.

Devin took the cup away from her, tried a taste, grimaced, and finished it in a gulp. The cup was put to one side, and he stretched out on the bag, pulling Sydney with him matter-of-factly. She faced the fire, with the heat of his body along her back, and wondered how she would survive alone once this was all over.

"Now we talk for a few minutes about nothing important, then you get some sleep." His breath puffed against her scalp, setting up tiny erotic impulses.

"What about tomorrow?"

"Tomorrow I'll go after Wallace." There was no tenderness now in Devin's voice, only a grim sort of resignation.

"Devin, it's not your fight. I don't want..."

Her words trailed away when she was lifted and turned, lying flat on her back with Devin hovering over her like an avenging angel. In the shadows thrown by firelight, his eyes glittered hard.

"It became my fight in LA when he attacked you. Hell, it was probably even before that. Sydney, I..." He hesitated, searching for the right words, not wanting to use the obvious ones. It was too soon, and her emotions were too fragile. Sydney didn't think enough of herself to believe anyone could love her as she was. "I care about you." He lifted a hand to her face, marveling again at the softness of her cheek, the delicate strength of her bones. "I know you don't trust anyone to fight your battles for you—"

"Dev—" Her voice broke. She thought she had herself under better control. "I do trust you. But I didn't want—" She lifted a hand to his face, to the lines and scars that were a legacy of a lifetime of fighting other people's battles, touching the red slash along his cheekbone from this afternoon. "You've already been hurt so much."

He trailed his finger along her dark eyebrow, touching the lines at the corner of her eye, before sliding his hand around the back of her neck, under her hair. Tugging gently, he settled her against his shoulder, cradling her against his body, offering what support she would accept.

"How about, we go after him together?" he offered, feeling deep within himself the resistance in her small body.

Together. It brought up so many possibilities. Friendship, companionship, understanding. Things he knew had been missing from her life for so long. It could be dangerous. He hopes leaving that would be far more difficult than anything she had been forced before to leave behind before. But still—

He felt her answer in the unconscious easing of tension in her body as she edged closer. Every nerve came to life within him and he was tempted to overwhelm her with kisses and caring. But not tonight. For now, he contented himself with pulling the top of the sleeping bag over them, settling her even more closely. Sleeping fully dressed was not his idea of a comfortable night, but it would be warmer, and far less tempting.

He doused the fire, and the night settled around them, easing into the corners of their world, taking away the pressures of the day past and making slight promises for a better day to come. Right now, with Sydney resting against him in complete trust, her breath stirring the hairs at the top of his chest, world conquering wouldn't be too difficult. He eased a hand along her back, seeking out the places she liked to be touched. There was more tension in her than seemed normal.

"I didn't, you know," she whispered, her words puffing against his neck.

"That statement covers a lot of ground." How could he feel like laughing, just because she was sounding seriously illogical again?

"The village. I never torched a village. Dad refused any job that included warring on civilians." Her words were strong, defiant, hurt. "You didn't ask, but you must have wondered."

"I didn't ask because I knew you couldn't do something like that. Rick Wallace is obviously the King of Scum. How could I believe what he said?"

"Devin, I haven't always been—"

He stopped her with a gentle kiss and hoped he could keep it from becoming more. The ease in her body was fast disappearing in stress. After a moment, her mouth softened beneath his, and he felt the tension leave her.

"Later on, we'll worry about what you've been, and why. For now, we worry about getting some rest." He spoke against her lips, enjoying the softness against his own, the sweetness of her breath, the heat of reaction he could feel just within his reach. "God knows I've been no angel, babe."

She didn't answer, instead sliding into sleep, trusting him to keep her safe, at least for now.

Devin settled her closer against his side. Warrior princess. So strong, so tough, so frail. If she ever realized how badly he wanted to wrap her in silk and keep her safe, she'd be tempted to kill him. Sydney brought out every protective impulse in his body. At the same time, she could bring him to a fighting pitch faster than anyone he had ever met. There would never be a boring moment with her. Now if he could just convince her they were meant to spend the rest of their lives together.

Chapter 15

Are you ready to tell me the real reason you went hauling ass down the mountain yesterday?"

Devin asked the question over his shoulder while searching among trails leading away from the combat site of the day before. Hat settled on his head, he crouched low to offer a minimal target to anyone watching from a higher point.

"I told you," she explained in a reasonable voice. "I thought I could take Rick by surprise. If not, my next plan was to agitate him into making a stupid move."

Devin knew the look he offered was cynical at best, but he didn't challenge her. The early morning light was not yet bright enough for easy tracking and he had to peer closely at shoe patterns before finding the one he wanted.

"Here we go. None of the older tracks belong to Wallace. These are less than twenty-four hours old."

Moving with automatic stealth, he followed the

tell-tale signs, ensuring they led the direction he wanted to go, before turning again to Sydney. She was staying where he had put her, against the mountainside, out of his way and out of sight of anyone overhead. Her hat had become a repository for tiny wildflowers. Any other time he might have laughed at her air of utter innocence. Now was no time for games.

"I don't want the reason you came up with for me, or even the one you told yourself. Why did you really want to meet your husband without me there?"

She flinched from the harsh note in his voice, her features sharpening out of the early morning softness. The growing light brought out subtle highlights in her hair and touched her cheekbones with gold. It also pointed out the shadows that had taken up permanent residence under her secret-laden eyes.

He didn't enjoy digging at her, or the pain she would have to face in self-discovery. Something was eating at her that helped to build the damned wall she'd erected around her inner self. Going over it, even through it, wasn't enough. This time he wanted to eradicate it once and for all.

"Did you hope for a reconciliation?" he asked, as nastily as he could manage. The question gained only a look of disbelief.

"Don't be an idiot. You seem to forget, I attacked him."

"Only after you knew I was there. Were you trying to keep me from hearing something?"

That struck closer to home. She flinched, but recovered quickly. "That's ridiculous. What else could you possibly hear? He wasn't exactly secretive."

"That's what I've been wondering. Wallace tried to tell me you were a mass murderer and likely to attack me in my sleep. The news didn't send me screaming for the hills."

He leaned on one hip against a convenient ledge, turning to get a good look at her. Sydney was running a blade of meadow grass back and forth through her fingers, keeping her face averted so that their eyes didn't quite meet. He noticed she kept herself carefully out of reach. Or so she thought.

Leaning slightly, he snagged her wrist, pulling until she stood between his legs. Her narrow shoulders offered a convenient resting spot for his forearms. Even seated, his head was higher than hers, and he marveled anew at how much strength of will could exist in such a small body.

"Let's start again." He pulled her closer, until she braced her hands against his chest to avoid leaning on him. He moved one hand down her back to spread out on the flare of her hip, holding her steady while enjoying the resilience of her flesh. The other hand slid around her neck, thumb under her chin to lift her eyes up. "What was so all-fired important that you had to face Wallace down by yourself? Was it just that you didn't trust me to let you take care of him?"

The mysterious confusion in her smoky eyes cleared, replaced by a look of discovery, as though she had just solved a critical puzzle. Her smile was small but real. "You have to admit, you do tend to take over, Devin."

It was said sincerely, with a touch of whimsy in her soft voice. A perfect delivery for someone who couldn't quite figure out how to explain that he was getting too pushy, without hurting his feeling. It was a masterful performance but Devin knew it was only a portion of the truth. Sighing, he slid his lower hand around until he cupped her bottom and pulled her into the V of his legs.

The contact was a blissful torture, particularly when she relaxed, tucking her head under his chin and sliding her hands around his neck. Thick coats kept him from feeling the softness of her breasts against his chest, but he could torment himself with memories.

"We need to get going," he said ruefully, resting his cheek on her head. "With any luck, Ty'll be shed of the alphabet goons today and he'll be up to help us."

She tensed again, lifting her head away from its proper resting spot against his shoulder. "Will you wait until he can come in as backup?"

This from someone who thought she could face Wallace alone? Devin shook his head at the paradox that was Sydney. "We'll see," he said, bending to nuzzle his mouth against her lips. "I think I missed my morning kiss."

It was an undemanding kiss, full of tenderness and promise. Sydney gave herself over to his care, though the tension of her mouth gave away her inner doubts. As though he had all the time in the world, Devin deepened the kiss, hunting for her response until she gave in, softening in his arms. For now, this much surrender had to be enough.

"It's no wonder you two haven't done anything con-structive if this is how you've been spending your time."

The familiar voice held a note of weariness. Devin tensed then turned his head, not releasing her. Ty sat on a boulder in the shadow of the mountain, looking like a schoolboy playing hooky. If you could disregard the rifle in his hand and the grim expression in his eyes.

"How long have you been there, Ty?" Sydney asked, heat beginning to rise up her neck.

His smile was pure evil. "Long enough."

"Where were you when we talked this morning?" Devin's eyes narrowed suspiciously.

Ty looked around for a minute then indicated a spot uphill, about a quarter mile away.

"As soon as I could get away, I started up here. Things were getting too weird down there, and your calls just weren't cutting it. Especially when I heard Sydney decided to take out after Wallace by herself."

"How'd you find that out?"

Devin's surprise was genuine. Sydney knew he had only given Ty short updates on what was happening. Ty nodded as he turned, indicating they should follow him.

"That's part of what's so weird. Some of the goons are up here, spying on you. Let's take a break. Maria sent some lunch for you." He led the way to a secluded area in the trees, where they could watch the trail without being seen. "Any more, it's hard to say who's on whose side. Then, yesterday, someone new came in, a Major Powers."

Sydney stiffened then shook her head, a wry chuckle escaping from between clamped lips as she lowered herself gingerly to the ground. Devin settled next to her, leaning back against a fallen tree and pulling her possessively against him.

"You know this man, babe?"

"He knew Dad," she said, looking off at a squirrel in a nearby tree.

"And?" Ty prompted, when she didn't continue.

She shrugged, trying to lever herself away from Devin. This wasn't the time to allow herself to be dependent on a man. He just pulled her closer. Actually, he made a pretty comfortable pillow, especially when she gave up and relaxed, letting her eyes drift shut. In the ensuing silence, the rumble of an empty stomach could be heard clearly.

"I've been lugging this around all morning." Ty reached for his backpack and began pulling out wrapped parcels as though they had all the time in the world to enjoy their picnic.

"Don't we have something to do, Devin?" Sydney asked, not bothering to open her eyes.

"Looks like Ty's brought fresh coffee. Can't pass that up."

"Maria was worried about you having to eat your own cooking, Dev. Besides, Sydney's about to explain everything."

Ty began to lay out a small feast of fresh fruit and sandwiches made the afternoon before. Although her mouth watered at the thought of coffee that didn't have to be filtered through her teeth, Sydney sat very still. She would not be bribed.

Devin held a mug of coffee under her nose and a sandwich in the other hand. "If I were cruel, I'd make you talk before I let you eat, since you only seem to tell us as much as you think we need to know."

"Since he's not really cruel, and I have control of the food, we'll let you eat while you talk. Wallace is headed straight for Far Canyon, but he's not moving too fast. We have enough time to find out what this is all about."

"I honestly don't know what it's all about."

She tried to move away from Devin again. This time, he let her, but a quick glance let her know when she had gone far enough.

"A month ago, I job-shopped for a small international firm and was taking care of the horse my sister took from her ex-husband. Whatever I had done in the past, that was my life at that time."

"Do you think coming to Stormhaven had anything to do with all of this?" Ty asked, genuinely concerned.

"No. I think I brought all of this to Stormhaven, but I can't figure out why. Since Rick is involved, it must have something to do with that last job I did with my dad."

Devin offered her a packaged hand wipe then a sandwich once she felt clean enough to eat. With a small stash of food nearby, he settled next to her once more. Supporting, not smothering.

"If not that job directly," she went on, unwrapping the sandwich, "then something else that happened between all of us. I just don't know what." She took a small bite of sandwich and chewed slowly, her brow furrowed.

"Does this have something to do with why you baby-sit companies instead of coordinating missions?" Devin asked quietly.

"Maybe. After Dad died, it just wasn't the same. Actually, even before he died." Sydney traded her sandwich for the coffee. Now that she had started, she was determined to finish. "That job we took, when we rescued Jamie and his group from that village in Central America, was the last one. That was sort of a favor to an old client of his. Since Rick was in charge of the group that was in trouble, Dad felt sort of responsible. Rick worked with him at one time, but Dad didn't think he was stable enough to keep him on." She sipped at her coffee, wetting her throat.

"It was pretty much as Jamie said. The men were out of control even before they went in. Drugs should never be anywhere near a job. If you have that sort of a problem, you shouldn't do that kind of work. It gets you, and the people around you, killed too easily. As far as we knew, that's what happened down there. Rick and some others got wasted, and there was an accident. A car went out of control and ran into a lot of buildings before crashing with Rick, and I think one or two of the villagers. I honestly thought Rick was dead."

"Why did he wait so long to come after you?" Ty passed a bag of orange sections to her. They were cool and easy to eat, even while she was concentrating on her story.

"That's only one of the questions," she said between bites. "I want to know is why he's being so intense about all this."

"Obsession is not all that strange," Devin pointed out.

"Maybe, but it's not like I'm a great candidate for obsession. He never contested the divorce, never looked me up. Why now?"

Devin looked at her, an eyebrow quirking and a strange glow in his predator's eyes. But he said nothing.

"I'll bite," Ty said agreeably. "Why now?"

"Big help you are. I don't know. The best I can come up with is that I called someone, while I was in LA, who may have gotten in touch with Rick."

"Couldn't Rick have known where you were already?"

She shrugged, looking away. After a moment, she bit at her lips, pulling them in between her teeth. When Devin's hand slid under her fingers, she held on, reaching for control.

"I didn't leave for Singapore just because it was a good job. It was, but mostly Dad needed time to himself, with Wendy. She was the first woman he let himself get close to. They were so happy together, and I think I loved her almost as much as I did Dad, if you can put a qualification like that on love." She took a deep breath, pushing emotions out of the way so she could continue.

"Wendy was about my size and we were always snitching clothes from each other. Sometimes we couldn't remember who actually owned what. There was a dark blue hooded jacket I wore a lot when Dad and I were in town. After Wendy moved in, she sort of appropriated it. Since I was going to a more tropical climate, I left it with her.

"That day, she and Dad had gone into town. It was

blustery, and they were at a nursery, so I doubt she put the hood down. I used to tease her about being cold-blooded." She tightened her hold on Devin's hand, edging closer to his warmth.

"Anyway, the house blew up that evening. When the police found two bodies in the living room, they assumed I was with Dad, and that's what was in the papers.

"Erik called me before anyone else could and told me to stay in Singapore. Since Wendy had no family, he waited to straighten out the confusion. By the time he talked to the police, the media had a new tragedy to suck off of.

"I didn't actively try to stay hidden but I didn't look for attention either. Too many people knew me from before. It isn't really good for a mid-level security clearance employee to be recognized as the daughter of a mercenary."

"How in the world did you ever get a security clearance?" Ty asked, pouring out the last of the coffee.

"From the beginning, Dad had friends of a sort in Washington. They helped me establish a new life. He also had enemies, and he really didn't trust either bunch. That might be part of the problem now. Even after he retired, they wanted him to come back and work for them. I got a visit from one of them after the explosion. Sort of a quasi-sympathy call: 'So sorry your dad is dead. Want to work for us, little girl?' I did the same thing he always did and avoided a direct answer. That way, my name's buried in a file in DC, instead of being erased, which could also leave questions."

"So when I asked my old friends about you..." Ty murmured.

She smiled. "I wonder if we have the same friends?"

"They just said you existed and had no further information on you."

"We have different friends. Mine knew who you were. They helped me find you after I picked up Mosby."

They all laughed. It was too ludicrous not to.

"Rick didn't have friends, but he had contacts who might have noticed a file either closing or disappearing. Particularly if it was one they were supposed to be watching. Which brings me back to the same question. Why?"

"How did Rick even know you were still alive?"

"I kept myself out of circulation by following certain rules. When I settled in LA, I broke one of my rules by staying in one place for too long with Mosby, then broke another one by calling one of the old group to get a contact at a company for the place I was trying to straighten out. I didn't think he would have stayed in touch with Rick."

"Was Rick behind what happened in LA?"

"The phone tip? It had his stink to it. Especially if he's into the drug world now. I don't know about all of it. That was the work of more than one person."

"Maybe he has friends."

"If he had 'friends,' he wouldn't be doing this so penny-ante. He would be coming down on me like a ton of bricks. Rick was always good at overkill. Trashing that village to cover up his disappearance was more his style than subtle irritation."

"Are you talking about some kind of organized crime?"

"Once I accepted the idea that he hadn't died, the only thing that made sense was that he'd gotten in with another group. If he stayed a merc, I would have heard about him. Drugs make sense. It's not like we're talking about Einstein here, after all. Dad did all the planning. Rick was just one of the flunkies who was clever enough to always be in the right place when the kudos were handed out." She rested her chin on her upraised knee. "I guess I did kind of go underground after our house blew up," she said, feeling the memories threaten to move in on her.

"And now this," Devin said quietly, putting the sandwich back in her hands.

"Now this," she agreed, eating because she had to, not because she felt hungry. "Powers has been after me to work for him, but he was never real blatant. Just showed up from time to time, when he was 'in the area.'"

"There's significance to him being here now?"

"Of some sort, although I can't figure it out. If he came after the other group, we're probably stuck in the middle of Washington politics. Powers never thought much of keeping slime alive on the off chance they might be useful later. He once told me he found it difficult to carry on a conversation with a slug."

They'd finished eating as they talked and made short work of clearing up, throwing bread crumbs and orange rinds out for the birds and stuffing the trash into their backpacks.

"So where does this leave us?" Ty asked, settling his

backpack more securely and reaching for his rifle. "Up the eternal creek?"

Sydney let Devin help her up as a wave of weariness washed over her. Why did he think she would know when it would all be done? She didn't ask. Leaders didn't whine.

"How did you get away, Ty?" she asked instead.

"Yesterday, Powers called a meeting of the alphabet goons in my living room. He had everyone in there, including the guards, and there was too much yelling going on for them to notice anyone leaving."

"That's convenient," Devin muttered, watching Sydney closely. For a moment there, she'd looked as though she couldn't go on. Now she seemed to be in control of herself, and the situation, whether she wanted to be or not.

"Maybe too convenient. I wish I could figure out what Powers wants." Sydney fell into step next to Devin, apparently content to let Ty lead the way. "The man's a spy because he likes to be sneaky. If we're being maneuvered—"

"You think he let Ty leave?"

She turned on him, angry words trembling on her lips, then drew a breath. With the release of air, she regained her composure, and more distance. "Possibly. Guess we'll have to play this hand out to the end."

They followed the trail through an increasingly beautiful mountain morning. Ty and Devin moved soundlessly, never straying far from the trail but never allowing themselves to be a clear target.

Granite and spruce gave way to thicker trees, and they

soon overlooked a canyon of incredible beauty. The rippling silver of falling water could be seen in the distance, through thick pine trees. Lush bright green, far below them, emphasized the trail of the water as it wound through the canyon.

Sydney followed in a contemplative haze, taking note of the surroundings but not worrying about direction. Letting someone else set the pace and direction seemed strange but she was in no mood or shape to argue with them. It was better to just trudge along, trusting in a small way, while she sorted out everything that had happened.

There was something she needed to tell Ty now, before they caught up with Rick, and she didn't really look forward to the discussion. At least the surroundings would be peaceful. The opportunity came later in the morning.

While Devin scouting ahead for a better way into Far Canyon, Ty joined her on a log. He settled with a sigh, letting some of the watchful tension go out of his shoulders while he stretched the aches out of his long legs.

He groaned, tilting his head back to loosen an ache in his shoulders. "Time was, I could hike this whole mountain double time and never feel it. I'd forgotten how rough it was to do this without a horse."

"Ty?" She hated to intrude on his rest, but there wouldn't be a better time. When he tilted his head to look at her, she went on. "How did you really feel about Lana leaving?"

The tall rancher shifted, to face her more directly, and pushed his hat back on his head. His brow furrowed as though he sought words for something he didn't understand. Lana had always been good at confusing people.

"Disappointed, more than anything else. I think I knew shortly after she moved here that it was a mistake believing she could be happy. It still shocked me when she left with no warning, no note, and took Mosby. Even though the marriage wasn't working out, I would have expected her to talk about it before she left. Part of me wanted to believe she was after the money she thought I had, but what you said at dinner, about her books, made me think. Maybe I should make an effort to find her and try to talk all this out."

"I don't think you can."

Something in her voice must have warned him. Ty tensed, his face going very still. When he didn't speak, didn't encourage her next words, she went on, looking away at the spot where Devin had disappeared.

"Rick said she told him where the ranch was, just before he killed her." She said it quickly, not believing in sugar-coating ugly truths. Not sure she could say more than that without breaking down herself.

The silence was absolute. Ty turned away slowly, lifting his hat, and resettling it, checking his rifle, re-adjusting the straps of his backpack. The actions of a strong man, overcome with emotion and not willing to let anyone know.

"Do you trust what he says?"

Something deep inside her stilled, like a small animal caught in the glare of a semi-truck. She felt the tension in her muscles, the slight pain as her nails sank into her palms, and welcomed the knowledge that her body, at least, was able to go on feeling. She wasn't all that sure about her mind.

Could she trust what Rick said? He had always used the truth as a convenience, giving her just enough to make his lies sound all that much more convincing.

"Why didn't I think of that?" Her voice shivered with self-directed rage.

"Because, Ms. Castleton, even you have occasional episodes of emotional overload," Devin said dryly from a few feet away. He'd waited, not wanting to intrude on what was obviously a private discussion.

"I let him manipulate me. That makes me so weak."

"It makes you so human." Devin traded places with Ty, reaching for her hands, turning her to face him. "After what you've been through, who would expect you to be able to sort out truth from lies? Sydney, you're not Superwoman. No one will hold it against you if you make a couple of mistakes. Except yourself, maybe. Let it go, babe. Let someone help you."

She let him hold her hands, let him pull her closer. It wasn't time yet to rest against him, to turn it all over to him. Soon, maybe. Not quite yet.

"I don't seem to have a lot of choice, do I?" She felt a smile move up out of the calmness centering in her being and spread over her face. The smile was returned by two tough, dirty men who looked like they could handle anything.

ೊ*ೆ*ೂ

In the end, it was ludicrously simple.

Devin had spent so much time in Far Canyon, he knew more than anyone, except possibly Charlie, how to get in and out without anyone else seeing you.

Wallace obviously believed he'd chosen an ideal defensible position. He had full view of every approach from below, and the only place above him was unclimbable rock. Or so he thought.

The rock face was steep, with many convenient hand and foot holds. Sydney made it up the last of the climb with help from both men. Devin chose a ledge wide enough for all of them to lie on at once, and slanted enough that, with care, they would remain hidden from the man below.

Rick was restless. He would settle for a moment, then spring up to stride back and forth across his small clearing, peering over the edge at the trails below him, then to either side. Some of the trails seemed well traveled, particularly one that went down to the valley below.

They pulled back after a minute, huddling at the back of the ledge and speaking barely above a whisper.

"He's getting edgy," Sydney noted, releasing her backpack and shrugging out of it.

"It's getting on to late afternoon. We should have been trudging up one of those paths long before this." Devin reached over to ease the pack off her shoulders, wishing he could take more of her burden away.

"Did Charlie actually leave that much of a trail?" Ty asked, pointing to an obvious path down the mountain. "It seems like he would have been more secretive."

"False trail, partner. Charlie's cave is farther into the valley. He walks over this trail from time to time to make anyone who comes into the valley think that's an easy way down."

"Clever," Sydney said, trying for a light touch. It was obvious she was affected by the idea of the disturbed recluse feeling he needed to worry so much about security.

"He is that." Devin shrugged out of his own backpack, pushing it behind them. "You'll have to leave your rifle up here, partner. Charlie doesn't tolerate long guns too well."

Ty secured his rifle behind their backpacks and checked the pistol he'd slid into a holster behind his back.

"Won't Wallace's rifle bother him?"

"Hard to say. I just hope Charlie gets spooked at so many people here and stays in his damned cave. Wish I could've gotten him down before this."

A small hand touched his shoulder, then his cheek. Sydney's eyes were soft with compassion, her expression mirroring the regret he felt. He felt that strange uprush of emotion coming through him. This had to be bringing back memories that hurt her, but she was trying to comfort him. How was he going to let her leave after they were through here?

Chapter 16

"Hello, Rick," Sydney said quietly, happy that her voice showed none of the fear that was almost paralyzing her.

Devin and Ty had argued with her plan, their voices no less insistent for not rising above a whisper. Finally, even Devin had to admit that the best and safest way for all of them was for her to come in behind Rick, distracting his attention while the two men closed in from the sides. As long as she did nothing to provoke Wallace, the brief period of time he thought they were alone wouldn't be too dangerous.

She didn't want to do this. After all the years of being her own person, of striving to be the son her father always wanted, she would have given anything to let someone else go in first.

When she'd faced Rick before, she'd still been confident about her own abilities. Now, she knew Rick was stronger than she was, and not quite sane. It was a frightening combination.

Rick wheeled, bringing the rifle up. Late afternoon sun glinted off the barrel in shades of dark gold. It was more of a long distance weapon, but would put a satisfactory hole in her at this distance.

"Getting a bit touchy there, are we?" She managed to maintain the note of gentle mockery as she slid down the last of the hidden path.

"Where'd you come from?" Rick's voice was that of a man on the edge of control.

"In the broad scheme of things, we all come from the same place." She continued the gentle, non-threatening voice as she edged closer, hands held away from her sides. "Most recently, I followed your rather clumsy trail up the mountain."

"Where's lover-boy?"

"He's still looking for a way into the canyon. I wanted to have a chance to speak with you first."

"Before I kill you?" With a smirk, Rick settled one hip against a rock. Her calmness affected him, at least temporarily, though he kept the rifle trained on her.

"That's what I wanted to talk to you about, Rick. What's all this about? You were never obsessive about me before."

"Of course not. Who could be obsessive about a homely, cold bitch like you?" He gestured wildly, his words slurring together. "All you ever wanted was to make your father happy. You tried so hard to be better than everyone else. You couldn't stand the fact that your sister was better in the sack than you were. That's why you walked out on me."

"As I remember it, I walked out on you because once you hit me, there was no reason for us to stay together."

"Bull. You couldn't take the competition."

"That's past. Why now?" Sydney leaned forward, getting more of his attention. Devin and Ty were closing in from both sides of the clearing behind him, moving with the grace of stalking cougars.

"You know too much." He hesitated, licking his lips, and the rifle wavered. "I can't let you tell him..." A crafty look came into his blank eyes.

She couldn't believe the changes that had come over him, as though he'd been hunted to the end of his endurance.

"What do I know, Rick?"

"Don't pretend!" The rifle came up again. "The village. How was I supposed to know she was his daughter?" He jerked his head, as though he heard something out of her range of sound. "Can't let him find out."

"Who?"

"Stupid bitch. Quit playing games with me."

If he had raised his voice, she would have had more warning. In one practiced move, Rick slid the strap of the rifle over his shoulder and drew a long knife from the holder on his back. He rushed at her, deadly in his madness.

Devin came in low and silent, his hands his only weapon.

At the last minute, some survival sense must have

warned Rick. Sidestepping, he turned, and the knife scored along Devin's arm.

Blood welled from the slash and Devin rolled, coming to his feet in a fighting crouch, a knife in his own hand. When Sydney moved, wanting to clobber Rick over the head with a rock, Devin spared her a moment's attention.

"Ty, keep her back."

Thinking to use the moment to his advantage, Rick rushed in, waving the bloodied knife. He'd learned to fight in some of the uglier spots in the world. But Devin was a far worthier opponent than Rick had faced in years.

Soon both of them were marked with blood. The fight went on, punctuated by stifled curses and the panting grunts of men at the limit of exertion. Restrained by Ty, Sydney could only watch, her pistol held uselessly in a solid two-handed grip. The men were too close together to risk a shot.

Rocks rattled behind them, startling Ty into looking away from the conflict.

"Son of a bitch." He released Sydney, pushing her to one side and moving to the back of the clearing. "Charlie. Go back, man. Everything's under control here."

The man, coming down the sheer slope with the agility of a goat, was long haired and wild eyed. His clothing was mostly old military, sturdy but stained. He had no weapon but a serviceable hunting knife, held in one hand at a menacing angle.

Devin looked up then leapt away from the fight, moving to intercept the rushing man. Rick didn't bother to follow him.

Instead, he took a step back, dropped the knife, and slid the rifle off his shoulder.

Time stretched, everything happening at once but seeming to happen in slow motion. Devin dove back toward Wallace while Ty was trying to hold Charlie with one hand. Charlie pulled away from Ty as though the powerful rancher was a child. Fire spurted from Wallace's rifle muzzle as it raised.

It was like a white hot poker searing her arm. Sydney spun, fighting to stay upright, as the second bullet grazed along the top of her shoulders.

"*Nooooo...*" The anguished cry echoed in her head, along with the report of the rifle. Then another voice, a strange one, yelled wordlessly, and she heard Rick Wallace scream in agony before all sound disappeared.

CRECR

Major Frank Powers didn't look like a man who lived for the convoluted world of lies and counter lies. Medium height, with thinning hair and a thickening waist, he seemed more like a high school physics teacher. It was his pale blue eyes that gave him away. Shrewd and piercing, they studied everyone, analyzing and categorizing them while he bumbled through introductions and mangled names.

He was for the moment kept at bay by Maria's bustling anger. A doctor had been in the helicopter that swept up to the face of the mountain, hovering to drop help, then lift out the wounded. Ty was not hurt, but there was no way he was going to be left on the mountainside while so much was going on at his ranch.

As the chopper swept away, Ty had occupied himself with keeping Devin from hurting the doctor, who was trying to decide which of Sydney's wounds to dress first. He did look down, to see a swarm of camouflaged men converging on the twisted bodies at the bottom of the granite mountain. Someone was going to have to come up with some damned good answers. Fast.

The doctor wasn't good enough, in Maria's opinion, to work on Sydney unaided. They kept everyone else out of the room, sending Devin off with Ty to get cleaned up so the blood encrusted gash on Devin's arm could be tended. This ploy only worked as long as it took to dress Sydney's wounds, administer an analgesic, and prepare her to meet with Powers.

❦❦❦

"Okay, Powers, here she comes. Let's have some answers."

Devin's growl was dangerous, but the older man merely reached for his tea cup without looking up from a thick file. When Sydney appeared in the entrance, Powers glanced up, smiled, and indicated the chair next to his own.

Sydney walked into the dining room unaided, except for the invisible support of some tiny pills and years of keeping herself upright, no matter what. There were coffee mugs set in front of chairs on each side of the table, and

Powers was already seated at the head of the table. She took the seat he indicated near his own—fell into it actually, sitting very straight to avoid touching the back. Devin and Ty sat across from her, looking more like sulky schoolboys than hardened men of war. Powers had that effect on a lot of people.

"Well, my dear, you've certainly shaken up the troops. When you refused to work with us, I thought I'd seen the last of this kind of operation."

Sydney shrugged, concentrating on the coffee Maria was pouring for her. Soup was offered and refused. For once, food was not a priority.

"Did you really expect to do any good, facing Wallace on your own? Twice, I understand."

"She wasn't completely alone, Powers." Ty spoke up, while digging his hand into Devin's arm to keep him from lunging across the table.

"Nonetheless, I have no doubt who was in charge." Powers pulled a pipe out of his aged tweed jacket and began the tedious operation of filling and lighting it as he spoke to the two men. "She used to plan these super hero scenarios when she worked with her father. Unfortunately, the man encouraged her."

"Do us all a favor, Major Powers, and don't discuss my father. You still don't have the right to mention his name." It was a different Sydney who spoke, her eyes as rigid and icy as her voice.

"As I explained to you at the time, my dear, once your father was dead, there was nothing we could do for him."

"You mean, once you let someone kill him, you saw

the benefit for your damned schemes in not going after the man who did it." Holding her coffee mug steady with both hands and an overdose of will power, Sydney took a fortifying sip. "Now I suppose you're going to tell me all this worked out exactly the way you planned it."

"Good Lord, no. I never intended Wallace to get this far. He was supposed to be intercepted before he left Los Angeles."

"I understand he took off from Salt Lake City, not L.A."

"Precisely. We lost track of him for a while. When I heard about this situation, I got here as soon as I could."

"Not soon enough." Devin's voice was colder than his eyes. "A good man was lost because of your carelessness."

"I never planned for you to take off after Wallace yourself, Mr. Starke. He was never supposed to reach the ranch."

"How were you planning to stop him?" Ty asked, a thinly disguised sneer on his lips. "With the men who wanted to keep him safe so they could catch his boss?"

"The idea was to catch them all together, and take care of the whole operation at once." Powers drew on his pipe until the noxious blend was burning to his satisfaction. "We knew Sydney was here, and that she would be safe as long as she stayed put. I didn't count on her playing fox and hounds in the mountains."

"You must not know her very well, then."

"On the contrary, Mr. Starke, I know her better than you ever will. Sydney and I go back a long way, and her father before her. She is doing a grave disservice to her country by wasting herself on silly little jobs. Of course, I understand why she chooses those jobs."

"That's enough, Powers," she said through stiff lips.

"Your father raised you to finish everything you started. With your obsessive nature, you began to need a satisfactory conclusion to every project. That is, of course, not possible in the line of work you did with your father. However, when you take on minor assignments with specific, short-range, goals, it's much easier to pretend to be accomplishing something."

"Damn you, Powers, don't you ever quit?"

"I deplore waste, my dear. Not having you on my team is a waste of criminal proportions," Powers chided gently as he tapped out his pipe, then re-lit it.

Sydney turned her head, wincing at the mild ache that tried to be felt through the pain medication. Looking across the table, she tried to gauge how the men were reacting to Power's revelations.

More than ever, Devin's face was set in an unreadable expression. Next to him, Ty tried to send her an encouraging grin, but it seemed his smile account was overdrawn. All he managed was a weak lift to one side of his mouth.

Devin wouldn't look at her. Sydney stared at him, willing him to raise his head, to turn his all-seeing predator's eyes in her direction. When he did look up from the table top, it was to glare briefly in Powers direction. Never at her.

So it ended, as the poet said, with a whimper, not a bang. Of course, Devin would be thoroughly disgusted with her by now. Her feeble attempt to control Rick, and protect the other two men, had resulted in the death of someone who mattered to Devin. Whatever he may have felt before was obviously gone now.

To cap it off, Powers was making her out to be some kind of a latter-day Mata Hari. As though it wasn't bad enough for Devin to hear her ex-husband extol the charms of another woman.

"Major Powers, yesterday Rick said something about Lana, my sister." Might as well use the old coot for information, as long as he was here bothering her.

"Oh, yes, that." His soft-looking face folded into a wrinkle of disgust. "It seems your sister, for some reason, was in Utah instead of Southern California, where she was supposed to be. Wallace tracked her there." The pipe wasn't drawing to his satisfaction. A quick rap on the table solved the problem. He didn't seem to notice the tension of the other three people. "Beat her rather severely before my men could get there." He poured more tea into his cup, added sugar, sipped appreciatively. "She's in Los Angeles now, with McFarley."

"How bad is she?"

"Eh? Ah, Mr. Randolph, I almost forgot, you were married at one point. Do forgive me." Powers pulled a large, snowy-white handkerchief from his pocket, dabbed gently at his nose and refolded the cloth. "She was bruised, perhaps scarred in the face. Nothing critical, but I believe she got quite a scare. I'd told her to let my men know when she was leaving. Of course, she wouldn't listen. That seems to run in the family."

"Enough games, Major." Sydney shifted, trying to find a more comfortable upright position. What she wouldn't give to be face-down on a bed right about now. "Why was Rick after me?"

"He told you, my dear. That wretched little village you and your father tried to save."

"The time Rick faked his death."

"Precisely." Powers ceased his fussy mannerisms as his voice became crisp with authority. "Along with his own false death, he also caused the very real death of a couple of the villagers. One of them was the daughter of Ramon Cesara, a powerful figure in the Colombian drug cartel. Her mother had been a maid for Cesara's wife, and returned to the village to raise her daughter. Even though she was illegitimate, Cesara kept watch over her."

"So when Rick's vehicle went careening all over the village?"

"He ran over the girl before crashing into the wall. Ironically, he was planning to work for a rival of Cesara's. It would have been to his advantage to brag about the death to his boss at that time.

"It wasn't until he went to work for Cesara, after a rather hostile takeover, that he learned about the death of the young girl. Wallace was the only one who knew for sure about the death, but he apparently decided you and your father would figure it out one day."

"I see." Sydney drew a deep breath and tried to call up another reserve of energy. It wasn't there.

She did see, so much. All the deaths, all the years of hiding, because Rick Wallace had carelessly taken the life of what he would have considered a useless peasant girl.

The drugs were taking their toll on her, as they always did. This last effort had drained her until she could barely hold herself upright. Before total collapse, she had to be away from here. By now, Devin must be tired of playing nursemaid.

"Major, will you be pulling out tonight?"

"As soon as I finish this pipe. Did you need a lift somewhere, my dear?"

"Would it compromise national security?"

"I don't think we need to worry about that. You get your things together, and meet me out front."

No longer trying to meet Devin's eyes, Sydney levered herself very carefully from the table and left the room.

సించి

She was leaving. Again. All through the interrogation, she'd sat in that damned chair across the table from him and answered the old man as cool as be damned. As if she hadn't seen a man killed in front of her, didn't have wounds under the soft blue sweater. As if she hadn't cried out in ecstasy in his arms.

"You gonna let her go again?" Ty was shocked, unfortunately not speechless.

"It would be the best for all concerned, Mr. Randolph." Powers was collecting his paperwork, stuffing it into a battered, oversized leather briefcase. "People of Sydney's talents are rare and very valuable in our line of work. Unfortunately, they do not function so well outside of that work. Not for long periods of time, anyway."

"She was doing just fine until you got here."

"Do you think so, Mr. Starke? Perhaps temporarily. Do you think she would have stayed here indefinitely?" He read the closed expression in Devin's eyes like a billboard. "Precisely. Sydney is not yet ready to settle down. As long as she has that restlessness inside her, I mean to put her to good use."

He stood, extending a hand to Ty. A soft hand, well-manicured, without rings. The hand of a man who had never worked at much physical, because he was needed so desperately in other areas.

"We don't have time to talk at length on this visit, Mr. Randolph, but I want to tell you how much I admire what you are doing here. Any help you might need, get in touch with me. You should be able to figure out how."

He scuttled out of the room, a mousy aging bookkeeper who controlled more power than either of them could ever conceive.

"Who the hell was that?" Ty asked, falling back in his chair.

"I'm not sure, but I'm glad he's more or less on our side." Devin settled in his own chair, refilling his coffee with an air of someone expecting to spend the rest of the evening in conversation.

"He might not be on our side, once you take his prize agent away."

"Who says I'm going to?"

"You can't just let her go, dammit."

"Why not? Hell, you saw her, Ty. She sat there like a queen, giving that spider back as good as she got. He's right, she's not meant to live on a ranch the rest of her life."

"Neither are you. And don't feed me any crap about not wanting to get in the way of her career. It sure didn't stop you before, did it?"

"We never really discussed it."

Ty snorted, obviously disgusted. After a moment of contemplating the emptiness of his own coffee mug, an expression of unholy glee overtook his face.

"You're scared," he said, with the first real smile he'd shown since heading for the mountains to help Devin and Sydney.

"Scared? Of what?"

"You're scared Sydney wouldn't choose you over being a super spy, so you chased her away."

"That's the stupidest thing I've ever heard. She left. I didn't tell her to go."

"You didn't ask her to stay, you fool. Am I going to have to nursemaid you through this whole damned affair?"

"It's not an affair!"

"It is until you marry her."

Devin stopped as the forbidden image came to him. Sydney, his. With him every day. Ornery, bossy, irritating, infinitely precious, critical to his very existence.

ℰↄℰↄ

There was actually very little to pack, and no one,

apparently, to waste her time with good-byes. For once, putting aside her qualms, she downed one more of the magic little pills, hoping foolishly that she could numb the pain deep inside of her. He hadn't come after her, but why should he? What man would want to spend the rest of his life with a woman whose past was a web of lies and whose future extended only to the next assignment?

Tucking the carry-on bag under her arm, she took one more look around the bedroom. Her backpack would be with Powers, of course. There was no reason to waste any more time. Maybe there would be a bed on the plane. Squaring her shoulders, she let herself out of the cozy adobe house, heading for the clearing where the helicopter waited, blades idly turning.

"Where do you think you're going?"

She didn't dare look over at him. In the early moonlight, his face would be all angles and shadows, and his eyes would glitter with the strength of his will.

"I thought you were listening. Powers offered me a job. Good pay, lots of travel and adventure, great benefits."

"You don't want to go with him."

"How do you know?"

"I know you, Sydney." As gently as he could, he took hold of her arm and pulled her around to face him. "Whatever you were or did in the past, you left all that behind you. You've made a life for yourself."

"Doing what? You said yourself those were senseless jobs."

"To hell with your damned career. You've become a

different person. No matter what you try to tell yourself, you can't go back to that life. I've been around enough people who've gotten out to know that."

"So, what am I supposed to do? Stay here on the ranch and put you at risk of more of my past coming back to haunt me? I watched you change up there, Devin. You lost whatever peace you'd found for yourself, and it was my fault. Then Charlie—" With a wrench, she pulled away from him, continuing resolutely to where the chopper was beginning to kick up more dust.

Devin stopped her again, stepping in front and grabbing both arms. He held her gently, but with an unbreakable hold.

"Charlie made his own decisions. So did I." He hesitated, his face growing increasingly more tense. "If you leave, I'll have to come after you. I can't let you go alone."

She felt the glimmer of hope, creeping up through the drugged depression. "Why, Devin?"

"For one thing, you're damned careless about watching your back. I figure you'll need me in the field with you."

Was that really the hint of a smile on his face? "Won't that look a little funny, Powers' super agent with her very own cowboy watchdog?"

"If funny keeps you safe, I'll be funny."

"Why, Devin?" she asked again, more softly still.

"You're not going to make this easy on me, are you?" He drew a deep breath then let it out heavily. "Okay, dammit, I love you."

She stared at him blankly for a minute then twisted

away, oblivious to the pain. Once more, she stalked in the direction of the chopper, although now she went toward the sound as her eyes were blinded with tears.

This time, when Devin reached for her, she retaliated with a wrenching twist that tore at her back and should have left him writhing on the ground. Instead, he stepped toward her, pivoted, and in short order had her pinned against him. Lowering her carefully, he eased her onto the large, flat rock she'd once used for meditation. One arm slid under her back, offering a cushion.

"Listen to me, you little hellcat. I love you. When you leave this ranch, I will go with you, because I'll be damned if I'm going to spend one more night anywhere but in bed next to you."

His body pinned her against the rock, but there was no fear in her. She looked up at him with an expression of near hope that ripped at the soft spot that had been growing inside him. Still, she shook her head, pulling her lip in between her teeth in determination.

"Please don't say that, Devin. You're just caught up in the moment. In a couple of days or weeks, you'll wake up and find out you don't love me at all."

"So you want to leave now, before I change my mind?" At her firm nod, he snorted, settling more comfortably against her. "What makes you think I don't love you, honey?"

She tried to turn away and was stopped by his hand in her hair. Pride kept her from closing her eyes. Fear kept her from answering.

"Don't you think you're lovable?" He studied her face

in the growing moonlight. All angles and shadowed mysteries, he couldn't imagine not loving her. Or her loving him. "It's the scars, isn't it?"

"What on earth do you mean?"

"You don't want to spend the rest of your life looking at my scars and watching me limp."

"Don't be ridiculous." She tried to see into his face, but the moon kept getting in her eyes. A reckless abandon overtook her. "Devin, your scars have nothing to do with it. I've loved you since the night you held me in the truck and kept the—" She was stopped by a sudden increase in the weight against her.

"Say that again."

"I love you. That's why I can't stay."

"Can you stay until you get tired of looking at my scars?" he asked, a solution finally forming amidst the desperation.

"I'll never get tired of looking at your scars. If you're sure you can live with my past, can I stay around until you decide you're tired of me being bossy?"

"I think we can work on the bossy part." Avoiding the attack of her suddenly released hands he rolled, pulling her over on top of him to protect her back.

As their mouths met in a kiss of promise and forever, the dust kicked up by a departing helicopter blew across the field.

It was doubtful they even noticed.

About the Author

Mona Karel became convinced at an early age that her life would not really begin until she was about thirty five. She has no idea what precipitated that thought, but she claims she was a strange child. Until reaching that age, she led a peripatetic existence for many years, criss-crossing the country, working with horses and dogs—and waiting tables to support her other jobs. At thirty five, when many people are well into raising their families, Karel settled down to "real" work as a buyer and expediter. She married a high school teacher, which led to over twenty years in Southern California.

Karel can't remember a time she wasn't reading, though she doesn't remember much fun with Dick and Jane. Her preferred stories involved dogs and horses, and once she had gone through every horse book in the high school library, she started in on Civil War stories. They rode horses, didn't they? At that time Romance was swash-bucklers and Gothic. Karel preferred the stronger heroines and more subtle relationships of Mary Stewart, Helen MacInnes, and Andre Norton. Then Karel discovered Romance in the form of Silhouette, Candlelight, and RWA, and her life was complete. Karel has since retired to New Mexico, where she lives in the wind at 6,500 feet with her Salukis. When not writing or going to dog shows, Karel works at a solar-related firm.